DANGEROUS PASSION

Kara tapped lightly on the door and entered, closing the door behind her. Brent was pacing the floor.

"There you are," Brent said. "Sit down."

Kara sank into one of the leather chairs and waited.

"I saw Sidney Eastman in your office. What's up?"

Kara felt her face burn. "He was despicable," she said in a low voice. "I'm going to make sure he gets what he deserves."

Brent's eyes were cold, hard chips of amber. "I changed my mind. I don't want to hear it. Leave me out of your personal business."

"But, you don't understand what he said to me—"

"I said leave me out of it," Brent said, his voice rising.

Anger flashed through Kara at his tone and she stood up. "Is that all you wanted from me?" she asked coldly.

Brent came from behind his desk and walked toward Kara. "No, that's not all I want from you," he responded, his voice low and husky.

Her woman's senses responded involuntarily to his closeness. Brent caught her in his arms. Her pulses pounded . . . she couldn't stop the moan. Her lips were moist and slightly parted in preparation for his kiss. His mouth touched hers, his lips burning. They felt of barely controlled passion. Dangerous passion. Kara met Brent's gaze.

"No. That's not all I want," Brent repeated, releasing her.

BOOK YOUR PLACE ON OUR WEBSITE AND MAKE THE ARABESQUE ROMANCE CONNECTION!

We've created a customized website just for our very special Arabesque readers, where you can get the inside scoop on everything that's going on with Arabesque romance novels.

When you come online, you'll have the exciting opportunity to:

- View covers of upcoming books
- Read sample chapters
- Learn about our future publishing schedule (listed by publication month *and author*)
- Find out when your favorite authors will be visiting a city near you
- Search for and order backlist books from our online catalog
- Check out author bios and background information
- Send e-mail to your favorite authors
- Meet the Kensington staff online
- Join us in weekly chats with authors, readers and other guests
- Get writing guidelines
- AND MUCH MORE!

**Visit our website at
http://www.arabesquebooks.com**

HEART'S DESIRE

Monica Jackson

Pinnacle Books
Kensington Publishing Corp.
http://www.arabesquebooks.com

PINNACLE BOOKS are published by

Kensington Publishing Corp.
850 Third Avenue
New York, NY 10022

First Printing: July, 1998
10 9 8 7 6 5 4 3 2 1

Printed in the United States of America

Dedicated with love to my mother, Ustaine Talley
Who gave me the strength to follow my dreams

One

Kara Smith mustered every ounce of will in her body and soul not to sob aloud. She knew the sound would upset her mother. Kara smoothed her mother's damp curls and whispered softly, "Mom?"

Her mother's eyes opened, first filmed over with pain, and then overflowing with love for her daughter. The hospice nurse returned with the pain medicine. Kara's mother sighed gratefully as the potent painkiller took effect.

The pastel colors in her mother's bedroom dimmed to tones of gray in the darkened room. A faint sickish and antiseptic smell replaced the familiar warm, floral scent of Kara's mother.

The nurse sat in the easy chair across the room. Kara was grateful for her presence in the wee morning hours. Kara had called the hospice panic-stricken when her mother gasped for air, her breathing erratic and weak. She tried to prepare herself for the inevitable, but faced with the reality of her mother's death, she wasn't ready—she would never be ready.

It was her mother's death watch, the last vigil. Kara's body trembled. How could she bear it? Now, she would be truly alone.

"There is something I want you to know," her mother said suddenly, in tones stronger than she'd used for weeks.

Startled, Kara flinched. Her mother's eyes were lucid and clear.

For a moment, hope coursed through Kara. Would it not be tonight? Immediately, she felt ashamed of her hope. She was selfish, cruel. A few days more in her beloved mother's presence meant prolonging her mother's pain and suffering a few days more. Death was the release her mother prayed for daily.

"It's about your father."

My father! Kara thought. Her mother had always said he was dead. When Kara was younger she'd wondered why there were no pictures of him around the house, no mementos, never any reminder or hint that he once shared her mother's life. Her mother had become tight-lipped and silent when she'd asked about him as a child.

Kara stopped asking as she got older. Whatever her mother's secrets were, they were in the past and best left alone, she decided. Her father was a ghost, buried in the past and long forgotten.

Her mother squeezed Kara's hand with unexpected strength.

"He's a great man, your father," she said.

Is a great man? Kara thought. Was her mother going to tell her he was alive? Fear curled within her, warring with her overwhelming grief.

"I want you to know of the blood running through your veins. I want you to know him." Her mother's eyes took on a strange intensity. "Tell her to leave," she whispered, nodding toward the nurse.

Kara glanced at the nurse who had already stood up to go. When the sound of the door shutting reached her ears, Kara's mother relaxed against the pillows and breathed in deep, gasping breaths.

"Mom, this is not necessary—" Kara started.

"Let me finish," her mother cut off Kara's words. "I loved him more than life itself. I would have died for him.

But what he needed me to do was easier than dying, Kara, my love . . ." she said in a rush of exhaled breath.

Kara shook her head in protest, not wanting to hear more.

"He was right," her mother continued. "I wasn't good enough. I would have held him back. He had a plan and a mission, and he's achieved all his dreams. I was so dark, so uneducated, poor, and pregnant. He never would have achieved his dreams with me. So, I gave him the greatest gift . . . I gave him what he wanted and needed. We got out of his life."

Her mother paused, her dry, withered, brown fingers picking at the snowy white sheets. Pain filled her mother's eyes, but it wasn't the familiar physical pain.

Kara choked and gathered her mother's frail, emaciated body in her arms.

"You're good enough for anybody and everybody, Mom. You've always been there, and you gave and gave, and even when you had nothing left, you would find the strength to give some more. Whoever this man was, if he wasn't there for you when you needed him, he wasn't good enough for you." Kara's voice was low and fierce. She hated this man—her father.

"But, Kara, you don't understand. You are blessed to have his blood running through your veins. I want you to know him, Kara. Promise me you'll at least learn about him after I'm gone. He's Congressman . . . Sidney Eastman."

Kara's blood froze when she heard the name. Then it pumped hot, fast, and furious through her heart. Congressman Eastman, politico fat cat, presently the favorite spokesboy of the conservative majority powers. Some people called him a sellout, most people called him worse.

This was the man her mother had protected, mourned, and loved all these years? Kara was incredulous, then a fury greater than she had ever known shook her. She looked at her mother lying back exhausted among the pillows, gasping for breath with the effort it had taken to speak those words to her daughter. Tears ran down her mother's withered cheeks.

Kara remembered the years of struggle her mother had gone through, alone . . . always alone. Mom had provided for her, and wanted to give her more when there was never enough. Then, when things had just gotten a little better, her mother had finally gone to the doctor about the pain. It was cancer—and it was too late.

Kara murmured the words of reassurance and comfort her mother needed to hear, but the man would pay. Kara vowed it, with all the grief and resolve in her heart welling up to a surge of fierce hatred. She would know him all right! And one day, Congressman Sidney Eastman would be sorry—so very sorry.

Brent Stevens took a stiff swallow of his scotch and surveyed the noisy cocktail party. He hated functions like this. He was here in a semi-official status as Congressman Eastman's surrogate and had just completed his business with one of the congressman's largest contributors who was throwing the party.

A jar at his back shook him, and scotch flowed over his fingers, disappearing into his immaculate white shirt. Brent swung around to face two soft breasts that had been momentarily pressed against his back.

They belonged to a woman with an exotic, but softly beautiful face. Her black hair was pulled back in a sleek chignon, and her lips were full and moist. She had flawless deep brown skin, a shade somewhere between chocolate and cinnamon. It would feel like velvet, he thought. Coffee-colored eyes sparkled up at him.

He couldn't look away and dismiss her as he already had

dismissed countless come-ons from women since the party started. Totally appealing and somehow familiar, she was delicious.

"You spilled your drink," she said, her voice low and cultured. "I'm so sorry."

Brent nodded but she made no move to leave his presence.

"My name is Kara Smith," she said, and sipped her champagne. She glanced around the room, then focused on him. "Are you planning to stay here much longer, Mr. Stevens?" she asked.

So, she knows me, he thought. He searched his memory for a moment, but couldn't place her. Brent decided to join her in the game. She excited him. With a mental shrug, he said with an amused twist of his lips, "Not if I can find something more interesting to do."

Her shell-pink tongue darted out and moistened her lips. It wasn't a nervous gesture, but a slow, provocative, studied one. Matching wine-tinted fingertips traveled caressingly from her chin and brushed her right nipple. He saw the nipple harden visibly through the golden lamé fabric of her clinging cocktail dress. Brent felt himself harden in response. She was hot. So hot. He started a slow burn. Her scent intoxicated. He moved imperceptibly closer.

Her figure was lush and rounded, voluptuously feminine, not like the tightly coiled, fashionably thin and athletic women he was used to. He was interested—definitely interested. Brent put his hands in his pockets and waited for her to make the next move. She didn't fail him.

"I know of some much more interesting amusements," she cooed. "Expensive amusements," she added.

Brent raised an eyebrow. So, that's it, he thought, money is what she's after.

Then, her fingers circled her other nipple lightly and rubbed, hardening it to match the right one. Brent's fingers curled in his pockets in response. He hadn't reacted this strongly to a woman's brazen advances in years. She was obviously very special . . . and experienced.

She moved her fingers from her breast and rested them lightly on his arm. "Let's go," she said. He raised his eyebrow again at her abrupt invitation.

He hoped she wouldn't cost him too much. He glanced down and gazed at her nipples. His taut body vibrated with anticipated passion. What the hell, even if her cost was high, she was worth it.

Brent reached for her the second the limousine door closed. She curled into his arms like a kitten. He rubbed his thumbs over her still stiff nipples and groaned, pulling her closer to him. Her head tipped up to his, her full lips smiling an invitation. He bent his head, and covered her lips with his own. Sweet and ripe, her lips were surprisingly tender. Drugged, slow kisses deepened into deep, throbbing passion. Their tongues entwined, he heard her give an incoherent moan, and trailed kisses down her neck.

He pulled the deep neckline of her dress down, exposing full, round, perfect breasts topped with large chocolate nipples. Lowering his lips to her breasts, his hand moved slowly up the silken pantyhose of her inner thigh. Her body stiffened, and he lifted his head to look questioningly at her.

"We're going a little fast, don't you think?" she asked, her voice low and husky. "I've always enjoyed my treats better when I've eaten them slowly . . . and savored them."

She gave his thigh a promising squeeze and withdrew slightly. Brent nodded in agreement. He drew a deep breath to steady himself. She was right, he needed to slow down. This night promised to be memorable.

He got a suite at the Crown Palace. The anticipation she skillfully built within him indicated she was worth it.

A consummate pro, he thought. Brent appreciated prowess in whatever capacity he found it.

She hesitated at the threshold of the suite. Her hands tightened on her purse, and she touched her hair. Nervous, Brent thought. Taken aback by her sudden apparent loss of brazen confidence, he set his briefcase by the elegant phone stand and picked up the phone, pressing the button for room service.

"We'll have champagne—your best, and fresh strawberries. Are you hungry?" he asked the woman standing awkwardly in the middle of the room.

She shook her head. What was her name anyway, Carol, Karen? He loosened his tie and ordered a steak, and added some giant shrimp in case she changed her mind. The woman still hovered.

"The bathroom is that way, I believe," he said. She gave him a look of relief and scurried off.

Brent dropped to the sofa and pulled off his shoes. He was tired. The situation made him uneasy. Casual sex had never been his preference, and he'd certainly never needed to pay for it before. He wondered what he'd gotten himself into. The woman's sudden change of attitude made him wary, as delectable as she was. If she decided to leave, that was fine with him.

Hunger rumbled in his belly and he wished they would hurry up with the steak. The overly fancy hors d'oeuvres at the cocktail party hadn't appealed to him.

Brent clicked on the TV in the living area to a twenty-four-hour sports channel and leaned back. He heard bath water run. He couldn't even remember her name. He thought he'd seen her somewhere, and that bothered him, also. He shrugged away his uneasiness; if she were significant, certainly he would have remembered her. The sports channel soon hypnotized him.

A few minutes later, he was savoring the succulent steak when her quiet entrance startled him. He'd momentarily forgotten her presence. Brent stifled a sigh. She was beautiful, but right now he didn't feel like dealing with her. Brent cut and chewed another bite of steak and watched her pour a glass of champagne to the brim.

She carefully picked a strawberry and sat in the love seat facing him. She sipped her champagne and silently watched him. She would occasionally dart nervous glances toward the phone. He wondered if she wanted to make a call.

At least she could tolerate silence. He gratefully speared a leaf of his Caesar salad. He had finished the salad when he looked at her again, and his breath caught when he saw her licking the strawberry. She gave him a tiny mischievous grin and her little pink tongue curled around the apex of the strawberry.

She teased that strawberry. She nibbled at it with her perfect white teeth. She licked it with passionate hunger. That strawberry seemed to beg to be devoured.

Brent's attention riveted to her lips, and his passion returned in a rush. When she finally bit into the strawberry, he caught his bottom lip between his teeth. He wanted her. The feeling was strong and insistent. Brent tightened his muscles and willed himself not to move toward her.

He watched and waited, his breath coming fast, while her confident, forward smile returned. She stood and the white hotel robe fell off her body. His mouth dried, and everything but her faded away. Everything but the beauty revealed before him was forgotten.

She guided him toward the bedroom, and feverishly rubbed her naked body against his. Brent groaned, his clothes suddenly stifling him. Pulling his shirt out of his slacks, he had an impulse to rip it off and let buttons fly.

Brent's fingers grazed his wallet in his back pocket and he remembered. He extracted two crisp one hundred dollar bills and dropped them on the dresser. Brent had no idea of the going rate. He had never had the need or desire for anonymous sex before, but he had never felt this sort of desire either—so wild and strong, sweeping reason away.

She stood by the bed in proud, utterly feminine nudity, staring at the money on the dresser.

"Is it enough?" he asked, reaching for his wallet again.

She raised her arms to him. It was more than enough invitation. He gathered her in his arms and lifted her to the bed. Her velvety skin, her soft curves invited him to explore. A clean, soft scent clung to her and rose up from her secret recesses.

Brent explored her, delved inside her, tasted her, and soon her soft gasps and breathed sighs matched the rhythm of his skillfully stroking fingers and lips.

She looked exquisite, delicate and innocent even in her ecstasy. He could wait no longer. Reaching out for the necessary protection, he applied it in one smooth movement. He guided himself to her velvety, furled doorway, and started to enter heaven with a single, smooth stroke.

A barrier stopped him. The woman stiffened and groaned, this time in pain. He couldn't believe it. Bewilderment and fear were reflected in the woman's eyes. Brent was aghast. It was incredible. He didn't know what to do, so he snorted, rolled off the bed, and stalked into the bathroom.

He turned the shower knob to as cold as he could stand it. The woman was unmistakably, beyond a shadow of a doubt, a virgin. Why? Why would she want to pass herself off as a prostitute?

Her looks were more than deceiving; the woman was obviously mentally unbalanced. Passion had canceled out his usual cool reason. She wanted something from him other then sex. He saw it in her eyes. Brent frowned under the cold, stinging water, and felt a momentary dread. He shook off the feeling and stepped out of the shower.

Brent took his time toweling himself off. He resolutely

tied the belt around the hotel robe. He really didn't want to deal with this. He knew in the back of his mind that once he saw her again—despite her virginity, despite his doubts, his uneasiness, and his usual clear-headed logic— he would still want her. He wanted her now. When Brent returned to the hotel bedroom, he was almost relieved to find that she was gone.

Two

The room spun around momentarily as Kara stepped out of the shower, and she leaned against the bathroom door frame, dizzy and dehydrated. The shower had been as hot as she could stand it, but she still didn't feel clean.

Trudging to the kitchen shedding droplets of water from her naked skin, Kara shivered. She left the kitchen lights off and opened the refrigerator door. The chill, dank air from the refrigerator matched her mood. Goose bumps rose on her skin, as she lifted the gallon jug of icy spring water and gulped it until she gasped and sputtered.

Starting to put the jug back in the refrigerator, Kara reconsidered. Carrying it back into her bedroom, she curled up, still wet, into her clean, crisp cotton sheets. Shame replaced her initial numbness. She couldn't believe what she had done. She'd tossed away her entire upbringing and the beliefs she'd once held so dear. She'd thrown herself at Brent Stevens and offered up what she once believed was her most precious possession, her virginity.

It simply hadn't been necessary to go as far as she had gone. She would have gotten what she needed regardless. There was no reason to allow him to bury his face in her most secret . . . shamed heat and remembered passion burned over her body.

She'd denied her feelings for so long. She'd denied the part of herself that craved, wanted, and needed the touch

of a man. At the cocktail party, when she felt his desire—
her own need became a roller coaster sweeping her carefully laid plans before its mad run. She couldn't stop. She
was out of control. The golden boy, Brent Stevens, wanted
her—boring, unattractive, not-too-bright Kara Smith. And,
God, how she wanted him. And from within her someone
new had emerged . . . someone brazen, beautiful, and daring.

That person had snatched Brent up as if he'd belonged
to her. He *had* belonged to that other Kara, if only for a
moment, and now it tore her up inside. He would never,
ever be hers again. Soon, Brent Stevens would hate her.
The thought hurt her already. But the plan was in motion
and she would endure the pain. Enduring pain was something she was getting good at lately.

Memory carried her back to the evening she'd seen Congressman Sidney Eastman on a popular talk show. She'd
watched him closely to see if any reflection of herself was
echoed in his light, almost-white skin, his blue eyes, and
his distinguished gray hair. His answers to the moderator's
questions had been glib and uninformative. He'd looked
relaxed and confident, tossing off easy one-liners. All the
bitterness buried within Kara's heart had welled up.

Congressman Eastman was her father, and it was all his
fault. Her doubts and loneliness, even her mother's
death—became all wound up in Kara's mind in a mael-
strom of bitterness and blame, underlaid with a sort of
longing. And for once, Kara hadn't denied her feelings.
A plan had come to her, unformed and unfinished. Get
close to the congressman and punish him for what he'd
done to her mother, punish him for what he'd done to
her. Find out what he needed and wanted. Find out his
desires and refuse them, deny him, destroy him. Let him
find out how it feels to have desire denied. Let him feel
what her mother felt. Let him feel the agony she felt now.

After her mother had died, she'd collected the substan-

tial insurance benefit and put the house on the market.
It sold quickly. She left the small town of Tyrone, Georgia,
and the even smaller religious sect in which she had been
raised, for Washington, D.C.

Kara applied for a job in the congressman's office. Not
for a moment did she ever doubt she would be hired. The
office manager offered a position as a file clerk.

Kara learned her job, did her work, and observed the
congressman's dynamic office. Nobody noticed her, a
quiet presence in her customary oversized navy suit with
her hair pulled back in a bun. She never saw the congressman.

Brent Stevens was Congressman Eastman's administra-
tive assistant . . . the congressman's right hand, and the
head, heart, and soul of the office. Kara watched him, his
competent way, his loose, easy stride. His crooked grin and
husky voice had been her undoing. Brent Stevens was attractive, charming, and confident; he was everything she
wasn't. He was everything she wanted and everything she
wanted to be.

Brent Stevens never really noticed her. Kara was just another pair of hands to file papers to him, a minute cog in
the machinery that ensured the smooth running of his
office. Always polite and courteous, his eyes were ever focused on the next problem or goal.

Her problem was that she noticed him all too much.
Kara noticed his smooth café au lait skin, the laugh lines
around his mouth, and his unexpected grin. She noticed
his light brown, almost amber eyes that changed with his
moods, the shadow on his clean shaven face that darkened
faintly as the day wore on.

Kara frowned at the realization that after months of
planning and preparation, she'd allowed her emotions,
no, her hormones to run away with her. Brent Stevens was
nothing but a stepping-stone. A stepping-stone to bring

her closer to her father, and a step closer to her father's downfall.

Kara glanced at the papers scattered across her dresser. She had gotten what she wanted, and she wouldn't give up. *Was it worth it? Was she crazy? Shouldn't she just get on with her life and let this obsession go?* Kara shook away the cobwebs of doubts. It might cost her now, and would surely cost her more in the future, but it was worth any and all cost. She would know her father and make him pay. Sleep claimed Kara, and her last thought was that when she woke, she would finally confront Brent Stevens and make him give her what she wanted.

Brent went through his briefcase a third time, and this time he couldn't deny the fact—the papers were gone. There was a feeling in the pit of his stomach that he supposed he'd feel while dropping from the third story of a high building. What would he say to the congressman? The thought of the outcome if those papers fell into the wrong hands—or if the media got hold of them—made him queasy.

There was a knock at his office door. His secretary never knocked, and unexpected visitors were announced. While Brent hesitated, another knock sounded.

"Come in," he called out.

The woman from the previous night appeared in his doorway. She wore a baggy, dark blue suit with a skirt that fell almost to her ankles. Her hair was pulled back in a severe bun. Her lips were held tight and firm.

Shock rippled through him at the sight of her. She looked the very cliché of the dowdy secretary. Except in the cliché, the frumpy secretary let down her hair and transformed into a stunning siren. Apparently, this woman had it backward.

Brent remembered all too well the soft feminine curves

now hidden by the ugly clothes she wore. But the clothes did nothing to hide the sultry, sensual aura she wore like perfume. He remembered the cascading waves of her hair once he'd released it from its loose, classy chignon on the previous night. He remembered her lips, relaxed with passion, moist, full, and lush.

He couldn't stop his body's involuntary response to her. His hands wanted to touch her, his lips wanted to taste hers again.

Then Brent saw the sheaf of papers she held in her hands. His eyes widened, and inner alarms went off. Suddenly, it all fell into place. The woman had seemed familiar because she worked at his office. But she was a file clerk, and he'd had no reason or opportunity to deal directly with her. She was the one who took the papers, she was the only one who had any opportunity. But why? He took a sip of coffee and stared at her with what he hoped was a calm gaze, and he waited for her to make the next move.

She stepped toward him and laid the papers on his desk. He didn't reach for them.

"I've made other copies," she said.

Brent said nothing.

"It's quite a coincidence," she said, "that Congressman Eastman's appointment to the Banking, Finance and Urban Affairs Committee came at almost the same time you accepted this large personal loan on the congressman's behalf."

Brent remained silent, but he could feel the pulse ticking in his jaw.

"It's even more of a coincidence that the loan is signed by Skippy Randall, eldest scion of the Randall family, an old banking family and primary shareholders in the Americabanc Corporation.

Every muscle in Brent's body was taut, but he waited in silence for this woman to show all her cards.

"These papers prove that the congressman was influ-

enced by corporate money on the very eve of his committee appointment! Where did all the money go? What is
the congressman supposed to do in return for the payoff?"

Brent had heard enough. "The papers prove nothing,"
he said. "We didn't keep the money."

"Of course," she said. "I'm sure the media will be glad
to hear it." She crossed the room and started to pick up
the phone.

"What do you want?" Brent asked. She stopped and
slowly turned.

"I want the job you have open for a legislative assistant.
I applied for it, and I couldn't even get an interview."

Brent lifted an eyebrow.

"And?" he asked.

"I get the open LA position with a contract signed en-
suring my job security for the remainder of the congressman's term—you get all the copies. And no one will know
about our little secret."

"Don't worry about my qualifications," she hastened to
add. "I've studied the banking industry inside and out."

The woman was mad. Brent remembered how much he
had wanted her last night. His pulses raced even now at
being near her, even in the unattractive costume that dis-
guised her beauty, even with her attempt at blackmail and
her ridiculous demands.

"When do I start?" the woman was saying.

He snorted with laughter. "Start? Lady, you're out of
your mind. I'm calling security right now to get to the
bottom of this."

The woman looked alarmed. "No," she choked out.
"All I have to do is make a call and my friend will send
copies of the papers to these addresses."

She handed him a list. Brent glanced at it and his heart
sank. All the major and minor media. They would have a
field day. It would be a mess for the congressman, with all

the hearings, investigations, and indictments going on now. And the mess would all fall into his lap.

He rubbed weary fingers over his eyes. What had he gotten himself into? He needed time to figure out what to do. Who was this woman and what did she really want? She could be dangerous. She was certainly crazy. The job she said she wanted would keep her close and placate her until he learned her true agenda.

"You'll start tomorrow," Brent said.

The woman looked surprised, then triumphant. She dug in her purse, pulled out a contract and handed it to him. He unfolded the paper, smoothed it out, and read it.

"I had it drawn up by a lawyer," she said.

Brent nodded and reached for the pen she handed him. He signed it and when she moved to grab it, he moved it out of her reach. The scent of fresh mown grass and sunny meadows assailed his nostrils. He remembered that scent. He remembered how incongruous he'd thought that scent was on a prostitute. He had expected her to wear something heavy like Giorgio or Red. The memory of how she'd deceived him sent pure fury through him.

"Blackmail sometimes has an ugly way of rebounding on the perpetrator," he said. Brent wanted to strangle her. He wanted to shake her until she begged him for mercy.

Kara's eyes grew wide and her complexion grayed. She made a quick move and the contract was in her hand.

"Tomorrow," was all she said before she left the room.

Tomorrow. Brent's thought echoed her word. Tomorrow she would regret she'd ever decided to play games with him. But first he needed to know her background, her motives, and most of all, whether she was dangerous to the congressman.

But when Brent picked up the phone to start the investigation, he found himself dialing the number of his old friend, Stone Emerson, instead of the feds he'd originally intended to call. Stone had a detective agency in Atlanta.

Brent wanted to deal with this woman himself. He would take care of her personally. Brent didn't bother to analyze why the thought gave him pleasure.

Kara's taut muscles relaxed when she finally stepped into her apartment. It had been hard to work after her ultimatum to Brent Stevens. Anxiety alternated with excitement, fear with exhilaration. The effort to do her work and remain outwardly as quiet and efficient as usual had been almost physically painful. A hot bath would feel great.

The doorbell rang, and Kara wondered who it could be. Her words to Brent about a friend having a copy of the papers she took from his briefcase had been a bluff; she didn't know anyone in Washington. She opened the door hesitantly. A woman stood in the doorway with a wide smile and a bottle of wine.

The woman wore her hair in dreadlocks, with a colorful scarf holding them back from her face. She wore brightly colored ethnic scarfs around her waist and at her neck. Heavy gold hoops hung in her ears, and she wore a ring on every finger. Tall and slim, she looked fashionable in a simple outfit of khakis and a white T-shirt.

"Hi! I'm Taylor, your next-door neighbor," she said, proffering her free hand. Taylor smiled and walked past Kara into the apartment.

"You're K. Smith. I saw your name on the mailbox. I've been meaning to stop by and say hi since you moved in. Do you have anything to open this with?" she asked, holding out a bottle of wine.

Kara shook her head no.

"Let's go over to my place then. By the way, what does the K stand for?"

Taylor walked out the door obviously expecting Kara to follow her.

Kara decided to take the course of least resistance. She

followed Taylor with the vision of a hot bath fading away.
"K stands for Kara," she answered.

Kara looked around Taylor's apartment. "I love your
apartment," she said. They were sitting on a soft futon
covered with hand-knitted and crocheted throws in bright
primary colors. The apartment smelled warm and green
with the profusion of plants. White shelves filled with
books, crystals, bright rocks, and other unnameable and
intriguing objects covered one wall. The place radiated life
and light.

Taylor wielded the corkscrew on the wine bottle with
expertise. She poured two large glasses of wine, and
handed one over. Kara took it and stared into the wine's
golden depths. She rarely drank anything alcoholic.

"Hungry?" Taylor asked.

"Not right now," Kara murmured.

Taylor got up and grabbed a bag of ready-made salad
from the refrigerator, poured it into a bowl, and shook
sunflower seeds and croutons over the leaves, and topped
the salad off with dressing. Kara lifted the wine to her lips,
and sipped. It tasted bitter and strong. She tried not to
sputter. It was an acquired taste, like coffee, Kara thought.

Taylor returned with her salad.

"I hate to cook," she said. "And I'm a vegetarian. You?"

Kara looked at her. "Yes, I'm a vegetarian, too." She
took a bigger sip of wine and smiled. She supposed her
answer wasn't really a lie, from now on she'd be a vegetarian. She'd always wanted to try it, but her mother said God
gave man the animals to eat.

"A vegetarian next-door neighbor. That's fantastic,"
Taylor said.

"I love to cook, too."

"Oh, girl, I'll buy the ingredients and you can make the
dinner anytime."

Feeling warm and relaxed, Kara noticed her glass was

half empty already. This wine was a quickly acquired taste. She liked it. Taylor refilled both of their glasses.

"Your space should reflect your soul," Taylor said.

"Your space should reflect your soul," Kara repeated slowly. "My space has never reflected me."

A solemn look crossed Taylor's face. "I felt that as soon as I walked into your apartment. You've never really had any space of your own have you?"

Kara hesitated. "I've always had my own room," she said.

"But it wasn't allowed to be yours. Everything was dictated by other's needs and wants. You've never been allowed to be you, or to find out who you really are. You're covered by layers and layers of . . . debris and masks, and it's hard for me to even discern who's underneath."

"How can you possibly know this?" Kara asked, poised to flee.

Taylor gulped her wine. "I'm sorry. Sometimes I get carried away and talk too much—or too soon. I'm very psychic. I get a feel for people right away."

Psychic, Kara thought. That word was heavy with connotations for her. She had always been taught that divination and any hint of the mystical would bring any practitioner or follower directly under the power of Satan's minions. A year ago she would have fled the room without hesitation. But now, she made no move. She couldn't feel any evil in this room or in Taylor, only concern and warmth.

Kara took another sip of wine and sat on the floor in front of Taylor. She'd decided when she moved to Washington, it was time for a new attitude to go with her new life.

"Ever since I was a child I could sometimes see colors surrounding people," Taylor said. "I knew things about people. The scariest thing was when I would think something had happened already and I would say something, only to discover such a thing never happened—yet. If I was certain, if I had seen it, it always came to be. I soon learned to keep my mouth shut."

"What do you know about me?" Kara asked.

"Only what I said. And I felt a strong need to go over and see you this evening. I don't know why."

Kara got up and poured the last of the wine into her glass. She'd always been so shy, a loner. Yet she was comfortable in the presence of this stranger, as if she'd known Taylor for years.

"Can you see my future?" she asked. Kara had a sudden intense longing to see what lay ahead on the path she had chosen.

"I don't tell fortunes," Taylor said.

Disappointed, Kara said, "I wanted to know if I'm making the right choices. "I'm going through a lot of changes right now."

Kara darted a glance at Taylor. She sat quiet and alert, waiting to hear more. Words started to tumble out of Kara. She never confided her deepest emotions to anyone, not even her mother, but she told Taylor everything.

Taylor was an ideal listener, attentive and responsive, also sharing her own goals and aspirations. They had started on a second bottle of wine when Taylor said, "You know what we both need?"

"And what is that?" Kara felt relaxed and ready for anything.

"Shopping! We need to go shopping."

Shopping had never been high on Kara's agenda. Her mother had always said shopping was a vain activity, and time that could better be spent in the Lord's service.

Taylor looked at Kara's navy suit. "Honey, I hope you don't take this wrong; you're really attractive, but if that's what you wore to work today, you need some new clothes."

Kara laughed. "You're right, I do need some new

clothes. I've been studying the magazines and I was planning to get some this weekend."

Shopping with Taylor this evening, instead of alone, seemed like a real good idea. She could start her new job with a new look.

"If cash is the problem, I've got plastic. You can pay me back," Taylor offered.

"You're sweet, but cash is no problem," Kara said, thinking of her hefty bank account. She stood up, and wiped imaginary crumbs from the front of her skirt. "Let's go."

Three

It was ten-thirty in the morning, and still no Kara. Brent spread her personnel file over his desk. Her past attendance and timeliness had been outstanding, so where the hell was she? He drummed his fingers on his desk. Maybe she wouldn't show up after all.

Regret unsettled Brent. He should be relieved, the woman was a major problem, a complication he didn't need.

How would he explain Kara's sudden appointment as a key legislative assistant for the congressman's new commitment to the nation's finance industry and urban affairs? Kara Smith was a nobody, with no relevant job history and no credentials. The congressman put a lot of trust in Brent; they went back—way back. Brent stretched that trust to the limit with the move he had just made. He couldn't confide in Sidney, there was no way he could justify allowing those papers to fall into Kara's hands.

He'd made a stupid mistake, an emotional mistake; a type he rarely, if ever, made. Kara Smith had the goods on him. He'd underestimated her once, but he was going to make sure she paid for underestimating him also.

Brent had just picked up the phone to call Stone about Kara, when Jenny breezed in.

"I've missed you, sweetheart," she cooed. "Did you get that rest you needed?"

Frustration filled Brent. He really didn't want to deal
with Jenny right now. He'd broken off their engagement
weeks ago. She simply didn't get it. But, he was trying to
be as gentle as possible. Jenny was emotionally fragile. He
didn't want to hurt her, he just didn't want to marry her.
It had once seemed so easy. She was crazy about him, and
she fit into his life perfectly. Sunny, uncomplicated, and
very sweet, she was all the things he once thought he
wanted in a woman—and a wife. He just couldn't love her,
and he couldn't imagine spending his life with her.

"I feel pretty good," he answered.

"Wonderful. I hope you enjoy this freedom I'm giving
you. But like I said, I miss you. How about dinner tonight?
And then afterward . . ." Jenny gave a suggestive smile.

A suffocating feeling came over him and he loosened
his tie. He was going to have to talk to her *again*. When
was she going to realize it was over between them?

"Are you okay? Maybe I can get you something?" Jenny
asked, sounding anxious.

"I'm fine," Brent said, irritated at her solicitousness.
Her sensitivity to his every mood and facial expression had
once enchanted him. Now, his irritation only added to the
weight of guilt for breaking up with her.

Jenny came behind the desk and perched on his lap.
She lightly kissed his forehead. "I know what you need,
and I've come to give it to you."

She ground her bottom in his lap and Brent felt
alarmed—surely she didn't want to . . . right here in his
office? He'd started to gently push her away when she dan-
gled a key in front of his face. "I've made reservations for
lunch at the Crown Palace. And I've got us a room for
dessert."

She bent to kiss him. "I've missed you, sweetheart, it's
been so long," she whispered.

His office door opened. Brent straightened, softly push-
ing Jenny off his lap. Kara Smith was standing in the door-

way looking shocked—and looking totally different. Her short off-white fitted suit outlined her curves, and her high-heeled creme leather pumps accentuated her legs. Her hair was down, but instead of the soft curls he remembered, she wore a sleek bob gently brushing her shoulders. Her makeup was natural and professionally applied. She was gorgeous.

Brent reacted more strongly to Kara than to all of Jenny's wriggling and fevered kisses. He put his hands in his pockets.

Jenny smiled at Kara and held out her hand, "Hello, I'm Jenny, Brent's fiancée."

Brent stifled a sigh. What was wrong with the woman? Was he going to have to hit Jenny over the head with a sledgehammer to get through to her?

Kara shook Jenny's hand a little stiffly. "Kara Smith, legislative assistant."

"You didn't tell me you finally hired the new LA, sweetheart. Daddy will be pleased."

"He'll be thrilled, I'm sure." A tinge of sarcasm colored his voice. Jenny gave him a quizzical glance.

Brent noticed Kara staring out his office window. She looked unhappy and preoccupied.

"We were just leaving for lunch," Jenny said. "Why don't you join us?"

"I don't think—" Kara started to say.

"I'm sure Kara wants to get acclimated to the office," Brent cut in.

"Brent, she's got to eat. Don't worry, Kara, he's not a slave driver, just a workaholic. I insist you come with us," Jenny said.

Kara looked toward Brent. Caught in the middle, he shrugged.

Jenny grabbed her purse, "It's settled then. Kara, do you mind following in your car? There's no way all three of us will fit into Brent's Jag."

* * *

Dear God, here she sat in this fancy restaurant with this huge menu in front of her, filled with completely unfamiliar choices, with her sister and her sister's fiancé . . .

Kara took a deep breath and continued to pretend to study the menu. And with the man she was in bed with the day before yesterday, who was her boss, who if he crooked his little finger she'd feel hard pressed not to jump in bed with him again . . . Whoa there, Kara, get a hold of yourself. She took two more deep breaths and tried to focus again on the menu.

Back at the office, Jenny had quieted when Kara said she didn't have a car. They all drove over in Jenny's yellow Acura.

Her sister was a nice person. Brent Stevens was a dirty dog. Her mother had been right about the way of men in the world. They were lustful liars and cheats.

The waiter approached, his pen poised over his pad.

"Oh, I'll have the chicken marsala, and your marvelous chocolate cake for dessert," Jenny said.

"I'll have the grilled sirloin steak, medium rare, and house salad with oil and vinegar. No dessert, no potato," Brent said, handing the menu over.

They all looked at Kara.

"I'll have what Jenny's having," she said.

"I'm so happy Brent has hired someone near our age. He has a full complement of all these dour political types working for him. There's nobody I can relate to. This is so great."

Was she for real? Kara wondered. Gazing into Jenny's sweet, uncomplicated face, she saw her answer.

"Where are you from?" Jenny asked.

Kara noticed that Brent came to attention.

"I just came to Washington about five months ago from Tyrone, Georgia."

"Is Tyrone near Atlanta?" Jenny asked.

"About two hours."

"I really miss Atlanta. This is the first time I've really lived away. I went to Spelman, and you?"

"I never went to college," Kara answered.

The remark just lay there.

"You must have tons of experience in politics, then," Jenny said, obviously eager to ease the awkward silence.

"No . . . not really."

Thankfully, the waiter interrupted with their food.

Jenny kept up her chatter during the meal, not questioning Kara again. She must have picked up on how uncomfortable her grilling made Kara feel.

Jenny's light honey-colored face was open, her emotions were open, too, and easily readable. A short froth of brown curls topped her sweet-natured features. She glanced often at Brent with affection. In contrast, Brent seemed quiet and reserved.

"I have something to confess," Jenny said leaning forward.

Kara raised an eyebrow. Brent looked uncomfortable.

"I got a room for Brent and me after the meal. We haven't spent much time alone together lately. Would you mind driving my car back to the office, and we'll take a taxi back?"

The waiter interrupted the sudden silence and proffered the check. Brent reached out but Kara intercepted him.

"This is on me," she said softly, laying down a VISA gold.

Emotions warred within Kara. Brent had brought Kara to this very hotel. She'd left the money he paid for her services untouched on the dresser. She'd be damned if she would allow Brent to pay her for anything anymore.

Brent looked irritated. Jenny thrust keys at Kara. "Thanks so much. We really appreciate it."

Jenny beamed into Brent's face. Kara stared at Jenny's car keys. She stood up.

"I have a meeting in a half an hour, Jenny," Brent interjected before Kara could speak.

Jenny looked momentarily dejected, then contrite. "I guess these things happen," she said, regaining her sunny smile. "I was being impetuous, I should have checked with you first."

"Well, let no one say Congressman Eastman's daughter is demanding," Jenny continued, dimpling up again. "Here, let me take you and Kara back to the office right away."

Nausea struck Kara at being reminded again that Jenny was her sister. She could see a hint of herself around Jenny's eyes. And in spite of everything, she still wanted Brent Stevens. She wanted her sister's man in spite of his cheater's heart.

"I want to walk back," Kara said. "I usually walk everywhere I can and it's such a beautiful day . . ." Kara turned away before Jenny or Brent could say anything and moved toward the waiter to retrieve her credit card.

She needed to flee and let the sunshine and fresh air burn away the darkness inside her.

Back at the office, Kara received profuse compliments on her changed appearance. Her male coworkers did double takes and a new assessment appeared in some women's eyes. She didn't feel awkward. Kara's new look fit her like her skin. She moved differently, more smoothly somehow.

She stared at the attractive, confident woman reflected in the harsh fluorescent lights of the employee bathroom. Where had the old Kara disappeared to—so completely and suddenly? She shrugged and lathered her hands with soap. She'd gone too far to turn back now, she was finally going to get what she deserved out of life. And with that thought, an inexplicable icy tendril of fear curled up Kara's spine. And what was it that she deserved?

Brent hadn't appeared back at the office, and no one said anything about her promotion, so Kara took up her old duties. She knelt to file a stack of papers in the bottom file. Finally finished, she straightened up and turned . . . and bumped directly into Brent Stevens. He looked like a thundercloud. He grasped her arm with an electric touch. Kara gave a tiny gasp and he jerked away as if her flesh was furnace-hot.

"Come with me," Brent said, nodding toward his office. He spun around and Kara followed. She saw the office manager looking after them both with a very puzzled gaze.

He closed the door behind them. "What do you want?" he demanded in a low voice, palpable tension building within him.

"I want to do my job," Kara said.

"What do you want?" Brent asked again. The atmosphere resembled a gathering storm.

Kara opened her mouth and shut it again. What could she tell him that made sense?

"Let me tell you that every move you make will be monitored and observed. Whatever your motive, you will not be allowed to compromise the congressman or this office in any way. Are you clear on this?" Brent said.

Kara ran her fingers through her hair and looked out the window.

"Are you clear on this?" Brent's voice whispered near her ear.

She turned back to Brent, and smiled. "What are my job responsibilities?" she asked.

Her bright, false smile showed him that she wouldn't allow him to intimidate her. "I'm looking forward to starting my new job."

Brent looked disgusted. "What do you know about banking?" He gestured toward papers on his desk. Kara saw her name on her personnel file.

"The only job you've had is as a cashier in a hardware store?" Brent asked.

Kara nodded. Brother Jenkins had owned the store, and he'd always tried to get her to work more hours.

Brent snorted and rubbed his forehead. "To start with I want you to learn something about government and the Banking and Finance Committee." He pointed to a stack of books and reports. "I got these for you to go over. Study all that and give me a full report on your understanding. Have it on my desk in a week."

The pile was easily three feet high. Kara looked over the material, and smiled serenely.

"No problem, I've already covered most of these books."

Brent looked shocked, then irritated. A profound sense of satisfaction filled Kara at Brent's reaction.

"Where do I work?" she asked.

"There's an intern's office down the hall. It's empty right now," he said.

She followed him to a dank, windowless closet, presently used for storage. She glanced around and saw plenty of electrical outlets and a phone jack.

"I'll need something to write on," she murmured.

"I'll have Katey install a computer."

Kara set the books she carried on the floor. She'd closed the door after she followed Brent into the office, and suddenly the room felt stifling. Brent stared at her lips. Her tongue involuntarily moistened them in preparation. The atmosphere thickened, and her breath came faster. Brent moved closer. Her whole body tensed and vibrated in preparation for his touch.

She looked down at her feet, anywhere but at him, then heard the sound of her office door shutting. Kara exhaled with relief. She'd been holding her breath. With every woman's instinct she had, she knew whatever it was between them was out of control. It was crazy, but it wasn't going away.

Congressman Sidney Eastman stroked his chin and waited for Brent to explain his actions. Brent dreaded this moment because he still didn't have an explanation for why he'd hired Kara for the much coveted congressional legislative assistant position. He couldn't even rationalize to himself why he kept Kara's blackmail secret. She should be sitting in jail right now with a federal investigation underway.

"She used to be a file clerk for God's sake. Here she appears out of nowhere and you offer her a prized job for which you've received dozens of resumes and have been interviewing for two months!"

"I believe she can do the job," Brent said in a quiet voice to counteract the congressman's rising one.

"You *believe*? Boy, you better *know* she can do the job, because your rear is on the line with this one."

He rose out of the chair and stalked over to the bar in his luxurious Washington office.

Brent watched as Sidney Eastman returned to his high leather chair behind his desk.

He sipped his drink and regarded Brent. "You know, boy, I think of you as a son, and I was looking forward to having you as a son-in-law." He picked up a picture of Kara and sniffed.

"She's a fine specimen," he said. "I hope you didn't hire her for the obvious male reason, because my little Jenny will be more heartbroken than she already is."

His little Jenny needed to get a grip on reality, Brent thought. "If my judgment is in question, there's no need for me to remain in your employ. My resignation is tendered immediately."

Brent turned to walk out. "And don't call me *boy* again."

He never would have put up with a white man calling him boy. He didn't know why he'd put up with it so long from Sidney.

Sidney quickly moved between the door and Brent. "Now, bo . . . Brent, don't get all upset. I trust your judgment. It's been a hard week, with this controversy about congressional funds going on. And you know how I look out for my little girl."

Brent shrugged his hand off his shoulder. "Yeah."

Once he'd loved Sidney Eastman like a father. The man had given him the opportunity to earn everything he had now. But now, into his second term on the Hill, he was turning into someone Brent didn't recognize, someone who courted business and dollars before the needs of people.

For Sidney to hold onto his power, money was primary. In a congressional election it took millions just to campaign; to win took more. Brent could see the power intoxicating Sidney Eastman.

Congressman Eastman fit well into the ranks of the GOP. He was their darling; a conservative, well controlled and predictable, his prematurely silver hair and blue eyes projecting a fatherly reassuring appearance and excellent camera presence. The fact that he was African-American was merely icing on the cake; he barely looked tanned.

The Sidney Eastman Brent once knew and loved was slowly slipping away.

"You know I'd never want to lose you as the key member of my team," Sidney was saying, looking like a well-satisfied cat.

He fed the picture of Kara into the paper shredder. Brent watched her features being swallowed up. It seemed a harbinger of things to come.

Four

"The biggest furniture place in town," was what the radio announcer said about the store. After work, Kara wandered the array of displays, each one with furniture artfully arranged so they looked like dozens of miniature rooms on the warehouse floor. Nothing made her pause more than a few seconds.

She left feeling frustrated, not having the foggiest idea of how to proceed. She took a taxi downtown, and spied a tiny little Italian restaurant on the corner. Her stomach grumbling, she had the taxi driver let her out.

The decor was amazing. The owner had an astonishing array of objects scattered about and hanging from the walls. A life-size inflatable doll struck her eye first, and something that looked like an antique washboard in a tub stood in the corner. The eclectic clutter somehow achieved a pleasing energetic, funky atmosphere. She wondered how they did it.

A friendly blue-jeaned waiter came to take her order. Afterward she spied a pay phone in the far corner and had the urge to call Taylor. They'd had such a wonderful time shopping for her clothes, maybe Taylor could help her out on this decorating thing.

No, she wanted to do this for herself. Taylor hadn't had much input on her style of dressing, she'd thought about the look she wanted for weeks, and it was just a matter of picking up the right pieces.

She'd do the same thing with decorating her apartment. She simply had to find the right style that reflected her. The problem was she didn't think she was going to find it in a department store.

The next morning Kara received an abrupt call from Brent summoning her to meet Sidney Eastman. She had no time to prepare. She hesitated before she opened the door to Brent's office. She'd fought hard to get to this point, she couldn't be weak now. She'd face her father. Kara wiped the sweat from her palms on the skirt of her chic new olive suit and walked into Brent's office.

Brent looked up. "Come in and sit down."

Kara looked nervously around Brent's office for Sidney Eastman, but didn't see him. She sank into one of Brent's comfortable leather chairs and stifled an urge to nibble on her nails. The soft, low chair seemed designed to throw visitors off base.

Brent gave her an assessing look. Kara resented the impression he gave of judging her.

"Sidney Eastman wants to meet with us. He's eager to meet his new LA and look over the ideas and input you have on banking and urban affairs. You do have a briefing ready?" Brent asked.

Kara studied her nails. Funny, she had no further urge to bite them. "No, Brent, as you are well aware, I have no briefing for the congressman to review." She settled into her seat. "But that's your problem now, isn't it?" she asked.

Brent's eyebrows shot up.

Kara stood up. "I need to go to the ladies' room. When you're ready to go meet with the congressman, I'll be in my office." She swept out of Brent's office without a backward glance, in spite of hearing small choking noises coming from his direction.

In the employee's bathroom she applied a fresh coat of lipstick and surveyed her image in the mirror. She looked well groomed and attractive. She looked competent and smart. She could pull it off—she would impress Congressman Eastman and to hell with Brent Stevens.

Brent waited at her office door when she arrived from the bathroom. Kara smiled at him sweetly.

Brent looked on the verge of explosion. "The congressman is expecting us," he said.

Kara followed him into the inner sanctum of the office she'd never had access to before. Instead of the gray industrial-grade floor covering of the congressman's outer offices, her heels sank into a plush carpet of deep green. Chandeliers sparkled, and the art on the walls was traditional and tasteful. A portrait of the congressman dominated.

An elegant woman with beautifully coiffed blond hair greeted them and led them to a massive oak door. She swung it open and led them into a luxurious office. A large leather desk chair faced the picture window. Her father. For a moment Kara couldn't breathe.

"Kara Smith, this is Congressman Sidney Eastman," Brent said.

The chair swung around and commanding blue eyes met hers.

He exuded power. He ran his eyes slowly up her form until they fixed again on her face. Kara got the impression Sidney Eastman missed nothing, from the tiny scuff on her Italian leather pumps to the quality of her Versace suit. He took his time standing up. He walked over to her and his hand swallowed hers.

"Ms. Smith," he said. "You've caused quite a stir around

here with your sudden appointment as my legislative assistant. I can't wait to hear your ideas." He walked over to his bar and poured a drink.

"Would you like something?" he asked Brent.

"I'm all right," Brent answered.

The absence of an offer of hospitality to Kara was noted.

Sidney Eastman settled himself on the couch. "Sit down, you two," he said.

Kara and Brent sat in each of the matching leather wing chairs facing the sofa.

"Well?" Sidney asked Kara.

Silence hung in the air. Sidney appeared to relish the moment. Then Kara cleared her throat.

"There are some issues coming up that will give you substantial leverage with your constituency, but they might necessitate minor changes in some of the statements you've made regarding several issues."

Kara launched forth her spin on the Banking, Finance and Urban Affairs Committee's upcoming agenda, and the public statements he'd made in the last year regarding the issues he'd have to deal with.

She paused at the end of her dissertation and looked at both men. Sidney looked to be in the unfinished act of lifting his glass. His mouth hung open. Brent looked stunned.

"Well?" she asked, her challenge neatly echoing Sidney's initial question.

He finally took a sip of his drink. "Well, young lady, it seems as if you may have something there after all." He looked over at Brent. "You may indeed. Bring her to dinner tomorrow evening, seven thirty sharp," he directed Brent.

If he wanted her to come to dinner, he could at least have the decency to ask her directly. What if she had other plans? Irritated, Kara opened her mouth to refuse, but then snapped it shut. She wanted to get to know her family, didn't she? Congressman Eastman had just handed her the perfect opportunity.

That afternoon, Kara was immersed in research when a knock sounded and a head popped in her office before she could answer.

"I just wanted to meet for myself the woman who's the talk of the office." A well-built and attractive young African-American man walked in without waiting to be asked.

"My name is Dante Eastman," he said, offering his hand, his smile open and friendly in a light cinnamon face, sprinkled with chocolate freckles and closely cut reddish brown hair. He was of medium height, and his muscles were evident even under his casual dress of khaki slacks, sweater, and loafers.

Her brother. Just great. Anxiety started to color Kara's bleak mood, and she hoped it wasn't apparent. She took his hand and shook it in a brisk business-like matter.

"Kara Smith," she said.

Dante's grin widened. "I knoowww," he said, dragging out the word. "Former file clerk turned legislative assistant extraordinaire. My sister says you're wonderful. But then, she thinks everybody is wonderful."

"How is Jenny?" Kara asked, eager to change the subject from herself.

"Jenny is fine, but then you can see for yourself at dinner tomorrow. When I heard the man himself, my dad, issued the invite, I had to meet you. This is not an ordinary occurrence, you must be quite special."

Dante's facial expression was unchanged, but his eyes were suddenly sharp and penetrating. "I'll be there myself, even though I'm canceling a date," he continued. "The man wants us at dinner and he demands his edicts be obeyed, especially by his employees and children."

Kara had no idea what to say.

"Well, it was nice meeting you," he said, turning to the door.

"Umm, nice to meet you," Kara answered, offering her hand. Dante took it, holding it a little too long. He gave her a very male, appreciative look. "I'm looking forward to seeing you there."

At seven sharp, Brent pulled up to Kara's apartment building to pick her up for dinner. As usual, the pit of his stomach ached when he saw her. She'd changed to a black dress that clung to every curve as she moved. The dowdy persona she'd assumed to trick him had completely disappeared. Brent's fingers tightened, and he felt momentarily disappointed that the steering wheel wasn't her neck.

She got in and gave him a cool nod. He pulled off, repressing the adolescent urge to burn rubber. The familiar clean, fresh scent she wore lingered. Tension vibrated in the air. He glanced out of the corner of his eyes and saw her lick her lips. Brent had a sudden memory of those lips caressing a strawberry at the hotel and he almost ran off the road.

"Do you want me to drive?" Kara asked. She looked alarmed.

Brent ignored her. What he wanted to say wasn't appropriate to express in front of a business colleague. He shot an exasperated glance at her.

"Keep your eyes on the road," she said, pursing her lips. "I want to get there alive."

Images of violence spun in front of Brent and he could actually feel his blood pressure rise.

"If you say another word, there will be no guarantee of that."

She sniffed, but was thankfully silent. Kara didn't seem fazed by the silence. She dug around in her handbag for something, and when she didn't find it, she let out a soft sigh. Brent's jaw tightened and a pulse throbbed there.

They were waiting for him and his protégée at the congressman's house. He dreaded arriving. The way things were between Kara and him couldn't go on. Someone would pick up on it. For the first time in his life, he was making a mess of things. He was usually so clear—others depended on him to make the hard decisions. This woman had made mincemeat of his emotions, and possibly even his career.

He pulled into a pancake house parking lot. "We need to talk," Brent said.

"We'll be late," she said.

"So?"

"The congressman said seven thirty. I hate to be late for anything."

Brent went around and pulled open her door. Kara hesitated, and Brent had the profound impulse to drag her from the car. Fortunately she decided to get out.

Once inside the restaurant, Brent said "Coffee for two," without even bothering to open the menu.

"I don't see what we possibly have to talk about," Kara said.

God, he wanted to strangle her.

"We need to talk about how I won't tolerate your lies and subterfuge a moment longer. We need to talk about how if you don't come clean about why you wanted the position this second, you're history, you're fired."

He finally had her attention.

"But, you signed the contract," Kara said.

"The hell with the contract. It won't hold an ounce of water in court."

"I'll have the papers released," she said in a voice so low he had to strain to hear.

The papers she had connived to steal from him.

"You won't get the chance, release the papers and I guarantee you won't see the light of day again," he snarled.

Kara's eyes widened. "Are you threatening me?"

"I don't need to threaten you. I have the force of the law behind me."

"Hmm. The force of the law," Kara echoed. "How will the force of the law feel about the way you virtually handed me papers compromising your employer? After dozens of guests at the cocktail party saw us leave? After being observed in a heated embrace by the limousine driver for an obvious sexual liaison as he chauffeured us to one of the best hotels in Washington? After being observed checking into the same hotel with me under your name with your credit card? Possibly the force of the law would excuse your carelessness that night, but I doubt Congressman Eastman would."

She had a point. His own actions had gotten him into this mess. He couldn't help but feel grudging admiration for her intelligence. Checkmate. Brent ran an impatient hand through his hair and smiled wryly.

"It looks as if you've got me there. Maybe we will need to work together a little longer, at least until I get to the bottom of this."

"There is no bottom. Like I said, I simply needed an opportunity. I don't see why you have an issue if I'm doing my job properly."

Brent didn't say anything.

Kara asked with an edge of anxiety in her voice, "I am doing my job satisfactorily?"

"Much too satisfactorily. How do you expect me to believe a file clerk with a high school education whose only other job was as a hardware store cashier could understand the inner workings of the government so effectively?"

She actually glowed. "Thank you, I studied hard."

Brent rolled his eyes heavenward. She drove him crazy.

"I think we should go. We're going to be very late," Kara said.

Brent sighed and gathered up his keys. As usual, an encounter with Kara Smith left him thoroughly frustrated.

Five

Kara stood with Brent at the doorway of a lovely old Georgetown brownstone, her father's house. A plump and stately African-American woman outfitted in full gray housekeeper regalia answered the door. Impressions of dark polished woods, and navy blue and cream colors, struck Kara as the housekeeper ushered them quickly through the Eastman home. Even Kara's unpracticed eyes appreciated the quiet opulence of the furnishings and the subdued traditional elegance of the decor.

When they entered the sitting room, all eyes turned to them. Sidney Eastman walked over to them.

"You're late," he said. He turned to his family. "I wanted you all to meet the person my AA promoted to be my banking and finance LA from the rank and file. Rank and file clerk," he repeated. He smiled at his own pun. "Rumor has it, he's considering the janitor to manage my reelection campaign."

Kara's eyes widened at the put-down Sidney Eastman didn't even bother veiling. Her father wasn't a very nice person. Kara felt Brent tense like a silent panther, waiting, watching, muscles coiled, ready in an instant to make the kill.

A woman glided over before Brent responded. "My name is Tiffany Eastman," she said, offering her hand to Kara.

Since Kara's mother had said her skin was too dark for the congressman, Kara had had a mental picture of Sidney Eastman's wife as a light, bright bourgeois society matron. That picture was shattered by the beauty of Tiffany Eastman.

Her features were striking and markedly African. Creamy, mahogany, flawless skin accentuated the woman's ageless beauty. Her neck was long, and her bearing regal. She appeared reserved and quiet, but not shyly so; Kara had the feeling she would speak up if she had something to say. How could Sidney Eastman marry this woman and be as colorstruck as her mother described?

Kara shook Tiffany's proffered hand and allowed her to lead her to the sofa. Jenny grinned welcome at Kara, than draped herself over Brent. Dante was standing in a corner with a cell phone against his ear, deep in conversation. He nodded at Kara and Brent.

Then, the housekeeper pulled open the double doors that led to a formal dining room, and announced, "Dinner is served."

Kara sat between Tiffany and Dante. "How are you liking our city? My husband said his new LA was from a small town in Georgia," Tiffany said.

"I love it, Mrs. Eastman. I especially enjoy the shopping." Kara indicated her suit. "Lord and Taylor has a fantastic customer service department, they call me when something they think I'll like comes in."

Tiffany's eyes brightened. "Call me Tiffany. You have discovered my weakness, I love to shop. I go to Lord and Taylor's all the time. Have you checked out Niemann's? They're famous for accessories."

"I love their stuff." Kara pointed to her shoes and scarf.

"You look great," said Tiffany. "We have to go shopping sometimes."

"That would be wonderful. I need to do some decorating, too."

"I must give you Anthony's number, he does a wonderful job. He did this house, but he does interiors for all styles and tastes. He's adamant about the space reflecting the dweller. He's really into Feng Shui lately."

Kara had no idea what Feng Shui was, but decided not to ask. "I'd love the help, I just don't know where to start."

Tiffany looked up the table toward Jenny who was gazing adoringly into Brent's face. "Poor Jenny trapped up there with all that politics talk. Brent's in love with politics. He's ambitious, too. I see him eventually carrying on the congressman's legacy."

"The legacy of kowtowing to business and special interests with money to fling around?" Kara asked.

There was a pause. Kara groaned inwardly. She'd have to watch her mouth. After being careful about whatever she said her entire life, now her tongue had a mind of its own and her mouth was starting to get her in trouble.

"I'm surprised to hear that coming from a staffer that he's just hired," Tiffany said. "But it's refreshing to see that Brent and Sidney are starting to hire people with minds of their own."

Tiffany leaned over to Kara and whispered. "Don't lose your opinions, but it might be wise not to be so open about them."

Kara nodded, mortified. The congressman's wife was giving her advice to be discreet. If she only knew how much Kara had to hide.

The first course was bouillabaisse, a French fish stew, full of several different kind of fish, shrimp, lobster, crab, mussels, and clams flavored liberally with wine, garlic, and basil. It was wonderful. Kara decided right then her new vegetarianism would include seafood.

Prime rib followed. It smelled so mouthwatering that Kara decided to let her vegetarianism go for special occasions. Dinner with her new-found family was special, even if they didn't know who she was.

"You're awfully quiet," Dante said.

"The food is delicious. I haven't been able to get my face out of my plate," Kara said, smiling.

"I'll tell the cook you enjoyed the meal," Dante said.

Kara wondered what it would be like to live with cooks and housekeepers taking care of all the mundane chores of life. Pretty good, probably, especially if they ate like this everyday.

"How are you settling in our city?"

"I've settled in well. Everyone seems to have the impression that I've just arrived in D.C., but I've been here for over five months."

"Everyone is wondering how you got that LA position. They're saying your prior position of file clerk hardly qualifies you. But then you must have some other qualifications that they don't know about, perhaps some hidden assets." Dante commented as his eyes lowered to gaze at her breasts.

"What everybody says about me and my qualifications doesn't concern me in the least." She turned a baleful eye on Dante. "And I really don't care about your opinion of my assets."

"Touché, prickly lady," Dante said. "Please accept my apology. I'd like to make up for my errant tongue with lunch tomorrow." There was no hint of apology in his grin.

Kara had never heard a young man say touché before or refer to his errant tongue. Her brother was a piece of work. She'd like to get to know him, but lunch would be a mistake. He seemed too interested in her sexually.

"No, I can't." Kara softened her refusal with a smile.

"Another time," Dante said.

"Another time," she echoed, regretting the promise even as she uttered it.

After the meal, they returned to the sitting room for coffee and tiny tarts and cakes.

Jenny hovered over Brent, positively oozing devotion. Kara smiled refusal when the housekeeper offered her cake. All the food she had eaten started to nauseate her. She kept her eyes carefully averted from Brent and Jenny.

She noticed her father stood aloof from his family, sort of like a king surveying his subjects. The phone rang, and when the housekeeper returned from answering it, she whispered in Sidney Eastman's ear.

"I have to leave," he said, addressing himself only to Brent.

Brent murmured goodbye and Sidney exited the room, not even saying goodbye to the family or Kara. His departure went totally unremarked on. Kara thought it strange that Sidney Eastman thought the only one important enough to say goodbye to was Brent, and that the family seemed to take the entire exchange for granted. Kara didn't think this was normal behavior, but what did she know about family?

Dante moved over and sat on the hassock by the chair she was sitting in. Before he could say anything Tiffany came over and gestured for Dante to get up and let her sit by Kara. He obeyed quickly, giving Kara a little wave goodbye.

"I wanted to tell you how much I enjoyed the meal," Kara said.

Tiffany waved her hand. "I'll tell our chef you liked it." Tiffany's eyes darted toward her daughter and Brent. "I'm going to ask Jenny to go with us on our shopping expedition," Tiffany said.

"That would be nice," Kara answered. What else could she say? That she felt uncomfortable around Brent's fiancée?

"I'd like Jenny to get to know you," Tiffany said. "She doesn't have any close friends since we moved to Washington. She was so involved with her engagement and her upcoming wedding, but now that Brent's called the wedding off . . . I feel a young woman should have other interests, don't you?"

"They're not engaged?" Kara asked.

"No, Brent broke up with her about a month ago." Tiffany cast a worried look at her daughter, who was grinning up in Brent's face across the room. "I'm afraid she thinks everything is going to be fine, that Brent will come to his senses. She's had a crush on him for years."

Kara was at a loss for words. Tiffany was confiding in her about her daughter, and Kara didn't want to hear more.

"Jenny seems like a nice person. She's so friendly."

"She's a sweet girl. I'm proud of her. But, Kara, I wouldn't mind her having a little of your spirit and self-possession. We all know that Brent did the best thing in the long run. She needs to move on. I think being around you will be good for her. She's all excited about your arrival. She's been talking about you nonstop all week."

"Oh?" Kara couldn't imagine why.

"I believe you're the youngest staffer Sidney's ever hired into a senior position. Do you mind if I ask your age?"

"I'm thirty."

"Jenny's twenty-three. You're older than you look, I'd have guessed early twenties, certainly no older than twenty-five."

Tiffany had just dropped in her lap the opportunity to get to know her family. She should be grateful, but she had mixed feelings. Jenny was obviously still in love with the man Kara was attracted to, she'd probably have to fend off her brother's advances, and she couldn't stand her father.

Brent Stevens was who she wanted to get to know better. Her own thought shocked her. Her sister's ex-lover. Kara saw Jenny smile up at Brent, and felt her stomach turn. She wouldn't allow that fact to escape her again. She'd gotten this job to be close to her father and his family, and already she was losing her perspective.

Kara and Tiffany carried on light conversation about shopping and the decorating plans she had for her apartment. Kara glanced at her watch; it was getting late. She looked toward Brent to see if he was ready to leave. He was engrossed in conversation with Dante with Jenny snuggled into the crook of his arm. Jenny intercepted Kara's look, and disengaged herself.

"I've neglected you tonight, but I haven't seen Brent for so long. I hope we can finally spend some time together this evening." Jenny looked toward Brent, her need for his attention plainly written on her face.

Brent approached, with Dante following close behind. "Ready to go home?" he asked Kara. As panic filled her at the thought of being in the small car with him, her eyes fell on Jenny's hand clinging to Brent's arm.

"Dante, would you mind taking me home?" Kara asked. "I'm sure Jenny wants to spend more time with Brent."

Brent shot an incredulous look at her and Jenny's face brightened. "Why, that's considerate of you, Kara."

Brent looked uncomfortable. "No, I brought you, I'll take you home," he said.

"Man, that's *okay*," Dante said pulling out his keys, grinning. "It must be my lucky day. Kara, let's go."

The next morning, Kara woke up much later then she usually did. She'd planned to spend the weekend studying banking practice in regard to real estate. She'd showered and settled into her books when her doorbell rang. It had to be Taylor, she'd forgotten completely that she'd promised to cook brunch for them both this morning.

"Is he gone?" Taylor whispered when Kara opened the door.

Kara blinked.

"I understand," Taylor continued to whisper, backing away from the door. "Some other time."

"What are you talking about?" Kara asked. "Get in here."

It finally dawned on Kara what Taylor meant as she closed the door behind her. "You thought that I brought someone home." The thought appalled her, remnants of her strict religious upbringing, notwithstanding her actions with Brent.

"I saw that hunk walk you in. He's built. Honey, he made me catch my breath."

"That's Congressman Eastman's son, Dante."

"You mean he's—"

"My brother." Kara finished the sentence for her.

"And he doesn't have a clue."

Kara shook her head.

"Watch out. He was looking at you like he wanted to eat you up."

"I know." Kara sighed.

"Your brother, yuk! That's too kinky for me."

Kara laughed and threw a cushion from her sofa at Taylor. "Don't even go there."

"You're getting awfully chummy with the congressman's family. Isn't all this kind of fast?" Taylor asked.

"I can hardly believe it. His wife Tiffany basically came right out and asked me to befriend Jenny. Dante wants to ask me out, and Tiffany wants me to go shopping with her."

"You're practically part of the family already."

Kara ran her hands through her hair, a pained expression on her face.

"Lighten up," Taylor continued. "Things couldn't be better. What about your father?"

Kara lifted her head. "I don't have a father, I have a sperm donor who abandoned me and my mother at the time we were most vulnerable and condemned us to a life of . . ."

Kara's words trailed away.

"A life of what? Kara, you told me about the strict and sheltered way you were raised, but that has to do more with your mother's choices than any decision your father made. It sounds as if there was a lot of love in your home between your mother and you."

"Yes, there was love. But there was also lack. We never had enough of anything. And in hindsight I hated the demands put on me. Sitting for hours in those hard chairs at the meetings, knocking on stranger's doors, never celebrating anything, being different. I hated it all."

"So why did you do it?"

"I felt I had to. I had it drummed into me from infancy that if I didn't comply with all the rules and requirements, God would reject me totally, that He would kill me. I thought that if I didn't do what my mother wanted, she would reject me also."

"That's pretty heavy." Taylor walked over to the couch and sat next to Kara. "I always thought God identified his own by their love."

"He does," Kara answered.

'Fear is the opposite of love," Taylor said. "When someone acts hatefully it's always because of fear. Human fears of not having enough, of losing, of being denied. When you obey because of the bad things they'll do to you, instead of being secure in love that they'd never harm you, I'd say that's fear."

"Fear," Kara whispered. She reeled a little, absorbing the implication. She was amazed at the magnitude of the insight Taylor had granted her so casually.

Taylor looked around. "Where's the food?" she asked.

Kara and Taylor were in the middle of making nut pancakes for breakfast, when there was a knock on Kara's door.

Kara frowned; she didn't know anyone in Washington except people from work.

"Aren't you going to see who it is?" Taylor asked.

Kara looked out her peephole and she saw Jenny's tearful face. She immediately pulled open the door.

"Come in, Jenny. What's wrong?"

"I'm so sorry to bother you. I don't know your phone number, but Dante told me where you live. I hope you don't mind."

"No, of course not. Come in, and sit down."

Kara drew Jenny to the sofa and sat down beside her. Taylor followed, proffering orange juice, which Jenny took gratefully.

"This is my neighbor Taylor," Kara said. Jenny nodded and smiled.

Then tears welled anew in her eyes. "I can't tell my mother this, but I had to talk to someone. I hope you can help me. It's about Brent," Jenny said.

Six

Taylor choked on her orange juice at Jenny's words. Kara wondered why Jenny would turn to her about a problem she had with Brent.

"Do you want me to leave?" Taylor asked, having recovered from her coughing spell.

"No, please stay, maybe you can help me, too." Jenny twisted her handkerchief, leaning toward Kara.

"I thought you could help me because you have it so together. I try but—I mean . . . Oh, he doesn't want me!" Emotion overcame Jenny and she collapsed into sobs. Kara handed her a fresh box of tissues.

"Last night I tried everything to get him to want me. But it didn't work. He- he . . . said he had to go, he had to get up to meet his friends to play basketball early in the morning!" Jenny let the last words out in a wail.

Kara looked toward the door. She wanted to escape her own apartment.

"If only I was as sexy and experienced with men as you are," Jenny continued.

Kara was speechless. Taylor snorted, and Kara darted a look at Taylor. She could do without the sound effects.

"Please help me. I would just die if I lost Brent!" Jenny cried with a fresh outbreak of sobs.

Kara thought Jenny's mother had said she'd already lost Brent. "Did Brent break off your engagement?" she asked.

"Not really. I think he needs a little space. If I could get him into bed, everything would be all right. I just know it!" Jenny choked out between her sobs.

Something sounding vaguely similar to a snicker echoed across the room. Kara looked sharply at Taylor, who was gazing at Jenny with innocent, angelic concern.

"When I tried to touch him, he—"

Kara found her voice. "We don't need the details." But Kara had to try to help her sister. That other Kara, the sexy, daring one, came naturally. When sexual sparks flew between her and Brent, that was the way it just was. She never tried to do anything, or be any way other than herself. She looked at Jenny, at a loss.

"Let me go get my cards," Taylor said, and left the apartment.

"She wants to go get her tarot cards," Kara explained. "She wants to read your future," Kara added in answer to the question in Jenny's eyes.

Jenny looked blank. "What does that have to do with anything?"

"She's really good, I think it may help," Kara said.

Taylor came back into the apartment with her cards and sat on the floor across from Jenny. She shuffled the cards and asked Jenny to hold them cupped in her hands. As Taylor spread the cards, Jenny waited eagerly.

Taylor stared at the cards and bit her bottom lip. "In abandonment, you will eventually find your strength," she intoned. "But heartbreak and desolation lie on the road ahead of you. A dark woman stands in the way of what you believe you want. Your fulfillment lies down a different path."

Kara couldn't believe her ears. Heartbreak, desolation, a dark woman? Taylor was tripping.

"But what does that mean?" Jenny asked.

Taylor shrugged. "It means what I said."

Kara wanted to kill Taylor.

The silence that followed grew uncomfortable. Kara twirled a long strand of black hair around a finger. Jenny stared at the cards. Taylor looked away.

Jenny cracked her knuckles and Kara winced. Jenny looked guilty and clasped her hands.

"Well, I better go," Jenny said. She gathered up her purse and walked toward the door.

"Thank you for the reading," she said. Taylor nodded and Jenny slipped out the door.

"That was cheerful. Couldn't you have said something to make her feel better? And you mentioned a dark woman! You had to spell it out for her, didn't you?" Kara said.

Taylor shrugged. "I can't control the way the cards fall. I read 'em like I see 'em."

Kara sighed. "I would just have liked to help Jenny feel better, that's all."

"With all you told me that's heating up between you and Brent, there's no way you're going to make her feel better."

"Jenny's so innocent and naive, she's like a child."

"I thought she was kidding when she first came over," Taylor said. "But she really has no clue."

"I know. I hate the thought of hurting her."

"Then don't. Lay off Brent."

"I'm not on Brent," Kara snapped.

Taylor got up in a smooth motion and headed back to the kitchen and the neglected pancake batter. "Then let the cards fall where they may," she said.

A week had passed, and the Federal Reserve chairman would be making a statement at a key meeting of the Banking, Finance and Urban Affairs Committee tomorrow. Kara had already called Velma and made sure the hearing was on Sidney Eastman's schedule. She'd thrown herself into preparing for this hearing, her debut.

Kara reviewed all the advance statements available for the hearing and prepared a list of questions and comments for the congressman that aligned neatly with his previous stance on the issues. She had her briefs in hand and she was ready. Kara would take her seat behind the congressman and march with him into the heart of the U.S. legislative process.

Kara gathered up her materials and walked to Sidney Eastman's office.

"Velma, I'm here to meet with Congressman Eastman before the committee hearing, as scheduled," Kara said.

Velma looked surprised. "He already left for the committee meeting."

"I'd better hurry to meet him there," Kara said, turning to leave.

"Kara, Bob Wilson went with him to the hearing."

The room spun for a minute and Kara shook her head slowly.

"Bob Wilson went to the Banking, Finance and Urban Affairs Committee hearing with Congressman Eastman," she repeated to Velma.

It was more a statement than a question, but Velma nodded anyway. Kara detected a hint of pity in her eyes. Fury built within her and she whirled, heading straight to the chief LA, Tim Redman. He was on the phone and he bid her sit down.

Kara's attention was riveted to a desk that had been empty yesterday. Instead of being clean and barren, it overflowed with papers. The trash can was half-full and a computer was in place.

Tim hung up the phone and turned to Kara. "How can I help you?" he asked.

"Velma tells me Bob Wilson went with Congressman Eastman to the Banking Committee hearing."

"Yes, and he took the new LA, Davis Stanhope, with him."

Kara was silent for a moment, struggling to get control of her emotions.

"Davis Stanhope?" Kara asked.

"Brent just hired him for the LA banking position."

Tim leaned back in his chair and watched her, enjoyment plain on his face.

"Thank you for the information," Kara said sweetly.

She didn't bother to knock before she burst into Brent's office. He was deep in conversation with another man. They looked up, startled at her entrance.

"What the hell do you mean by hiring someone for my job?" Kara demanded.

"I'll tell you what, Brent, this can wait until later," said the man, making a hasty exit.

Kara threw the briefing notebooks on Brent's desk. "You know the time I spent preparing for this committee hearing, and you didn't say anything—you just went and hired another LA behind by back! You—you monster!"

"I'm your superior," Brent said quietly. "I'd call speaking to me like that insubordination. You're immediately suspended—one week, no pay—and your probation is extended three months on your return."

"You can't—" Kara started to sputter.

"I can and I will. I won't have lack of discipline and displays of temper in this office."

Kara took a deep breath and looked at her shoes. "I'm sorry," she said. "I was out of line. It's just that I worked so hard on this, and I was looking forward to taking a part in the legislative process.

"I'm not clear on my job responsibilities," she continued. "I thought you realized I was working on the briefing for this committee hearing."

Brent sighed. "Banking is an intricate field. The legislation is complex. Right now there's a lot going on and there's media attention. I need someone next to the congressman who knows banking and the Hill inside and out."

"I believe I would be competent."

"Stanhope has a law degree, and three years of experience in corporate banking practice. He worked as chief LA for Congressman Avery for two years and has been on the Hill for the past six years."

"We had a deal," Kara said.

Brent slapped his hand on the desk. It sounded through the room like a gunshot and Kara flinched. She approached Brent, standing within a foot of him. She saw him tense, saw the pulse ticking in his jaw. She faced him. He looked down at her, at her lips, and fire flickered in his eyes.

Kara lifted her head, her lips mere inches from his. She could feel Brent's breath coming faster, his eyelids starting to lower.

"Will you reconsider that suspension?" Kara asked in a low voice.

Brent's eyes snapped open. The fire in his eyes turned to frost.

"This job means a lot to me, and I did apologize for my actions," Kara said.

"The suspension stands," Brent said, moving away from her.

"That's a clear violation of the contract you signed," she said pulling it from her jacket pocket.

"A guarantee of uninterrupted employment," Kara read. "You realize, Brent, when I release details about the loan to the media, I suspect Sidney Eastman will find your actions very hard to understand. If I were you, I'd seriously rethink that suspension threat."

Brent's eyes narrowed and his lips thinned. "I thought about it. You're suspended for insubordination. Now get out of my office before I fire you."

* * *

Kara lay on her couch in front of the TV. Her hand
hovered between the bag of chocolate chip cookies and
the bag of chocolate kisses. She chose the candy because
she was too lazy to get up and get the milk she'd want to
go with the cookies. There were three days left in the whole
week she had free to decorate her apartment and finally
get around to exploring Washington. The only problem
was she hadn't gotten dressed since she took off her
clothes to go to bed Friday.

She told Taylor she didn't feel good, which wasn't exactly a lie. She felt pretty miserable. So what if Brent suspended her. He was such a jerk. She hoped he spent all
week worrying if she was going to release the papers and
get *him* fired. Kara sighed over the growing mound of foil
wrappers from the chocolate kisses. The reality was she
richly deserved the suspension, and he'd called her bluff
without a blink.

She unwrapped another kiss and popped it into her
mouth. He'd won the skirmish, but the battle was hers.
The war was hard fought, but the problem was, like what
happened in most wars, Kara was losing sight of the reasons for the conflict.

Desire for revenge on her father was fading, and motivation to get close to her father's family was quickly reced-
ing. The more she learned about Sidney Eastman, the less
she wanted to know him, much less have him acknowledge
her as his daughter.

Every time her brother Dante hit on her gave her the
willies, and the fact that Jenny was her sister made her
miserable. It complicated incredibly her already confused
and complicated feelings for Brent. Brent. What her heart
desired. More than family, more than excelling at her job,
more than . . . self-respect. She'd been the jerk.

And she'd spent two days of her week off overdosing on

bad daytime TV and chocolate. She sat upright, dizzy from the sudden movement. She'd shower and dress, she decided. She had shopping and decorating to do.

That evening, totally exhausted, Kara let herself into her apartment and collapsed on the couch. She looked around her dingy, brown apartment, furnished in roadside motel decor from a rental place, in disgust. She'd found all sorts of pieces she loved and wanted to buy. The problem was none of them went together, and she couldn't picture any of them actually in her apartment.

Salespeople had shown her layouts of the various styles, contemporary, southwestern, traditional, Victorian, but none struck a cord within her. And she'd thought it'd be so easy to fix up a place if she had money. Well, she had money, but apparently she had no taste—in furniture, anyway.

Resolve hardened within her and she dug around in her purse until she produced a card. She held it up with glee. DESIGN BY ANTHONY, it read. Tiffany had recommended him highly and her house looked great. Kara picked up the phone to make the call.

Kara felt drained of emotion as well as money. Anthony had left her apartment. It had been more like a therapy session then an initial consultation with an interior decorator. He'd spent almost two hours delving into what he called her inner desires and needs.

While Anthony was very interested in getting into her inner desires, the attention to her body she'd gotten used to since her makeover wasn't forthcoming. Outrageously handsome, with deep blue eyes, he had eyelashes longer than she'd seen on any woman. Styled platinum blond hair topped pouty lips and great creamy peach skin.

He'd given her the name and address of his hairdresser, his manicurist, and the woman who did his skin. She wondered what someone would get done to their skin, but judging by Anthony's complexion, whatever it was, it worked. She'd never met anyone quite like him.

He assured her that she would be overjoyed with her apartment when he was finished and she trusted him. They'd clicked right off like she had with Taylor. Her hand only shook a little when she handed him the check for the initial payment for his services. He'd better be worth it.

Seven

"What do you have?" Brent asked Stone Emerson, the detective he'd hired to investigate Kara Smith.

"Man, I couldn't find anything new on her," Stone said. Brent's fingers tightened on the phone receiver.

"You're kidding."

"No. It is just as she says. Born and raised in Tyrone, Georgia. She lived with her mother until she died, then she took the insurance money, sold the house, and moved to D.C. But, hey, this girl was overdue for a change. She and her mother had been members of a strict religious sect their entire life. Until Kara split, she was an exemplary member."

"Stone, are you sure? It doesn't fit her actions."

"I have documentation. Man, I really worked this one for you. I have interviews on tape. I know everything about this girl. And believe me, none of it is interesting. She's probably the last thirty-year-old virgin left in America," Stone said.

Technically, at least, Brent thought. "What about family connections?" he asked.

"What about them? When the mother joined the religious sect, she was estranged from her family. The girl had no knowledge of or contact with them. The father isn't in the picture."

"What happened with the father?"

Stone hesitated. "I don't know. People say he's dead,

but there's nothing officially recorded, and the birth certificate has no father named."

"Find out about the father. And see if she had any clandestine contact with her mother's family. Follow up on anything you get," Brent said.

He hung up and drummed his fingers on his desk. Kara checked out squeaky clean, but it just didn't add up. He would figure out her game. In the meantime, he'd make her his personal assistant.

There was no other way to justify her presence on the payroll. He'd been due an assistant for some while, but he'd put off hiring one. Kara Smith would do nicely.

He'd have to get himself under control. He wanted to throttle or ravish her when she was near. Kara maddened him, but that was no excuse. He had control; he had cool. He'd always treated women with consideration and respect. His two sisters made sure of that. What was wrong with him lately? Brent didn't believe in problems that couldn't be worked out.

An inner voice whispered, why don't you fire her, and let the consequences follow. You could handle it. No way could it be as bad as what's going on now. The woman has you whipped—your emotions gone haywire, you going along with her every demand. Kara Smith is red-hot poison. Fire her. Fire her now.

"No." Brent rubbed his eyes. He was a grown man. He was in control. Kara would do a good job as his personal assistant despite her temper. She was intelligent, organized, and a hard worker. He would get to the bottom of whatever reason she had for tripping, and they would work it out. He ignored the foreboding feeling that his world was getting ready to spin out of control.

When she returned to the office after the suspension, it was as if nothing had happened. Kara got back to work.

She was concentrating on a brief she'd pulled up on the computer when she heard a knock at her office door.

"Come in," she called out absentmindedly.

"I thought I'd drop by and see you again."

Kara looked up from her computer and saw Tiffany Eastman standing in her office. Flustered, she stood up.

"How can I help you?" Kara asked.

"I was in the area and I wanted to see if you were free for lunch."

Kara thought, nobody is "just in the area" of Capitol Hill. But you don't turn down a lunch offer from the congressman's wife. Her stepmother.

"I'd love to lunch with you, let me get my purse."

The other staffers watched them curiously as they left. They took a cab downtown to one of Washington's premier restaurants. Tiffany kept the conversation general and light. Kara's confusion increased, but she didn't question Tiffany about her motives for this lunch.

"Would you like a drink?" Tiffany asked after the maître d' seated them.

"No, thank you."

"I'll have a martini," Tiffany said to the waiter. "Double and extra-dry."

"We had such a good time at dinner a couple of weeks ago. I'm sorry I haven't kept my promise to you about shopping, but I've been so preoccupied."

The waiter brought the martini and Tiffany took a sip.

"I'm worried about Jenny," Tiffany said.

Oh, no, maybe she knows what happened between me and Brent, Kara thought.

"But that's neither here nor there," Tiffany said. "You know why I want to talk with you."

Kara tried not to show her panic. She knows Sidney Eastman is my father. What am I going to do?

"I know you're sleeping with my husband."

Kara started to choke on her water. Paroxysms of coughing shook her. People started to turn in their chairs and stare. A waiter rushed over with water. Another waiter ran over. "I can do the Heimlich maneuver," he said, and tried to grab her waist.

Even though she was still racked with coughing, Kara gave him such an evil look, the waiter backed off. She buried her face in her cloth napkin and willed herself to stop coughing. It didn't work. Tiffany looked shocked and faintly disgusted at all the commotion. Kara fled to the bathroom.

The coughing finally stopped and Kara turned her face to the cool wall.

"Can I help you, ma'am?" the bathroom attendant asked.

Kara shook her head no, and walked to the sink and splashed water on her hot face.

Tiffany thought she was having an affair with Congressman Eastman. My God, the man was her father! Not that she could tell Tiffany that. Shit, Kara thought. The word felt appropriate.

"Shit," she said. She'd never said the word aloud in her entire life.

The bathroom attendant looked alarmed, but Kara didn't apologize. She dried her face and hands and strode back into the restaurant.

Tiffany was working on her second martini.

Kara slid into her chair.

"I'm so sorry you believe that I'm having an affair with Congressman Eastman, but you couldn't be more wrong,"

Tiffany took a piece of bread and buttered it. "Honey, you aren't the first, and you won't be the last. But you seem like a nice girl. I thought I'd lay down the ropes for you. He'll never leave me, you know that." She took a bite of bread. "I'm starving. Oh, I ordered for you. Shrimp."

Kara's hands clenched. "I am not sleeping with Congressman Eastman. The thought makes me sick. Whatever made you think such a thing?"

Tiffany started her second piece of bread. "That's a novel response," she said. "But you weren't at all subtle about it, honey. My husband's AA hires someone preeminently unqualified for the LA position for which he interviewed candidates for two months. Then he hires someone else to actually do the job. So what are you actually on the payroll for, honey? I always wondered, does getting paid for it make it more satisfying?"

I don't have to take this crap, Kara thought as she started to rise from the table. But then, she saw a lone tear roll down Tiffany's cheek. Raw pain reflected in the older woman's eyes.

Kara sat back down. "I'm so sorry," she said.

Tiffany's composure broke and she reached blindly for her napkin.

"I honestly thought those days were over," Tiffany said. "Lately it was getting better at home, he was treating me with a little more respect. But then you came."

"Tiffany, I swear—I swear I'm not sleeping with your husband," Kara said.

"I'm tired of being a fool. I'm just—" Tiffany looked up, her voice breaking. "So tired. I've had enough."

She looked at Kara. "If you want him, you got him. I'm leaving him."

"Don't leave him!" The words were explosive and Tiffany looked wonderingly at Kara.

"Don't throw away all the sacrifices you've made, the marriage you've built. Stand your ground and give it a chance," Kara said. "I'm begging you."

"Why do you care?" Tiffany asked.

"I don't know why I care so much. Maybe I don't want you to throw away something that could be good for something that's not true. I'm not having an affair with Sidney Eastman."

It was as if Tiffany didn't hear her.

"I never did this before, you know," Tiffany said. "Looked one of his women in the face. But you had the gall, the nerve to walk into my home, to invade my sanctuary. I don't know why I trusted you then. I confided in you. I asked you to befriend my daughter." Tiffany was shaking with rage.

Kara wanted to admit to Tiffany that she wanted her daughter's ex-fiancé, not her husband. She wanted to tell Tiffany she was accusing her of having sex with her own father.

Kara opened her mouth and nothing came out.

Tiffany stood up from the table, disgust and condemnation replacing the pain once reflected on her face.

"Stay away from what's mine, or you'll be sorry," Tiffany said in a deadly whisper. Tiffany spun and left the restaurant.

Kara sat there in shock, belatedly realizing that on top of everything, Tiffany had stuck her with the bill.

Kara's nerves were taut when she got back to the office. What a mess. She was getting to know more about Sidney Eastman and his family than she ever wanted to know.

The phone rang. "I want you to meet me in my office, now," Brent said.

What now? Kara wondered.

"Sit down," Brent said when Kara arrived. He leaned back in his chair. "I've been thinking about your job responsibilities and I've decided to give you the duties of my personal assistant—"

"That's out of the question," Kara said.

"May I ask why?" Brent said, his fingers steepled, his brow raised.

"You hired me as an LA, and that's what I want to be.

You can't go yanking me from job to job with no good reason."

"There is a very good reason," Brent said. That telltale pulse ticking in his jaw gave away Brent's rising agitation. "I have to justify your employment in the congressman's office."

"Well, you should have thought of that when you hired that Ivy league graduate for my job. A degree is just a piece of paper. And we have a deal."

"I'm getting quite tired of hearing about our deal." Brent's voice was getting lower.

Kara knew that was a dangerous sign, but she was upset. It had been a trying day, and at this point she could care less about Brent's temper. Her own had reached the boiling point.

"And what makes you think I could be your personal assistant. I don't want to be a secretary. And how could we be up under each other all day? You drive me crazy."

Kara narrowed her eyes as she glared at Brent. "Personal assistant?" she continued. "You didn't have one before, so why do you need one now all of a sudden? Just how 'personal' do you expect me to be? Uh-uh, no, forget it."

She turned to march out the door and felt Brent's hand on her arm as he swung her around.

"Take your hands off me!"

Brent instantly dropped his hands, and looked toward the door.

"Be quiet," he hissed. "Sit down and just sh—be quiet. We can work this out," he said.

Kara dropped into a chair, and muttered, "I don't see that there's anything to work out. I'm not—"

"Not another word."

He sat in the chair across from her. He appeared to be hyperventilating and his eyes were closed.

"What's wrong with you?" Kara asked.

His eyes flew open. "I don't suppose you realize how

near you are to death at this moment," he muttered. "But, I want to be logical and reasonable about this. We will work this out without me doing time in prison. The only way you can continue in the employment of this office is to take the open position of my personal assistant. That's the only option I can come up with."

"You need to rev up your imagination then, because there's no way—"

"It's either that or you're fired."

Kara stood up. "We've been over this before. You can't fire me."

"It's done."

"You know what I'm going to do."

"I don't give a damn. Release the papers. I'm tired of this."

"You are despicable," she said. "Your word is worthless. You make me sick." And much to her chagrin, she started to cry.

Brent handed her a tissue. She blew her nose noisily.

"It's been a hell of a day," Kara said. "Tiffany Eastman accused me of sleeping with the congressman."

"What?"

Kara nodded. It was all too much.

Brent sighed and she walked into his arms. He folded his arms around her and held her close. No thinking. No debating. Just a rightness and naturalness that told her this was where she belonged. They stood there for long minutes. His heartbeat, the rhythm of his breathing, melded with her own. Kara willed this moment in time to freeze, and never stop.

A tremor went through Brent's body. Kara lifted her head and his lips touched hers. Gently, a question, a mere caress—she wanted more. Her need became his and the hunger of his kisses drove away any other thoughts. Their bodies fused. Hardness and softness strained to each other. Kisses deep and devouring, they became one with passion.

The din of the phone jolted Kara rudely back to the reality of the office. They jerked apart, both breathing hard. The phone rang again. Brent walked to his desk and hit the speaker.

"Jenny is here to see you," the receptionist said.

There was a pause. They didn't look at each other.

"Send her up," Brent said.

Kara was already out the door.

Eight

The only reason Kara wasn't suicidal was that she couldn't think of any method that wouldn't hurt, or at the very least make her nauseous. What else could happen today? Her stepmother unknowingly accused her of sleeping with her father, and she had been ready to throw down with the man her sister loved, in his office.

She walked into her apartment and kicked off her shoes. Satisfaction flickered as she surveyed her apartment. Coming home was a joy since Anthony had finished her apartment. He was a genius and worth every penny she'd paid him.

The apartment had an Oriental feel, not Far Eastern, but the atmosphere of ancient Constantinople or Moorish Spain. Anthony created an aura of an Eastern harem without making the place seem like a whorehouse. He used color liberally, deep jewel tones, ruby, emerald, and sapphire.

It suited her perfectly, though she never would have guessed it of herself. Anthony must be somewhat psychic, like Taylor, she thought.

She left her shoes in the middle of the floor and curled up in her favorite chair. She picked up the phone. She couldn't wait to call Taylor. It had been a hell of a day and she needed to talk.

"Hi, Kara," Taylor said, picking up the phone on the first ring.

"How'd you know it was me? No, don't tell me. Psychic, right?"

"You got it. What's up?" she asked.

"Psychic or not, I bet you won't believe what happened to me today." Kara rubbed her feet. She wished she'd gotten out of these stockings before she called Taylor.

"Come on. Give it to me," Taylor said.

"Sidney Eastman's wife took me to lunch and accused me of sleeping with him."

"You're lying," Taylor said.

"No, I swear."

"Why'd she think you'd sleep with your daddy? Gross."

"It looked fishy to her, me being promoted from a file clerk all of a sudden."

"Well, it is kind of fishy, but that doesn't mean you're sleeping with him. It seems like she'd first assume you're sleeping with Brent."

"I think she's paranoid over her husband. Apparently he has a history of affairs."

"Geez," Taylor replied.

"And that's not all. Brent kissed me today."

"At the office?" Taylor breathed.

"Yeah. I was so upset about Sidney Eastman's wife, I started crying . . . and one thing led to another."

"Umm, was it good?" Taylor said.

"You're not helping. Yes, it was very good. But, it's not right. My sister still has a heavy jones on him. And if we're in the same room for more than thirty seconds, we're at each other's throats."

"Sounds like love to me."

"Oh, please. And, he's going to make me his personal assistant."

"His personal assistant! Now, you're going to be with

him all the time. You better either put a bed in that office, or get a mop and bucket to clean up all the blood."

"No. I'm going to stop this before it starts. I'm going to have a talk with him tomorrow," Kara said.

"It is a little doggish, hitting on you at work."

Kara instantly defended Brent. "He never hit on me, most of it was either my fault or it just happened. I'm going to have to make sure it stops."

"It's a regular soap opera over there on Capitol Hill. I can hardly wait to see what happens tomorrow."

"I can," Kara said. "I think I'm getting an ulcer."

Kara got to the office early the next morning to prepare mentally for her first day as Brent's personal assistant. She started the coffee, then ventured into Brent's office to check his calendar.

Kara almost jumped out of her skin when Brent's chair swung around from the window.

"I'm sorry if I scared you," Jenny said. She looked tired, with dark circles under her eyes. She reeked of liquor.

"I wanted to check Brent's schedule for today," Kara said.

Jenny waved her hand toward Brent's calendar. "Be my guest. Brent told me you're going to be his assistant. Please sit down. I could use the company."

Jenny held a glass of orange juice in her hand. She took a shaky sip. Kara got Brent's calendar and sat down in the chair facing the desk. She watched Jenny with concern.

"I know Mom thinks you're having an affair with my father. I asked Brent about it, and he said you weren't."

Kara's fingers tightened on the calendar she held in her hands. "I'm not having an affair with Congressman East-man," she said.

Jenny shrugged and gulped down the rest of the orange

juice. She reached for an open quart carton of juice and refilled her glass. "Want some?" she asked Kara.

Kara shook her head.

"Mom's been through a lot with Dad," Jenny continued. "A lot of women throw themselves at him. I guess it's the power thing."

Kara wished she hadn't sat down with Jenny. She longed to retreat to her office.

"I'm adrift here in Washington," Jenny said. "I thought about graduate school, but I've put everything into this relationship with Brent, and then he postponed the wedding. We argued last night, and he told me again that it's over, that he's never going to marry me. I know a man needs his space and all, but I can't wait until this male phase of his is over and we can get back to normal," Jenny said.

Kara looked at her in disbelief.

"He used to treat me like a kid sister," Jenny continued. "When I got back from college I flirted with him outrageously. He would grin and keep on treating me like a kid. Then I let Daddy believe we had been more intimate than we really had been. I guess he said something to Brent, because after that, Brent treated me differently. He treated me like a woman, and things went on from there. But now . . ." Jenny paused, sighing.

"He's been so distant lately," she continued. "He avoids me physically. He avoids me when I try to talk to him, and he denies anything is wrong. I'm going to talk it out this morning though. He can't run away from me in his own office. Do you know what bothers me most, Kara?"

Kara shook her head; not only did she not know, she didn't want to know.

"He's never said I love you. I tell him all the time, but even when he asked me to marry him, he didn't say the words."

"Why do you want to go through with the marriage after

he's broken . . . ?" Tears gathered in Jenny's eyes, and Kara's words trailed away.

"I want to marry Brent more than anything in the world. I'd make a good wife for him. He's politically ambitious and I know that type of life. I would help him."

Kara shifted uncomfortably in her chair. "I don't know what to say," she admitted. "Would you like some coffee? I'm going to get some." Kara stood up.

Jenny came from around the desk and extended a hand and rested it lightly on Kara's arm. "Thank you for staying and listening to me. You helped a lot. I hope we can be friends. I need a friend here in Washington."

Jenny was the little sister she'd always wanted, and she was hurting. A rush of sympathetic caring tinged with remorse filled Kara, and she gave Jenny a hug.

"It'll be all right, just hang in there. If you need to talk, give me a call." Kara scribbled her number on her notepad and gave it to Jenny.

Tears filled Jenny's eyes and she nodded staring at the piece of paper as she sat down.

Shock and confusion flooded Kara as she left Brent's office to get their coffee. What was in that orange juice? Jenny reeked of liquor. It wasn't even nine o'clock in the morning yet. Kara headed to the employee breakroom and poured a mug of coffee.

Jenny needed this coffee more than she did. Kara stopped at her office and dug some breath mints out of her purse on her way back to Brent's office.

Jenny was leaning against the window, staring out, the glass of orange juice clutched in her hand.

"Brent—" Jenny started to say, as Kara came in.

"Brent's not here yet. Maybe you should reconsider talking to him until later," Kara said.

"Why?"

Kara took the glass of orange juice. "That's why," she

said, handing Jenny the coffee. "It's obvious you've been drinking, and Brent would pick up on it immediately."

Uncharacteristic hardness filled Jenny's eyes. "Why do you care?" she asked.

Kara paused. Jenny's mother asked her the same question yesterday. Because you're my sister, Kara wanted to answer. Because I've always wanted a sister more than anything, and you're what I pictured she would be like. Sort of. Because I want you to care about me, too.

Kara said none of those things. "You asked me to be your friend," she replied.

She laid the breath mints down on Brent's desk. "I think you should go before Brent gets here. Did you drive?" Kara asked.

"Yes," Jenny whispered.

"Give me the keys right now," Kara demanded.

Jenny meekly handed her purse over. Kara got Jenny's keys out.

"Come on," Kara said, "I'm calling a taxi."

Kara had the cab driver pick Jenny up in the back so they wouldn't see Brent.

Kara had never known anyone who drank alcohol, having grown up in a church that forbade it. Jenny's use of liquor to deal with her pain seemed pathetic and self-destructive. Regret washed through Kara in waves. Was she responsible for Jenny's pain, for her drinking? Would Jenny manage to get back with Brent if it weren't for her? Kara was the villain in this scenario and she hated it.

Kara touched her lips; the memory of Brent's kiss burned.

"Never again," she whispered.

When Kara returned to the office after helping Jenny into the cab, she expected Brent to jump all over her for being late.

"Good morning," Brent said. He didn't seem as confident and breezy as usual.

"The coffee is excellent this morning," he said. "Would you like to go get a cup before we meet?"

"No, I'm all right. I already reviewed your appointments today, there is an hour before lunch available to go over my job duties."

"There are some changes and my appointments have to be rescheduled, but first, sit down. We need to talk."

Kara sat.

"You're my employee. That fact makes my conduct reprehensible. I want to apologize to you. I wanted to let you know that what happened yesterday isn't going to happen again."

Kara bit her lip, and plunged in to say what she had on her mind. "Is there any chance you and Jenny could get back together?" she asked. "I don't want you not to get back with her because of me." Kara remembered Jenny's lost, pained eyes. "She loves you so much."

"I'm not so spineless that I'd need to use you as an excuse to extricate myself from an entanglement with Jenny. Anyway, I'd broken up with her before I met you." Then, Brent frowned and ran his hand over his hair. "Why am I discussing this with you?" He walked behind his desk.

"The congressman wants to meet with me ASAP. And I need to talk to Congressman Ridgeway's AA after lunch. Two lobbyists left urgent messages for me. I'll meet with them early this afternoon. Fit whatever appointments you can around that."

Kara stood and looked at him, bemused.

"Well? What are you waiting for? I'm having maintenance set up a desk for you outside my office. After you reschedule my appointments, you can move your stuff out. I almost forgot, I need you to get a briefing on Congressman Coffey's policies on the budget and economic policy to Bob Wilson right away. He's overwhelmed with work right now. Schedule a staff meeting for next week, we're overdue for one. The congressman likes mornings."

With that torrent of words, Brent picked up his suit jacket and walked out the door past Kara.

Kara snapped Brent's calendar shut and closed her eyes for a moment, praying that Brent would make up with Jenny. Her guilt wasn't relieved by Brent's words or the fact that she'd give almost anything for him to hold her in his arms again.

"If I go out with you today, will you promise to leave me alone?" Kara spoke in the phone in a furious whisper, all too aware of the office staffers going to and fro past her new station right smack in the middle of the hallway in front of Brent's open office door.

Kara wanted to slam the phone in the cradle. Dante Eastman had been calling her for the past week every hour, on the hour, begging her to go out with him. He wouldn't take no for an answer.

With the palpable tension between Brent and her at the office, and her coworkers avoiding her as if she were poison, Kara's nerves were stretched to the limit. Apparently rumor had it she was sleeping with the congressman.

Brent worked her hard. Kara didn't know how he'd coped without an assistant before. She got home exhausted every evening.

Jenny called every night, but Kara let the answering machine pick up. Apparently Jenny still couldn't get Brent into bed. Kara didn't know what to say to her.

Now, Dante was hounding her. Kara wondered if persistence ran in the family. She'd finally given in to Dante, anything to get him to leave her alone. She hoped he was a man of his word, and would now leave her alone.

"If you're going out to lunch, be sure you get back in time," Brent said, standing by her desk.

Damn, had Brent heard every word she said on the phone?

"Do you have the letter to Goldman drawn up?" Brent asked.

Kara nodded.

"Bring it in, I'm going to have to make some changes." Wordlessly she picked it up and followed Brent to his office. Without thinking, Kara shut the door behind her. Suddenly Brent's office seemed very small. She sank into a leather chair. Brent didn't go behind his desk. He picked up his legal pad and sat in the chair across from her.

"I've jotted down what I need to add to the letter. The first point . . ."

Brent's voice faded in the background. She could smell the Ivory soap she knew he showered with every morning. The thought brought an image of Brent in the shower. Golden skin, lean muscles, firm, round rear, heavy—she became aware of her breath coming fast and she crossed her legs, trying to banish the thought.

Brent was no longer talking. He was staring at her thighs. Heat shimmered between them. Tiny beads of sweat broke out on Brent's upper lip. Kara longed to kiss them away.

"Umm, what were you saying?" Kara asked. "I missed the last part."

Brent's lips were so firm and well shaped. She didn't like thin or overfull lips on a man. His lips were perfect. She involuntarily shivered as she remembered how and where he'd kissed her on their first meeting.

The room went silent again. Thick, heavy silence, redolent with ghosts of passion. Brent cleared his throat. He handed the legal pad to Kara.

"Here, take my notes, and make the changes accordingly." She reached for the pad, and their hands touched.

Electricity coursed through Kara and they stood there for what seemed an eternity.

"Okay," Kara stammered, and fled from the office back to her safe haven in the hallway.

He hadn't meant to listen, but he couldn't help but hear Kara promise a lunch date to some bozo on the phone. Whoever it was called all the time. He needed to learn when to give it a rest.

He replayed the image of Kara as she'd walked into the office with her graceful, catlike walk. Kara looked good in yellow. But then, everything looked good on her. When she sat down in the chair, her skirt had hiked up a few inches, exposing her creamy chocolate thigh. Her generous nipples showed through the bra she wore under her golden silk blouse. Brent remembered their sweet honey flavor. He wrenched his mind away from that dangerous memory.

He was going to do something about the dress policies in this office. Skirts should be below the knee, and women should wear those Cross-Your-Heart bras he saw advertised on TV. Those bras looked sturdy.

Brent had felt himself go rock hard. Did she know what she was doing to him? Fortunately, Kara had cleared out of the office quickly.

Whenever Kara came within ten feet of him, it took all his will not to ravish her. Jenny, on the other hand, had taken to more and more obvious sexual blandishments than when they were engaged, and he couldn't respond to her in the slightest. Making love to Jenny held the appeal of making love to his kid sister. That is, none at all.

And now, every time he turned around, Jenny was there. She'd start to cry, cling to him, and tell him how much she loved him, how she couldn't live without him.

Brent loosened his tie. This couldn't go on. Tonight he'd try again to make sure she understood it was the end and there was no going back.

Nine

Dante stared hungrily into Kara's eyes.

"There's something undefinable about you that excites my imagination," he said.

Kara looked away and stifled a sigh. She dearly regretted having lunch with Dante. It wasn't as if Dante was that bad, flowery talk and all. It was that he was her little brother, and he was hitting on her so hard it was freaky.

She'd gotten him to drop the lines long enough to learn he had a law degree from Howard University, and he had a new job in the public defender's office where he was already a shining star. He was on his way to becoming the next Johnnie Cochran.

"Just relax, and let it be. We belong together, you and me, why fight it?" Dante said.

Kara started to laugh. "You're full of it, you know that?"

Dante started to look offended, then he relaxed and took a sip of his ice tea. Chuckling, he replied, "Kindred spirits recognize each other."

"Don't give me that kindred spirit crap, you're the one who dumped the manure so deep we're going to have to wade out of it. I thought any minute you were going to give an ode to my armpits," Kara said.

Dante raised his hands, grinning, "I give up."

"Do you really?" Kara asked. "You said you'd lay off me if I went to lunch with you."

"My word is my bond. Although I had hopes of charming you so much, you'd have to go out with me again."

"I'd think you'd have women all over you, seeing the shortage of eligible, professional, attractive, single, African-American men."

Dante's smile widened. "That description is a lot to live up to. But thanks, anyway. That's all the more reason you should go out with me."

Kara shook her head. "I'm interested in someone else," she said.

Dante's smile faded. He leaned forward, his eyes suddenly serious and intense. "So what's the deal? Is it true what they say about you?" he asked.

Kara stopped her fork midway to her mouth. "Is what true?" she asked. She knew what he was going to say, but she wanted to hear it from him.

"That you're sleeping with my dad."

The words shook her, but she remained outwardly cool. She laid the fork down on her plate.

"No, it's not true. Is this what it's all about? You want to trespass on what you believe is your dad's territory?"

"You should give me a try. I'm younger, undoubtably I have more stamina. I can make it worth your while. What do you see in the old man anyway? Is it his money?"

This was getting ugly. "It sounds like you need therapy," she said quietly.

Silence hung heavily over the table. Dante rubbed his eyes. "What came over me? I'm sorry. You don't deserve this scene, even if you are sleeping with my dad. You're right about one thing. I probably do need therapy."

Dante looked so woebegone that in spite of the ugly things he said, she almost forgave him. Almost.

"I'm not sleeping with Sidney Eastman. Brent gave me the position—"

"Brent," Dante interrupted. "It's Brent, isn't it? Poor Jenny. At least she won't ride down the same road my mom does . . . those empty nights alone. At least Brent ended it when he saw something he liked better."

Alarm filled Kara at her brother getting it right, and so quickly. He was no dummy. A line from a TV show she had watched last night came to her—"Deny everything."

"I don't know what you're talking about," she said.

Dante looked amused. "Don't worry. It's none of my business. It's just if you and my father were together . . . see, we have a little competition going on."

Kara said what she thought. "Sounds sick to me."

"Believe me, it is," Dante said.

Kara was deeply disturbed when she left the restaurant. She didn't know what to make of Dante, except he was a man in pain. She hoped he'd get it together, at least get therapy. She took long strides out of the restaurant, and raised her fingers to hail a taxi.

Once in the taxi, Kara wondered what it was with her. Every relationship she tried to start with a member of her family turned disastrous. Her family. It was laughable. She had no family, had never had any, except her mother, who made sure because of their religion Kara was always on the outside looking in.

She thought about the plans that once obsessed her; the plans to extract revenge from Sidney Eastman for abandoning her mother. Revenge seemed small and petty, and . . . purposeless. After getting to know his children, Kara realized she was probably better off not growing up with him as a father.

She needed to concentrate on her own desires. She wanted to excel at whatever she did. She wanted Brent. Okay, so she wanted a lot, and getting even with Sidney Eastman wasn't high on her list anymore.

Taylor said family members were psychically connected, and impacted on each other throughout lifetimes. The effect Kara had on her family seemed uncanny. It was as if they recognized her and were attracted to her in some way—like a snowball, gathering momentum, barreling down the cliff. The problem was Kara was standing in the way.

Eight o'clock and Brent was just getting home. He tossed a frozen dinner into the microwave and popped open a Coke when the doorbell rang.

Jenny stood in the door swathed in a black fur coat. It was getting cooler outside, but it wasn't that cold yet.

"Aren't you going to let me in?" she asked in a husky voice.

"Come on in," Brent said. "I was just going to eat. Do you want a frozen dinner?"

She didn't answer and he took that for assent. He went into the kitchen and started rifling through the freezer.

"I've got about anything you'd want. Chicken, fish, beef, Chinese, Mexican, Italian," Brent called.

"Come out here," Jenny said.

"You want a Coke?"

"Brent, come out here." Jenny started to sound impatient.

Brent went back into the living room and paused. Jenny was standing there buck naked with the fur coat puddled around her feet.

"Jenny! The window's open," Brent said, hurrying to close the blinds.

He heard a sniffle behind him and dreaded turning around. Jenny cried more than should be allowed by law. He was getting tired of it.

"What's wrong, now?" he asked, trying to keep the irritation out of his voice.

Jenny had sunk into the coat on the floor, sobbing. Brent got on his knees and tried to pull the coat over her.

"Calm down, Jenny. What happened to your clothes?" A horrible suspicion struck Brent. "Have you been assaulted?" he asked.

She sobbed louder. "I'm going to call the police," Brent said, rising.

"No!" Jenny cried out.

"I know it's hard, but we have to call the police. Don't worry, I'll stay right beside you through it all."

"I haven't been raped," Jenny cried. "I was trying to turn you on!"

"Oh," Brent said.

"It's no use," she sobbed. "It's just no use."

Not knowing quite what to do, Brent got Jenny some tissues and sat beside her until she quieted down. Finally she lifted her tear-streaked face.

"You're not gay, are you?" she asked hopefully.

Brent's eyes widened. "Noooo," he answered. He'd never been asked that one before.

"Then it's me, isn't it? I knew it, it's me. I'm so skinny and ugly."

"Jenny, stop it," Brent said. "You're not skinny or ugly. You're a very desirable young woman."

"But," she said bitterly. "There's a but in there somewhere, isn't there?"

Brent nodded. "It would have been a mistake for us to marry," he said.

Jenny started to sob again.

"Don't do this to yourself. You said you've had a crush on me ever since you were fifteen. That's not love, baby, that's hero worship. I'm not all that."

Jenny stood up and drew the fur coat close to her.

"Yeah, you got one thing right. You're not all that." And then she stormed out of the apartment.

Brent wished he'd given her something to put on, a sweatsuit or something. He was worried about her. He started after her, but heard tires squealing and the flash of her yellow Acura streaking by. He sighed. Jenny was a big girl. She'd be all right.

That night Kara stretched voluptuously in her new bed with four high posts and a canopy draped with diaphanous white fabric. Aretha was playing on the CD, and scented candles burned.

She and Taylor had gone out for Thai food and it was great. She'd never had Thai food before, they were trying a new cuisine every week.

Aretha came to an end and soft jazz came on. She wanted more Aretha but she was too lazy to get up, and she couldn't reach the remote. She blew out the candles beside her, and her thoughts drifted until they rested on Brent. She'd wondered what it was like, the love between a man and a woman. Brent had given her a taste, but her body longed for the real thing.

Memories of Brent's lips tasting her all over burned in her mind. She imagined Brent's hands touching her everywhere, and running her hands over his satin skin, so like hers, but different. Touching that part of him that was so different.

How would it feel plunged into her to the hilt? How would it be if he shuddered his completion within her, spilling his warm seed deep in her womb, while she held him tight in her arms? How could this be a mortal sin when it would feel so right? So right . . . Kara thought as she finally drifted off into sleep.

The ring of the phone jarred Brent out of a sound sleep. He blearily looked at the clock. Four thirty-seven A.M., and who the hell could it be? The phone rang again and he grabbed it. "Hello," he croaked.

It was Sidney. "Jenny's been in a terrible accident, get down to Memorial Hospital now," he barked.

"How is she? Is she all right?" Brent asked, but the phone was dead. Sidney'd already hung up.

He sat on the side of the bed with his head in his hands. Guilt rocked him. It was all his fault. He should never have been so blunt. Jenny was fragile.

He groaned and pulled on a pair of jeans and a sweat-shirt.

Bright, harsh, fluorescent lighting greeted Brent when he arrived at the hospital's emergency room. He was es-corted to the private room reserved for VIP's where the congressman and his family waited. Tiffany's face was turned to the wall and Dante was bent over his mother. Brent went to Sidney, who was seated in the middle of the room staring at a magazine.

"How is she?" Brent asked.

"She's in surgery. Her injuries are grave. Abdominal trauma and internal bleeding. Possibly some trauma to the spinal cord."

"My God," Brent said.

He sank into the chair next to him and the waiting be-gan.

Several hours later the surgeon walked in. "She'll prob-ably make it," he announced, wasting no time getting to the point.

Tiffany started to cry and Dante buried his face in his hands.

"What about her spinal injuries?" Sidney asked.

The surgeon looked somber. "We won't know if she suf-fered significant cord injury or if it's just swelling for sev-eral days, maybe weeks. We just have to wait. And pray," he added.

Then he seemed uncomfortable. "Someone else wants

to see you," he said to Sidney. He looked toward Tiffany. "Not here though, please follow me."

Sidney Eastman looked to Brent, and for once Brent saw his calm, dignified exterior start to crack. "Can he come with me," he asked. "He . . . he was her fiancé."

The surgeon nodded and Brent and Sidney followed the surgeon to a small room where two men, obviously plainclothes policemen, waited.

"We have bad news, Congressman Eastman," one of them said. "You may want to sit down," Sidney remained standing.

"What do you have to tell me, gentlemen?" he asked in clipped tones.

The detectives flipped open a pad. "It was a bad accident, Congressman. Your daughter was mighty lucky. Three cars were involved. There were two fatalities—a thirty-one-year-old man and his infant son."

"I'm sorry," Sidney murmured automatically. Brent was silent, sensing the worse was to come.

"Your daughter's blood alcohol was twice the legal limit."

"It's not possible," Sidney said, his lips barely moving.

"She crossed the meridian into oncoming traffic. The family she hit didn't have a chance. The fatality's wife survived, and she wants to press charges to the full extent of the law."

"No," he said.

"The doctor says your daughter's likely to be all right, and I'm glad. But you'd better get her a damned good lawyer."

The detective walked to the door, the other one following. He turned with his hand on the knob. "Congressman, I don't see how you can keep the press off this one. Prepare yourself."

Sidney's face crumpled, and he looked old and defeated.

"What am I going to do?" Sidney Eastman asked. "What am I going to do for my baby?"

Brent's heart went out to Sidney and the Eastman family. He was sick with worry over Jenny. But he couldn't get the echo of what the detective said out of his head. Jenny's blood alcohol twice the legal limit . . . a man and his infant son dead. The wife left alive, her family wiped out in an instant.

"Everything will be all right," Sidney was saying. "I'll get the best lawyer possible. Cecile'll handle the press, there's no one better. My little girl is going to be okay, isn't she? My little girl's going to be fine."

Brent nodded, a sinking feeling within him. There was no way he was going to tell Sidney Eastman and his family that he'd rejected Jenny prior to the accident. That it was his fault. Visions of a dead father and son flashed in front of Brent. All his fault. All because he dumped Jenny Eastman.

When Kara got to the office the next day, Brent wasn't there, phones were ringing off the hook, and Velma, Cecile, and her assistants were scurrying around like ants.

"What's going on?" Kara asked Velma as soon as she could corner her. Velma was one of the few people in the office who was cordial to her.

"Didn't you hear? There was a horrible accident and Jenny Eastman's in intensive care at Memorial Hospital. It was on the news this morning that Jenny was drunk and killed a father and his baby son."

Blood drained from Kara's face, leaving her ashen. "Oh, no," she breathed.

Kara had to show her credentials to get past security and get on the same floor where Jenny was. They wouldn't let her see Jenny or give her any information, but eventually they ushered her into the room where the family waited.

Tiffany saw her first. "You have the gall to show up here. How could you?" she shrieked. Tiffany appeared ready to launch herself at Kara, and Kara shrank away.

"You'd better get her out of here," Dante said, looking at Brent.

Sidney Eastman didn't look up. He sat in a corner, his head in his hands.

Brent grabbed Kara by the arm and led her out of the private waiting room, none too gently. "Your timing is poor," he said. "I'm surprised they let you in, only family is allowed."

"That's the point," Kara said, breathing deeply. Brent looked confused.

"What do you mean?"

"Nothing. How—how is Jenny?" Kara asked.

"She's in serious but stable condition." Brent said. "It appears that she's going to make it, but we don't know yet if she'll walk again. Her spinal cord may be injured."

Kara bent her head and shivered in reaction.

"Whatever possessed you to show up here?" Brent asked. "It's really not appropriate."

Kara shook her head, not trusting herself to speak. It seemed as if she was forever on the outside looking in. Brent was right. She didn't belong here.

"Jenny means a lot to me," Kara said. "She asked me to be her friend. I never was a very good friend, but I cared. Please call me if there's a change in her condition."

And Kara walked away without looking back.

Ten

It was 9:00 P.M. Kara was finishing up for the day when Brent walked passed her desk into his office. Kara followed him, prepared to go over his next day's schedule with him. They'd fallen into a routine in spite of all the time he spent at the hospital with Jenny.

"How is she?" Kara asked Brent.

Brent sighed and rubbed his eyes. "Stable for now," he said. "There's still no response from her muscles below her waist."

"How is she taking it, Brent?"

"Surprisingly well. Everyone's giving her as much support as they can. She hasn't been told about the full ramifications of the accident. Stacey Bailey, the widow, is pressing charges."

"How awful," Kara said.

"Tomorrow, I want you to meet with Tom Handley, he's a lobbyist who's extremely important to our team. I have a standing appointment with him this time every month. And clear my calendar as much as you can. Jenny says she needs me to spend more time with her."

Kara nodded.

"You look exhausted," she said. "Take care of yourself or you won't be able to take care of Jenny."

"I'm more hungry than tired. It's been so hectic, I forgot to eat. I haven't had anything since breakfast."

He picked up a letter opener on his desk and fingered it. "Want to go out and grab a bite with me?" Brent asked.

"I'm very pleased with your work performance," Brent said. Kara and Brent sat in a bright, crowded sandwich shop. Their sub sandwiches, chips, and drinks were scattered about the table in the booth they shared.

"You've taken a huge load off me. I honestly don't know how I could have made it at work since Jenny's accident without you."

Kara glowed from Brent's praise. "Thank you. It means a great deal to me to hear you say that," she said.

Brent took a bite of his sandwich. "We got off to a pretty bad start. Do you ever wish you could go back and rewind the scene, and do it all over again?"

Kara grimaced. "All the time," she said. "I especially feel bad about our rocky start. It was my fault."

"Please, no guilt. I'm carrying a big enough load for both of us," Brent replied.

Kara looked away. "I doubt that." She put down her sandwich, unable to eat another bite.

Their eyes met. "We both know the feeling," Brent said.

Kara leaned forward. "We can't rewind all our tapes, but we can rewind our personal tapes with each other. I'm sorry for manipulating you for a better job. At the time, I didn't see a better way." She paused. "It was stupid."

"Apology accepted and tape rewound. I'm sorry, too," Brent said. He caressed her hand, then suddenly withdrew.

"I need to go say good night to Jenny," he said.

"Give her my best wishes." Brent's eyebrows raised a fraction. "It's sincere. She doesn't deserve to be hurt."

"It was terrible, what I did to Jenny. I had no excuse, I've always realized that she's fragile. I've been pulling away from her so hard, putting my own needs ahead of . . . everything."

Brent looked momentarily distraught. "If it wasn't for me she wouldn't have been drinking that night," he continued. "She's never drunk anything but an occasional glass of wine before."

Kara remembered the orange juice Jenny had fortified with strong liquor one morning, but she didn't contradict Brent.

She reached out and clasped his hand, wanting to give him comfort more than anything in the world. "Nothing is ever all the fault of any one person, rather a combination of decisions, actions, and circumstances. You know I share your pain and guilt."

"We can't rewind that particular tape, but we can go forward. When Jenny is well, I'll hopefully make it clear to her that she's free to find the love she deserves," he said. "In the meantime, I can't continue hurting her, emotionally or mentally."

Brent's fingers trembled a little as he withdrew his hand. "I have to go. And thank you again for your help at the office." Brent paused. "It's as if this huge weight has been lifted by getting this stuff between us out in the open."

Kara nodded. She knew exactly what he meant.

Anthony picked up Kara in a red Corvette. Kara paused to admire the car for a moment. "Oh, my," she said.

"And you'll look mighty fine in it. Jump on in."

They were going out to meet a few of his friends and go to a show and dancing. Kara had never been to any live show, much less dancing.

She'd consulted with Anthony over what to wear. He had a dress delivered by the time she got home from work. She felt obligated to wear it, since he'd gone out of his way to buy it for her. The problem was there wasn't much of it. She wore an attractive coat, sort of like a coat dress, because she wouldn't take it off anytime soon. Well, maybe once she was sitting down.

"How'd you like the dress, honey?" Anthony asked.

"It's nice, but honestly—I hope it's going to be warm where we're going."

"Very warm. You got it, baby, so you should flaunt it, that's what I say."

Kara didn't know about all that, but he was entitled to his opinion. She really liked Anthony, even though he was unusual. She'd never met any guy before who was so comfortable with his feminine side. He'd call her and they'd chat. She loved his offbeat sense of humor.

She'd have to get him and Taylor together. Anthony had invited both of them to a party at his place last weekend; he'd said there'd be lots of men there. She'd tried to get Taylor to go, but Taylor had rolled her eyes and muttered something about how she liked her men "straight-up." Kara didn't get it. She ended up staying home because the last thing she needed was another man in her life. Brent was complicated enough.

Anthony was just a friend and she needed a change, it seemed lately that all she did was work and worry. Going dancing might be the break she needed. They pulled into the parking lot of a huge building. It was almost ten.

"It's late, did we miss some of the show?" Kara asked.

"Honey, the show doesn't start till midnight."

That was odd. Well, if she got tired, she'd take a taxi home. She could feel the music thumping and vibrating out to the parking lot. This was exciting.

The huge warehouse-like structure had all the flashing lights and shifting bodies that Kara had seen in places like it on TV. Anthony led her to the bar.

"What do you want to drink?" He shouted to make himself heard over the music.

"A glass of wine," Kara shouted back.

Anthony left and Kara sat on a bar stool, her coat securely in place. Her eyes gradually adjusted to the dim light. She was surrounded by some of the best-looking men she'd ever seen in her life. A few women were scattered here and there, but not many. She looked on the dance floor. The men were dancing with each other. Something is wrong with this picture, Kara thought.

All the sermons about sodomites she'd heard came to mind. Hmm. She liked Anthony. She didn't care about his amorous preferences, as long as they weren't directed at her.

He came back with her drink. "I told you I've led a very sheltered life," she said. "You realize that you've surprised me with all this." She gestured around the club.

Anthony gave her a wicked grin. "I know, girlfriend. Wanna dance?"

She finally took a taxi home at one in the morning, and left Anthony happily gyrating on the dance floor. She'd had three glasses of wine and danced with fabulous-looking men until her feet were sore. The show consisted of men dressed up as women who had the nerve to look better than she did. Well, almost.

When she walked into her apartment, she collapsed on the bed, not even taking off her makeup or brushing her teeth. It was sort of fun for one night, but she sure couldn't take it as a regular diet. Maybe once every five years.

When the alarm went off, she couldn't believe it. It felt as if she had just laid down in bed, a steamroller ran over her, and then this irritating sound buzzed in her ear. She slapped the snooze button. It must have been malfunctioning, because two seconds later it went off again. She gazed blearily at the clock; it was time to get up. She couldn't believe it, she thought again.

Now, she truly knew the meaning of the phrase "to drag into work." She was working on her third cup of coffee

and fielding two calls at once, one from a committee LA
and another from a political action committee represen-
tative. Velma interrupted saying, "Brent's on line three
with an urgent message."

Kara said she'd get back to the LA, and transferred the
PAC person to Cecile. She hit the button on line three.

"Jenny's in critical condition," Brent said.

Kara inhaled and let her breath out slowly. "You said
she had pneumonia, but I had no idea that it was that
bad."

"It's a strain of bacteria the antibiotics aren't touching.
She's not conscious anymore, and they're talking about
putting her on a ventilator."

Brent's voice had a ragged tone she'd never heard before.

"I've been here three days straight. And with this
news—"

"You've got to have a break. Go home for a couple of
hours, take a shower and a nap. Get some decent food to
eat."

"What if—"

"There's no what if. You're completely exhausted. I can
hear it in your voice, you're near collapse."

"No, I can't leave now."

"You're being ridiculous. Jenny's own father and
brother haven't spent as much time in the hospital as you
have. You're not going to make her better by your will and
presence. You're not God."

"All right, I'll go home for an hour," Brent said, capitu-
lating. "Will you meet me there?"

Kara hesitated.

"Could you bring me something to eat?" he asked.

"I'll be there," she said, against her better judgment.
Brent needed her, the mere fact he'd asked proved he was
at the end of his rope.

"There's a key under the front mat. I'll be home as soon as I speak to Jenny's doctor."

Kara balanced the paper bag of groceries on her hip while she searched for Brent's key and let herself into his townhouse.

It was decorated in the bleak bachelor style of black leather and chrome. It looked somewhat like a hotel suite, no pictures to relieve the white expanse of the walls, no curtains to soften the window blinds. The only personal touch was a cluster of pictures on the mantle.

Kara moved closer and studied them. Brent with a couple of women who looked so much like him they could only be his sisters, an old eight by ten of a beautiful woman that must be his mother. There were pictures of Brent and the congressman. Absent were any pictures of him and Jenny.

Kara entered the kitchen, which looked as if it had hardly been entered, much less used. She peered into the refrigerator. A bottle of ketchup, one can of beer, a jar of pickles, and leftover petrified pizza. The freezer overflowed with frozen microwave dinners. Brent was not likely to starve, but God help him if the electricity ever went out.

Kara shook her head and took out her groceries. She was going to make her favorite comfort meal, the meal her mom always made when things weren't going great. Meatloaf and mashed potatoes with cornbread and overcooked greens on the side. Pure bliss. Kara wasn't going to make the effort to clean the greens, overcooked fresh green beans with a touch of salt pork would have to suffice. She hummed as she worked. If she was going to sacrifice her new vegetarianism, the meal should be worth it.

It was a couple of hours later when she heard Brent let himself in. She'd dozed on his sofa while dinner cooked.

A smile touched Brent's lips when he saw her. Kara straightened and yawned.

"The place smells great. What's cooking?" Brent asked.

"Meatloaf," Kara said.

Brent made a slight face. "Meatloaf?"

"It'll be good. Go take a shower. It's going to take a few minutes for me to set dinner out."

Kara set out the dishes and put the meal on the table. She heard the shower running and shivered. She had a dream that went like this, her serving dinner and Brent in the shower . . . the memory brought heat to her face.

A few minutes later, Brent sauntered out comfortably dressed in a sweatsuit with a towel around his neck.

He surveyed the food. "Usually I eat a fairly healthy diet. I'm trying to cut back on the red meat," he said. "Real butter in those potatoes?" he asked.

Kara nodded.

"Good."

Later, much later, Brent leaned back in his chair, eyes closed. "That has got to be the best meatloaf I've ever tasted. It transcends meatloaf. You should open a meatloaf restaurant." He opened his eyes. "I'm serious."

Kara grinned at him, then she yawned.

"Brent, you should lie down for a good nap with all that heavy food in your stomach."

His smile faded. "I've got to call the hospital."

His face was drawn and gray when he returned from the phone. Kara was afraid to ask the news.

"They put her on a ventilator," Brent said.

Kara was speechless, shocked. She never believed it would actually come to this.

"The congressman doesn't want me to come back right away. He wants a few hours himself." With a twist of his lips, Brent said, "He's organized shifts."

Brent rubbed the back of his neck and stretched. "I'm going to bed." He turned to Kara. "Come with me," he said.

Kara's heart pounded. "No, we can't—we said—"

"I don't want to be alone now," he said.

Neither did Kara.

She followed him wordlessly to the bedroom. Brent stretched out on the bed, then curled into a fetal position. Kara kicked off her shoes and lay beside him. The beating of their hearts and the rise and fall of their breaths were the only sounds.

"If Jenny dies, I'm the one responsible. I don't know what I'll do."

Kara gave him what he needed; she listened.

"Jenny came over before her accident. She was nude under a black mink coat. I didn't understand what she wanted. I guess I turned her down. Then, I told her I didn't want her. Ever."

Kara laid her hand on his and Brent intertwined his fingers with hers, turning toward her. He reached to Kara and tried to draw her to him. She resisted.

"No, not right now, not like this," Kara said.

Brent withdrew. "Are you leaving then?" he asked.

"I'll stay."

Brent gave a grateful sigh, and in a few minutes his breathing became deep and regular. Sleep claimed him.

Eleven

Kara awoke disoriented. She was nestled with Brent, spoon fashion, his body curved around hers. Her skirt had hiked up around her hips, and Brent's arm curled over her, his hand cupping her breast, his thumb over her nipple. Incandescent red numbers on the clock beside the bed proclaimed it to be 2:23 A.M.

Brent stirred and his breathing changed. Kara sensed he was awake. Hard pressure deepened against her buttocks where she pressed intimately against him. Her arousal was instantaneous and intense. Brent's thumb eased a slow circle around her nipple.

Her moan was involuntary. Brent rolled over her, his knee easing between her thighs. Kara's eyes adjusted to the darkness in the room. She pressed her femininity against his knee with a whimper and surrendered to whatever came next. Consequences were for another day. This was what her body had wanted for so long, with the man she wanted. She smelled the musky male scent of him, felt his heartbeat, and pressed her fingertips into the hard muscles of his back. The warm, heavy honeylike feelings between her legs weren't allowing her to think clearly. Once she let him love her, there was no going back.

"No regrets?" Brent asked.

"No regrets."

Brent lowered his head, his lips touched her and his kiss

sent spirals of ecstasy racing through her. Her body arched and writhed against his hardness, seeking it, wanting it, needing it inside her. His lips parted hers, his tongue urgent and demanding.

Kara's legs parted and she strained to him. Brent's hips ground against her, and he rained tiny kisses down the side if her neck, down her chest, tasting her, savoring her. His hand unfastened the top buttons of her blouse. His lips lowered toward her breast and then Kara's ecstasy was shattered by the ring of the phone.

Brent actually snarled. Kara curled her fingers into little fists and listened to the phone ring again.

"You better answer it, it might be about Jenny," she said.

Brent grabbed the phone with barely concealed savagery. Kara rolled off the bed and went into the bathroom. She splashed cold water against her face, and stared at her reflection. Her makeup was smudged, her hair was all over her head, and her lips looked swollen and bruised.

The moment was gone. Regrets were already starting to rear their ugly heads. Maybe it would have been better for them to get it over with, to release the pent up tension.

Kara shook her head. She was kidding herself. If they did it, they would simply want to do it again . . . and again. The attraction between them was too strong and lasting for it to be otherwise.

It would be the ultimate betrayal of Jenny, her sister lying in that hospital bed fighting for her life. How could they? Kara closed her eyes against the gathering moisture. She didn't want to walk out of that bathroom and hear Jenny was dead.

She washed her hands prolonging the inevitable. When she walked out of the bathroom, Brent was sitting on the side of the bed, staring into space.

"Is Jenny . . . ?" Kara couldn't say the words.

"No. That was the congressman telling me I was late for my shift. Jenny's taken a slight turn for the better. The

new antibiotics seem to be working. Her fever's down, her
blood gases look good. They're going to start weaning her
off the vent tomorrow if she continues to progress."

Brent stood up and faced Kara. "I should have never
asked you to stay," he said softly.

She covered his lips with a finger. "No regrets."

Brent kissed her finger. "I've got to go," he said.

"I know." Kara got her purse and found her shoes and
jacket. She slipped out quietly. She didn't want to say goodbye.

Sidney was gone when Brent arrived at the hospital.
Only Tiffany remained. Tiffany had barely budged from
her daughter's bedside since the accident. The hours
passed and the day lightened with the sun's rise. Tiffany
entered the waiting room where Brent was sitting.

"How is she?" Brent asked.

For the first time since Jenny's accident, the heavy lines
of worry eased from Tiffany's face. "She's much better.
Her response to the antibiotic is wonderful. Jenny's breathing well on her own and her blood is well oxygenated. Her
doctor's going to remove the ET tube and unhook her
from the vent entirely as soon as she arrives."

Tiffany sat beside Brent. "I've been wanting to speak
with you alone for some time. Now that Jenny's doing better, I want to talk to you about the broken engagement."

Brent moved uneasily.

"She's had a crush on you since she was a child. I've
found notebooks with your name written over and over,
and every variation of Mrs. Brent Stevens, she could think
of." Tiffany smiled. "You made her so happy."

Silence hung between them.

"After you broke up with her, she fell apart. Then, she
regained a modicum of normalcy by totally disregarding
reality. She's never been the most confident child. I don't

know why. I did everything I could. She told me that she wasn't good enough for you, and that was why you left her."

Brent looked away.

Tiffany took a deep breath. "The night of the accident she came tearing in the house. She changed her clothes and was going to leave. I tried to stop her, I tried to get her to talk because I could tell she was distraught. She said that you were never going to marry her. Then she said she wanted to die, ran out the door and drove away."

Brent felt as if someone punched him in the gut.

"When she regained consciousness the first thing she did was to ask about you."

Brent didn't want to hear more, but Tiffany continued.

"What went wrong Brent? Is there anything, anything Jenny could do to make things right between the two of you?"

Tiffany clasped her hands together when Brent remained silent.

"I don't know how she will take the rejection, now that she's lying in intensive care. I'm begging you, begging you, please just stand by her and make her happy until she's well again."

Tears streaked down Tiffany's face, and her whole body trembled. Brent folded her in her arms.

"I'll make it up to her, Tiffany. I'll take care of her," Brent said. It would be his penance.

Jenny clutched Brent's hand fiercely. "You're not going to leave me?" she asked in an intense whisper.

Brent felt uncomfortable. "No, I'm not leaving. I'm here for you now," Brent said.

Jenny gave a satisfied smile and sank back into the pillows.

Over the last few weeks, her physical condition had stabilized enough for her to be moved to a rehabilitation hospital. She regained some use of her legs, and with a grueling physical therapy regimen, she'd probably walk again.

As her trial date approached, her lawyers said there was nothing to worry about. Brent didn't quite trust their reassurances. They spoke according to the money they were paid.

Brent went to see if there was anything he could do for the woman who lost her husband and child in the accident. Of course there wasn't, short of resurrection. She told Brent she forgave Jenny, because she was a Christian and Jesus forgave her continually. All she wanted from Jenny was justice, she said.

Sometimes Brent wanted to shake Jenny because of her blithe unconcern for anything but her own plight. Granted, her situation was extremely tough, but at least she had her life, and her doctors assured her she would walk again if she'd only work hard enough.

"I asked if you would get me some ice cream?" Jenny said, interrupting Brent's reverie.

"You have physical therapy in ten minutes. The last time you ate right before a session you got sick and couldn't go on. Do you think ice cream is wise?"

"I'm so hungry. How can I go to my session if I'm weak and hungry? Please, Brent."

Brent started for the door. He never could change her mind once she decided she wanted something.

"And, Brent, get me a sandwich, too, okay?"

Brent shook his head as he went to the kitchen.

Jenny didn't last five minutes into the physical therapy session before she started complaining she was feeling nauseous. She begged Brent to take her back to her room.

Brent lifted her into the bed. "Jenny, do you truly want to walk again?"

"What kind of question is that? Certainly I want to walk again."

"You've been told repeatedly that it is all up to you. You know how important your physical therapy is if you're ever going to walk. You refuse to cooperate almost every day. What sort of life are you going to have if you won't work for what's important to you?"

Tears welled up in Jenny's eyes. She spoke so softly Brent had to strain to hear her. "If I was all right, you'd leave me."

Brent bit his lower lip. "I'm here for you now. You have to fight Jenny. You have to get better." He caught her hand. "Do it for me."

"Hold me, Brent."

He held her for a while.

"Brent, why don't you call the nurse and see if my therapist is available for a session later," Jenny said. "I feel much better."

"Brent, someone named Stone Emerson left an urgent message for you to call him," Kara said.

Brent nodded and walked past her desk into his office.

Stone answered the phone on the first ring. "What's up?" Brent asked.

"I got a hot lead on Kara Smith," Stone said. "Her father."

"Tell me what you have."

Stone hesitated. "It's very hot, Brent, I want to make sure before I release any information. The only reason I called you so soon is that you told me to tell you as soon as I had absolutely anything on her."

"Okay, man, get back to me as soon as you can."

Brent rubbed the back of his neck. What if something did come out about Kara, and he had to get rid of her? He'd miss her sorely. It was more than that her work was excellent and she had made herself practically indispensable. Her presence, her nearness, was intoxicating. If he ever made love to Kara, it would be more than an affair.

He almost wished Stone would do his dirty work for him. He'd never let her go voluntarily, but having her here was tearing him up inside.

Kara had the flu. She was lying on the floor, flat on her back, and Taylor was carefully arranging crystals on her body.

"Are you sure this is going to work?" Kara asked.

"Positive. The energies from the crystals will align with the flows of your internal energies through your chakras and heal you," Taylor said. "Now if I screw up and lay these crystals wrong, I'll make it worse, you'll get pneumonia and die."

Kara glared at her. "That's not funny."

"Be still. There. Just lie there for a while." Taylor put on some New Age music and lighted some scented candles.

She returned and sank down beside Kara, settling into the lotus position.

"How do you feel?" she asked.

"Like I have to blow my nose," Kara answered.

"Hold on a little longer. The healing is for all three of your bodies, physical, emotional, and mental."

"I especially need the mental," Kara said, starting to chuckle.

"Actually I sense you need the emotional healing more. If Brent is truly your soul mate, you can't ever lose him."

Kara's lips tightened. "I can't talk about Brent now, it's hard enough at the office—"

"Quit," Taylor said.

"I can't quit."

"Why are you holding on so hard to the congressman and his family?"

"Taylor," Kara said warningly.

"I need to say this. You're my friend and I love you. I believe you need to hear this. You told me you released that obsession to destroy the congressman, so why are you still entwined with his family? Tiffany suspects you of sleeping with her husband, and Dante does, too. Except Dante wants to sleep with you, too. Do you think the father and son have a pattern of that? Sharing women?"

Taylor took a breath. "I digress. Look, everyone in this family hates you, and you've had nothing but problems since you met them. This is not healthy, Kara. Come clean. Tell these people who you are or get out of their lives."

"How can I announce I'm Congressman Eastman's daughter? It would be disastrous."

"Believe me it will be more disastrous if you keep traveling the road you're on."

Twelve

For weeks Brent had been leaving the office every day to go to the rehab hospital. He told Kara that Jenny was doing much better and starting to respond to therapy. Soon she'd be discharged from the rehab hospital to go home and resume outpatient physical therapy.

Kara heard this news with mixed emotions. On one hand, she was thrilled that Jenny was improving. On the other hand, her guilt increased when she realized that one reason the news made her happy was that Jenny might soon be able to relinquish her dependence on Brent.

Every day at the office was bittersweet agony. She loved being close to him, working with him. Sweetness was the electricity that shot through her at every accidental touch, the way his eyes rested on her hungrily when he thought she wasn't looking. Agony was the guilt that accompanied their intense attraction. Agony was that Kara wanted, needed his touch so very badly.

She should run away, quit, leave this unbearable situation. She just couldn't. Was that what it was with Brent? Weren't they both taking the safe way out? Kara's mind shied away, and she leaned toward her computer, trying to stave away the introspection and become engrossed in her work.

Brent approached her desk; he'd just returned from seeing Jenny.

"How's Jenny doing?" Kara asked, a little too brightly.

"Come into my office. I want to talk to you," Brent said, not quite meeting her eyes.

Kara hated the way their glances slipped away from each other lately. As if the sight of the other was intolerable. She followed him into the office, and carefully left the door open.

"Is there something wrong?" Kara asked.

Brent leaned against his desk. "No, Jenny's fine, taking her first steps. But what I want to talk to you about has to do with you and me."

Kara's heart beat faster. She suspected she didn't want to hear this.

"This isn't working out. I mean your employment here as my personal assistant. Our continued close contact is . . . difficult."

"I thought you said you were pleased with my work."

"I am. You know it's not that." Brent looked fully in her eyes. Their eyes held, and Kara's heart turned to butter.

God, she wanted him. A wanton Kara took over and she wanted to toss him on the desk and rip his pants off. Brent was talking. Kara had to force herself to refocus on what he was saying.

"We can't work this closely. It's hard on me and I think it's hard on you, too. It's like having candy you love in a dish in front of you, but you're not allowed to taste it."

Kara approached Brent. "Let's taste it then," she whispered.

Brent started to reach for her then his hands clenched into fists. "No. No, not only would it not be right here in the office, it wouldn't be fair to you right now, with Jenny so dependent on me. And once I tasted you, it wouldn't be fair to me. I'd know what I would be missing," he said.

Kara shuddered and dropped her head. "I'm sorry," she said.

"Don't be sorry, never be sorry," Brent said fiercely. "Neither of us is to blame."

"Do you want me to quit?" Kara asked. Then, before he could answer, she said, "Please don't ask me to quit. I love working in the congressman's office, and you know to what length I went to get a good job here."

"I know. Katey has said she wanted the position as my personal assistant. Could you consider filling the office manager's slot? It's a supervisory position, but as efficient and bright as I've discovered you are, I doubt you'll have any problems."

Kara steepled her fingers and brought them up to her lips. Office manager. She'd be taking her old boss's position and she'd be supervising a dozen people. A dozen people that didn't have a lot of respect for her. Could she do it? Working so closely with Brent wasn't working out. It was only a matter of time before she'd have to leave. But she couldn't. Not yet.

"I'll do it. When do I start?" she asked.

Brent looked relieved. "Immediately. I want you to work with Katey a couple of weeks to get a feel for the job."

"What are you going to do for an assistant in the meantime? You need one," she said.

"I can get someone from a temporary agency. It's just a couple of weeks."

"All right. I'll finish up and pack up my desk," Kara said.

Brent sighed and walked behind his desk after Kara left the office. He was relieved he didn't need to hassle with Kara over his decision. She must have realized that it simply wasn't working. Every time he saw her he had to fight an inner battle with himself not to go after what he wanted.

He hadn't minded going with the flow before he met Kara. Marrying Jenny seemed like a good idea, she was the congressman's daughter, a man he'd worked with for years. The congressman seemed to expect it when Jenny hinted to him that Brent had compromised her. He hadn't touched her, but it could have been worse, at least Jenny was good-natured and even tempered. She loved him. But it simply wasn't enough. He started feeling caged and confined. He couldn't imagine spending his life with her.

Once, Brent had thought he would grow to love her with all the passion he'd read about in books or seen in movies. Or he would think that the affection he felt for Jenny was love, and all the other was simply fiction, or Hollywood plot devices. He'd never felt mind-consuming passion before, so maybe it didn't exist. Or so he believed until he met Kara at that cocktail party.

The ring of the phone interrupted his thoughts.

"It's Stone. I thought I'd give you an update on my progress, it's been a while since I've gotten back with you."

Brent took a deep breath. "All right. What do you have."

"A hot lead," Stone said. "I can't seem to pin it down though. I still need concrete evidence."

"But what's your lead?"

Stone paused. "It has to do with a connection between Sidney Eastman and Kara Smith. I can't confirm anything now. I'd be in lawsuit territory. Understand?"

"I understand, but I'd sure like a hint off the record. We've been friends a long time, Stone."

"Okay, I'll tell you this. Kara Smith may be more involved with Sidney Eastman than we think."

"His wife thinks they're having an affair. But that can't be true. I always know about his affairs," Brent said.

"Don't get set on any theory, Brent. I'll let you know as soon as I track down hard evidence," Stone said.

Kara's new position as office manager was a cake walk compared to what she dealt with as Brent's assistant. She almost pitied Katey when she started her new job duties. They were taking another protracted coffee break at the legislative cafeteria.

"I wanted the job as Brent's assistant, primarily because of the money," Katey said. She looked at Kara out of the corner of her eye. "Why did you make the switch?"

Kara set down her cup of coffee. She'd dreaded this conversation. She knew Katey was dying to ask, but she'd taken pains to keep the conversation on an impersonal level.

While Kara hesitated, Katey said, "I'm not being nosy. I thought there might be a problem I don't know about."

"No, there was no problem. I'm interested in learning all facets of legislative office administration," Kara said.

Katey chewed on her bagel. "Being an LA, getting to work closely with Brent, and now being an office manager, you do get around."

"Maybe I'll try constituency services next."

"It sounds exciting, all that moving around, but I couldn't take the effects on my paycheck," Katey said.

Kara couldn't resist. "What effects? I've never taken a pay cut," she said.

Katey looked as if she was going to choke. Kara stood up and brushed crumbs away from her burgundy Chanel suit. "Shall we go?"

Katey drew Kara aside after they'd met in the employee's restroom. "Why didn't you warn me?" she whispered to Kara. "The man's a robot. I'm doing double the work without getting twice the money. I'm asking for a raise."

"Would it have made any difference if I warned you? Sit down and talk to Brent about the money though, he's very reasonable."

"I'll do that," Katey said. "By the way, have you heard the news? One of the freshmen congressmen is being censured for nepotism. He hired his own daughter to work in his office with campaign funds and tried to cover it up. With the hearing going on about campaign and legislative fund mismanagement, they're going to string him up over this one."

Kara's heart pounded. "I hadn't heard," she murmured, then quickly changed the subject. "Chin up, the job'll get easier, especially once Jenny gets out of the hospital."

"I can't get over that girl. When Brent isn't at the hospital with her, she's calling him every five minutes. I don't see how he gets anything done. Maybe we should move this office over to the hospital and put her bed right up under him."

Kara smiled weakly. Going back to her desk she thought about what Katey had said about the freshman congressman. Nepotism. Right now legislators were being squeaky clean with their campaign and office budgets. Hearings were ongoing and the attorney general was appointing a committee to look into the matter. More than one head would roll, and it seemed this congressman's head was first.

Kara's hands trembled and she clasped them together to hold them still. This was the edge she sought. The chance to bring Congressman Sidney Eastman down, to ruin his chances for reelection and his hopes for a Senate seat. The chance to finally lay her mother's spirit to rest.

When she was going through her mother's things she'd found a letter from Sidney Eastman. The letter acknowledged her mother's pregnancy and instructed her mother to "get rid of it" or give it up for adoption. The check he'd enclosed was yellow with age. It was for a very substantial amount, but her mother never cashed it. Kara blessed her mother for never carrying out Sidney Eastman's instructions.

Kara thought she'd found forgiveness within herself, but anger blazed up anew as she remembered. Her mother fled Atlanta and went to stay with a distant cousin in the tiny town of Tyrone. Apparently Sidney Eastman thought the matter was finished, ancient history, his child aborted or given to strangers. He soon would learn differently.

Another Friday night. Kara put on three blues CDs and settled back with a cup of hot chocolate. The music matched her mood. She felt frustrated and stuck. The roadblocks to what she wanted seemed immovable.

Her new start on life was working. She was a young attractive woman in Washington, D.C., with money and a good job. So why was she so dissatisfied?

Kara shifted restlessly. No sex, that was it. She grinned to herself. That was a problem, because if she couldn't have Brent, she probably was destined to remain a virgin forever. Right now, she couldn't imagine participating in an act of such power and intimacy with anyone but Brent.

The ring of the phone broke her reverie; she knew it wasn't Taylor, because she was out. She wished it was her, because she could use some girl talk about now, but then again Taylor had heartbreak of her own to deal with. There were no signs of her current flame ever leaving his wife.

"Hello," Kara said.

"What's up, girlfriend?" Her spirits perked up immediately. It was Anthony, the perfect antidote to a funky mood.

"Nothing, another Friday night in front of the TV."

"Get up, get dressed. Have I got somebody for you to meet. Do you have that red dress I got you?"

"Anthony, I'm not wearing that dress in public again. I don't know about going out. I'm pretty comfortable."

"You're too comfortable, that's the problem. Lay down that chocolate and turn off those Aretha CDs. I got a man for you."

"I'm listening to the blues. And this man, is he

straight?" she asked. Taylor had tutored her in the proper terminology.

"Honestly, girl, would I turn you on to anything else? This man is so dynamite if he wasn't straight, I'd have him myself. He's Gino's brother, in visiting from Europe. We're supposed to take him out on the town but he wants companionship of the female variety. Now that I've told you all that, I know you're going to help me out."

"I don't know. I really don't want to go out."

"I'm going to put my foot in your behind if you don't get it into gear. You're as bad as Taylor, sitting around and mooning over some man you can't have. I'm picking you up in an hour. Wear something sexy."

Kara eyed herself in the full-length mirror. She wore a short black lace slip dress. She had seen it at Lord and Taylor the other day, and she couldn't resist. She topped it with the matching bolero jacket, checked her makeup again, and she was good to go.

There usually was no point in arguing with Anthony, and he was right anyway. She needed to get out. Not particularly to meet men, but to have a little fun. And if nothing else, Anthony was fun.

She needed to get on with her life, because things weren't working out with Brent. She winced at the thought and wished Anthony hadn't set up this blind date. She didn't want to meet any man and she had no great confidence in this man Anthony gushed over. If he wasn't gay, he was probably teetering on the edge.

She heard a horn honk, and knew it was Anthony—no great respecter of social graces. She picked up her handbag and headed for the door. For one night, she was going to put Brent out of her mind.

Anthony gave her the once over when she approached the car. "You look good, girl."

It was no small praise from him, the last word on women's fashions, hair, and makeup. "Thanks," answered Kara.

When they arrived, Anthony tossed the keys to the valet at the Maison Bleu, one of the best, and most expensive, restaurants in Washington.

"You did say this was your treat?" Kara asked, grinning at Anthony.

"Hell no, the way you throw around money I counted on you to pick up the tab."

"Yeah, right."

They were led to a secluded table. Kara had met Anthony's friend Gino before. He was extremely attractive in a loud, feminine sort of way, like Anthony. The man sitting next to him got up as Kara approached the table.

He helped her into her chair, his eyes crinkling at the corners with pleasure at the sight of her. "I'm Alex Scoretti," he said.

"The lovely Kara Smith," Anthony introduced her.

"Bella," Alex murmured.

This guy looked like the actor George Clooney, but better, more masculine and rugged. The husky Italian accent was to die for. Kara immediately started going through her mental files of women she could introduce him to. This guy got her matchmaker instincts abuzz. If he was straight, he would be too good to let get away.

"Alex is in the States for a medical conference in New York; he's a pediatrician," Gino offered.

And a doctor to boot, a pediatrician no less. He must like children. She wondered if Taylor dated white guys. Maybe technically an Italian from Italy wasn't white. Kara wasn't sure. Anyway, it wasn't like he was British or German.

"Kara works in government. She's a congressional aide."

Alex looked suitably impressed.

They all ordered the specialty of the house, Dover sole.

Alex was an easy conversationalist. They talked about art, current affairs, and European versus American culture, lingering over drinks after the meal.

When they stood up to go, Alex caught her hand. "I'm in Washington for a week to visit my family. I'd like to see you again."

Kara smiled at him. She genuinely had a good time. "I had a wonderful evening, Alex. I'm involved with someone right now, but I have a friend I'd like you to meet, maybe Saturday evening?"

Alex looked taken aback for a moment. "If she's anything like you, I'd be delighted to meet her," he said in that shivery Italian voice.

This guy was too good to be true. If Taylor balked at going out with him, Katey'd probably jump at the chance.

Thirteen

Sunday morning, Kara tore through her boxes of personal papers. Where was it? She finally brandished the old yellowed envelope in triumph. Taylor, who'd been sitting on the floor watching Kara's frenzy, shook her head.

"There it is. Written proof that Sidney Eastman is my father," she said, handing the letter to Taylor.

She opened the envelope and carefully removed the letter and the check. The five digits on the check caught her eye first.

"Hot damn! She should've taken the money when she ran. That man didn't need to know your mama's business," she said.

"My mother was a woman of integrity," Kara said.

"Hmm. You think this check is still good?" Taylor asked.

"No, I think there's some limit."

"I'd find out."

"I'm not trying to cash Sidney Eastman's check thirty years after the fact. Now, turn your greedy little mind from those dollar signs and read the letter," Kara said.

Taylor unfolded the paper and read the letter. "He was a cold bastard," she said after she finished.

"I know. I was 'it,' " Kara replied.

"I get a strong feeling that if you try to use this against Sidney Eastman, it'll boomerang back to you. Harm begets harm. Let it go," Taylor said.

"A few weeks ago you told me to come clean."

"Not like this. I was talking about honesty."

Kara looked into the distance. "It doesn't seem fair. He got off scot-free, and my mother—"

"Let it go. The choices your mother made have nothing to do with you now. You're free. Make your own life. Make it a better life than she had. That's what she would've wanted for you."

"I don't know," Kara said, chewing on her lip. "My mother was pretty dogmatic about her religion. If she knew what I was doing now, I know she'd be back to haunt me." Kara smiled. "Except even that would be against her religion, she believed that once she died, that was it."

"What? No heaven or hell? No afterlife?"

"Nope."

"I'm happy she's learned the truth now."

"How do you know?" Kara asked.

Taylor started to speak, and Kara waved her hand. "Never mind, I don't think I can deal with the idea of my mother the ghost, not right now."

Taylor gave Kara a gentle smile. "If she's available, I'll be sure to send her your love."

"If she's available? Please, Taylor. Anyway, what should I do about the letter?"

"I thought we were over that. Hold onto it in love, and the answer'll come. Just don't do any harm."

"I'm in love, Kara," Katey said over the phone. "I can't thank you enough for introducing me to Alex." Then she lowered her voice to a whisper. "Thanks for the makeover. I still can't believe how great you made me look."

"Why are you whispering?" Kara asked.

"He's still here. He's in the bathroom now. Gotta go."

After Katey hung up, Kara felt a warm glow at everything working out so well for Katey. She just hoped Katey knew what she was doing when she let him spend the night so soon. That guy was going back to Europe next week.

Kara rarely saw Brent at the office anymore. He didn't believe in staff or other routinely scheduled meetings. He thought formal meetings were an exercise of management ego, a waste of time better spent working. Information was disseminated through memos, informal meetings, and phone calls. His method seemed to work; things got done, the office ran smoothly, and staff never complained about the lack of meetings.

One morning through the supremely efficient office grapevine, Kara heard Jenny was out of the hospital. As soon as Kara returned to her desk after hearing the news, a large yellow note was pasted alongside two phone message slips. *Call Jenny Eastman ASAP, she's called THREE times,* it read.

Kara bit back an expletive. She did *not* want to deal with her sister. She didn't want to analyze her jumbled tangle of emotions. She wanted Jenny to like and respect her, but guilt, envy, and fear stymied Kara. Jenny still loved Brent, and she couldn't stand up to Jenny, woman to woman, and fight for her man. It wasn't like that. Kara gave up on the man she wanted because they were sisters. Blood. She had to do right. Kara reached for the phone.

Congressman Eastman breezed through in one of his rare visits to the front office. He stopped and spoke to many of his staffers, making his way gradually to Kara's little open cubicle. She cut short her phone conversation as he drew near. She'd just hung up when to her surprise he sat down in the chair next to her desk.

Her pulse fluttered. "Hello. Is there anything I can do for you?" Kara asked politely.

"I decided to drop by to see how you're settling into your new job. Jenny tells me that you're going shopping with her on Saturday," he said.

When Kara called Jenny back, Jenny'd begged her to go shopping. She shifted things around on her desk top. Nerves. She put her hands in her lap to still them.

"I'm looking forward to it," she said.

"Oh, good. With all the attention Brent is giving her lately, my little girl is walking on clouds." Sidney Eastman crossed his legs and picked up a crystalline paperweight Taylor had given her. "Yes, we know it won't last, but I'm grateful that my Jenny is doing well and is happy for now. My only problem is that she tends to be so trusting."

He set the crystal down and leaned toward Kara. "She trusts too much in back-stabbing sluts whose main goal in life is to get what my little girl had," he said.

Shock caused Kara to draw in her breath sharply. Her eyes narrowed, and she waited to see what the congressman had to say next.

"Brent's like a son to me," he continued. "I gave him his first internship in college. He's stuck it out with me ever since."

Kara's breathing quickened at Brent's name. She picked up a pen and started doodling on the legal pad in front of her. She was so angry, she didn't trust herself to say a word.

"He's got a good head on his shoulders. I trust his judgment quite a bit. Even when he's stuck his neck way out for you."

Kara's pencil made slow circles on the paper.

"I can't say I understand why he goes out on a limb for you, but my boy Brent always has good reasons," he said.

His boy? "What's your point, Congressman?" Kara asked.

"And here I am thinking I'm being so clear." He leaned so close to Kara she could smell his aftershave. "My point is this. If my little girl gets hurt, I hurt. So you better make sure Jenny suffers no pain of any sort. Not only will Brent feel the brunt of my displeasure, I'll make it a personal priority that you get everything coming to you, young lady."

He stood up and straightened his tie. "It's been a pleasure talking to you." He winked at her and strode away.

Kara resumed drawing slow circles. Her entire body trembled. Suddenly, the pencil's lead broke, leaving a large circular gouge in the pad.

Brent picked up the phone to call Velma. "I need to locate the congressman. Where does his schedule put him?"

"He's in the front office, Brent. He needs to be present for a vote in sixty minutes though," she answered.

"Thanks." Brent hung up, wondering why Sidney would come through the front office without checking with him first.

He headed for the front office. When he saw Sidney sitting beside Kara's desk it stopped him cold. What was he doing in Kara's office? He saw Kara staring wide-eyed at Sidney, apparently upset about something. It didn't appear like a business visit.

Brent watched Sidney get up, straighten his tie, and exit. He walked over to meet him.

"There you are," he said jovially to Brent, clapping him on the shoulder.

"I've got a few things to cover with you," Brent said, as they walked toward the office.

Sidney looked at his watch. "I've got a few minutes," he said.

"I saw you talking to Ms. Smith," Brent said.

"Ms. Smith? You know there's no need to be so formal," Sidney said, giving Brent a meaningful glance.

A chill coursed through Brent.

"You're mighty quiet," Sidney commented as they reached his office. Brent followed him in.

"I was thinking about something," Brent said. "Why did you stop by Kara Smith's office? I'm curious."

Sidney gave him a knowing gaze. "I bet you are."

Brent waited but he said nothing more.

It must be true, Kara was having a secret affair with the congressman. She was a sneaky, treacherous *fox,* he thought with sudden fury. She was playing it for all she had to get ahead in politics. He couldn't believe he'd started to trust her.

Brent ran a hand over his hair. "I suppose we should move on to the matters I needed to talk to you about."

Sidney's eyes were bright and assessing. "I was waiting for you to do that," he said.

After the congressman left, Kara reached into her desk drawer with shaking hands for her purse. Fear and anger twisted inside her. How dare Sidney Eastman threaten her. She turned away from the open end of her cubicle and took out the letter she'd been carrying in her purse ever since she had showed it to Taylor.

Kara reread the letter he wrote to her pregnant mother thirty years ago. Moisture filled her eyes and tears ran down her face. Tears of anger and humiliation. She remembered the vow she'd made after her mother died that he would be sorry.

Sidney Eastman had just taught her that the value of forgiveness wasn't much. Successful and arrogant, he was still making undeserved judgments and laying down commands. It would stop right here and now, and this time Kara wouldn't back down.

She stuffed the letter into the back of her file drawer in

her desk. She only needed to decide how to drop the figurative shoe on the congressman's head.

The intercom buzzed. Kara picked up and Brent said, "I'd like to see you in my office as soon as possible."

It didn't let up, did it? Kara asked herself. Brent hadn't called her since she started this job. The congressman must have spoken to him about her.

Kara nodded at Katey as she approached Brent's office. Katey was on the phone but she jerked her head toward the door, indicating it was all right for Kara to go on in.

Kara tapped lightly on the door and entered, closing the door behind her. Brent was pacing the floor.

"There you are," Brent said. "Sit down."

Kara sank into one of the leather chairs and waited.

"I saw Sidney Eastman in your office. What's up?"

Kara felt her face burn. Brent sure got directly to the point.

"He was despicable," Kara said in a low voice. "I'm going to make sure he gets exactly what he deserves."

Brent's eyes were cold, hard chips of amber. "I changed my mind. I don't want to hear it. Leave me out of your personal business," he said.

"But, you don't understand what he said to me—"

"I said leave me out of it," Brent said, his voice rising.

Anger flashed through Kara at his tone and she stood up.

"Is that all you wanted from me?" she asked coldly.

Brent came from behind his desk and walked toward Kara. "No, that's not all I want from you." His voice was low and husky. She could smell his scent, see the tiny pulse beating in his throat.

Her woman's senses responded involuntarily to his closeness. Brent caught her in his arms like a tiny, frightened animal. Her pulses pounded.

He shifted her so she was positioned tight against his hardness, her breasts flattened against his chest. He ground his hips imperceptibly against her. She couldn't stop the moan, the arching of her back, seeking to pull him inside her. Kara tilted her head back and lowered her eyes. Her lips were moist and slightly parted in preparation for his kiss.

His mouth touched hers, his lips burning. They felt of barely controlled passion. Dangerous passion. A tremor went through Brent and now under steely control, he raised his head, watching her. Kara met Brent's gaze.

His eyes looked lost and hurt. In no way did they match the passion Kara discerned in his body.

"No. That's not all I want," Brent repeated, releasing her.

Kara stumbled back a few steps to the door. She touched her lips, feeling numb.

Brent sat back down at his desk and busied himself with papers. He looked up a few seconds later, seemingly annoyed to find Kara still standing there. "You can go," he said.

She opened her mouth to say something, but no words emerged. Then Kara turned and fled.

That Saturday as arranged, Kara met Jenny in a popular coffee shop. It was a sunny, unseasonably warm late fall day. A perfect day for shopping. Kara's mood was in direct opposition to the weather. Kara ordered a double latte. She didn't have to wait long. Jenny approached, dressed in black leggings and an oversized black sweater. She had a black cane to match with a swan's head carved into the handle. She walked with a very slight limp.

Kara stood up and embraced Jenny. "It's great to see you looking so good."

"Thanks," Jenny answered, sliding into the booth. "I'll have hot chocolate," she said to the waitress. "I missed you," she exclaimed. "Though I completely understand why you couldn't come to the hospital with my mother carrying on. I don't know what her deal is. She needs to get over it."

"She's frightened," Kara said.

Jenny nodded, looking sad. "She has reason to be," she said.

They finished their drinks and headed for the mall. Four hours later, Kara had had enough. She thought she had shopping in her blood, but her sister had her beat.

"Do you want Chinese?" Jenny asked suddenly. "Brent likes Chinese," she added.

Kara wondered what that had to do with anything, but she was hungry. Jenny was already dragging her toward the restaurant.

She was surprised when Jenny didn't want to eat in the restaurant, but ordered an astonishing amount of food to take out.

After a long wait, they got their food, and Jenny hailed a taxi. Kara staggered to the taxi, laden with packages and Chinese food. She couldn't wait to get home.

She was looking at the passing trees, when she realized the taxi was heading away from her apartment.

"I thought I was going home," Kara said.

"Nope. We're going to meet Brent over at his place for dinner. I thought it would be a nice surprise for him," Jenny said.

It would be a surprise all right, Kara thought. "I didn't plan on staying out so late. I have other dinner plans tonight," she said.

"You can use the phone at Brent's to call and cancel," Jenny said cheerily.

"I don't want to cancel my dinner plans," Kara said.

Jenny glanced over at her and frowned. "I want to go to Brent's to eat."

"You can go to Brent's if you like. I'm going home," Kara said.

"No, you're not, we're going to Brent's," Jenny answered.

Maybe Jenny didn't understand, Kara thought. "My previous dinner plans are very important to me," Kara said.

Jenny's lower lip pouted. "You can reschedule."

"So where do you want me to drop you off?" the taxi driver asked.

"Where I told you earlier," Jenny said. She sounded quite firm.

Kara decided to take another tack. "I work with Brent all day, socializing together is a bit much, don't you think?"

"Oh, no, when Brent and I get together again, you'll see him all the time."

That statement effectively rendered Kara speechless.

They continued to speed to Brent's place and Kara's heart continued to sink. Jenny was set on having her own way. The easy, compliant girl Jenny was before the accident had disappeared. Was the stress of the accident, the arduous recovery, and now the upcoming trial allowing the true Jenny to emerge? Or was this what Brent had to deal with throughout his engagement?

They arrived at Brent's town house and Jenny hopped out of the car. Kara followed slowly after paying the driver.

"Come on, Kara," she called.

Jenny rang the doorbell enthusiastically. Brent opened the door, his smile melting when he saw them. Jenny bounded past him, chattering.

Kara saw shock, then anger cross Brent's features as he waited for her to reach the door. He stepped aside for her to pass.

"Welcome back," he said in tones only she could hear.

Fourteen

Jenny was already going through the cartons of Chinese takeout still in paper bags on Brent's dining room table. Brent took Kara's leather jacket. Their hands touched and it was all Kara could do not to snatch her hand away. Brent's lips thinned.

"Hey, guys, let's dig in. I'm starving," Jenny called out.

"I'll get the plates," Kara said, going into the kitchen.

Kara emerged shortly afterward with plates, silverware, and glasses.

"You sure know your way around Brent's place," Jenny remarked.

A slight strangled sound came from Brent to the left. Kara ignored it. "Town house layout is pretty generic," she said, starting to set the table.

Jenny shrugged. "I ordered enough to feed an army and I feel as hungry as one," she said.

Kara wasn't hungry and picked at her food. She couldn't turn her eyes in Brent's direction. The situation was too uncomfortable. Memories kept flashing through her mind. Her legs intertwined with Brent's. His lips on hers. No regrets, no regrets . . . It kept playing like an unwelcome tune in her head. She couldn't turn it off.

"You two aren't hungry?" Jenny asked as she refilled her plate.

"I don't have much of an appetite," Kara said.

Brent grunted something incomprehensible.

"I couldn't wait to get married to Brent and move into our new place. Mom wanted to hire a cook for us. But I thought I'd make sure the housekeeper I hired could cook," Jenny said.

Kara made a noncommittal sound. That was enough to encourage Jenny to keep talking.

"I wanted to have a pink wedding. But since it was supposed to be a December wedding, Mom wanted to go with red and white. She also wanted an evening wedding with a sit-down dinner. But I told her she would have to change her plans because I wanted a pink, early afternoon wedding."

Jenny stared at Brent. He looked away. Kara took a sip of soda and wondered what excuse she could come up with to get out of here. This was awful.

"Can you take me home now, Brent?" Kara asked. "I had some plans for this evening."

"I told you to reschedule your plans," Jenny said.

"I can't reschedule my plans at the last minute like this. I need to go home," Kara said.

Jenny pouted. "I was going to rent a movie and have popcorn."

At this point, Kara wouldn't have minded picking up one of the plates and popping Jenny over the head with it. But Brent was already getting up and reaching for his keys to take Kara home. She stood up and he draped her jacket over her shoulders, his hands seeming to linger.

She wanted to lean back against him and feel his strong, warm arms encircle her body. But all she did was draw the jacket over her arms. They walked to the door together. In unison they both stopped and turned toward Jenny who was still sitting at the table.

"Aren't you coming?" Brent asked.

"Uh-uh, I haven't finished eating. Bye!"

Brent looked grim. "I'd like to take you home now, Jenny, you can take the food."

"No, I'm staying," Jenny said cheerfully. "See you later."

Geez, Kara thought. Jenny was going to be a problem when Brent got back home. Brent's problem.

"That was an ordeal," Kara said, once she got in the car.

"What made you drop in like that? And with Jenny? Didn't we agree that we needed distance?" Brent said.

"That didn't seem to be the agreement in your office the other day," she said.

Brent paused. "I apologize for that," he said stiffly. "I should have had more self-control. It didn't seem fair at the time that I couldn't have what you're so generous with elsewhere."

"What do you mean by that?"

Brent frowned. "Where do you live anyway?" he asked. Kara told him and he did a U-turn.

"What did you mean when you said you couldn't have what I'm so generous with elsewhere?" Kara repeated.

Brent's hands tightened on the steering wheel. "We've been going through all this should we-shouldn't we stuff, all tortured with all this guilt and crap. And apparently you've had no problem giving it up to Sidney Eastman all this time."

"You think I've been sleeping with him?" she breathed.

"That's what I said."

"Did he tell you that?" Kara asked, remembering her conversation with Sidney Eastman at the office.

Brent looked uncomfortable, "Not in so many words."

"I bet not. He came into my office the other day and threatened me if I hurt his 'little girl' by carrying on with you."

Brent pulled up in front of her apartment. "Can I come up?" he asked. "We've got to figure out what's going on here."

"You got that right." Kara dug her keys out of her purse. Brent followed her, and stood closely behind her as she fumbled with the keys.

Taylor popped out of her apartment, dressed for a night out on the town.

"Hi, Kara," she said, eyes assessing Brent with appreciation.

"Brent Stevens, this is my friend Taylor Cates," Kara said. They shook hands and murmured greetings while Kara opened the door.

"Have a good time," Taylor called, as she walked down the hall.

"You, too," Kara replied.

Brent entered, filling the apartment with his masculine presence. He looked around.

"Nice. Looks exotic," Brent said, indicating the apartment.

"Your mother's decorator, Anthony, did it for me," Kara answered. "Would you like coffee?"

"Please." He sank into the overstuffed cushions of her sofa. Kara went into the kitchen and emerged a few minutes later.

"The coffee will be ready in a moment." Kara perched on the edge of a chair.

"I knew Tiffany was being paranoid when she accused you of having an affair with Sidney. She's been through a lot. It was inexcusable that I jumped to the same conclusion," Brent said.

"I don't know how people think I'd sleep with Sidney Eastman. It would be like sleeping with my father!" Kara blurted out.

Brent looked taken aback at her outburst, then he asked, "You mentioned Sidney threatened you? What did he say?"

"First he said Jenny was trusting, then he brought you up. He said he didn't know why you're doing so much for me. Then out of nowhere he said if Jenny gets hurt I'll be sorry."

"That's it?" Brent asked.

"Yes. He didn't get specific."

"Damn." Brent got up and started to pace. "I know when I first gave you the job as the banking LA he wondered about us, but I never thought he'd confront you before he'd say something to me."

"Maybe he thinks it's all right for you to get what I'm so generously spreading around," she said, a touch of bitterness in her voice. Kara stood up in a graceful movement. "I'm going to get the coffee," she said.

Brent was standing at the window staring at the winking lights of the Washington night when she returned. She set the tray down on the coffee table and walked to him.

They stood side by side in silence for a few minutes.

"I'm truly sorry I thought the worst, Kara. I should have talked to you first."

"It's okay. We're both under a lot of strain," she said.

"What are we going to do?" Brent said, almost to himself. His voice was so low Kara had to strain to hear him.

"I don't even know just what I'm going to do, Brent. There's more—more than what meets the eye happening here."

He finally turned to her. "I want to ask you something, and I want an honest answer. Promise?"

"Ask me. But I won't make promises I may not be able to keep," she said.

"Why did you go to such lengths to get a promotion? I know there wasn't any chance of your getting that particular job right then, but your smarts and willingness would eventually take you wherever you want. It doesn't make sense that you had to go to . . ." His voice trailed away. Brent met her eyes. "Where you took it with me that night in the hotel. Where you took it when you stole those papers."

Kara opened her mouth and closed it again. She wanted to trust him. But the words wouldn't come out.

"Does it have anything to do with national security?" Brent asked, his lips barely moving.

"Lord, no," Kara said. "This is personal. Between me and Sidney Eastman."

"I've known Sidney a long time, I believe I know all the skeletons in his closet."

"Believe me, you don't know all of them," she answered.

Brent mulled that over in silence.

"As far as the Eastmans are concerned, I'm starting to feel like a bird caught in a cage. Trapped and put on display with no way out." He rubbed his forehead. "I shouldn't complain. Like my mama used to say, I made my bed, so now I have to lie in it."

She laid a hand on his shoulder and felt a shiver go through him.

"Kara, it's agony, wanting you, knowing it would feel so right between us—"

Kara put her finger on his lips. "No regrets," she said.

"No regrets," Brent echoed and with a groan, he covered her lips with the strong hardness of his own.

His kiss was urgent, demanding. She couldn't think, she couldn't breathe. The world narrowed to the feel of Brent's lips, his hard body, and the sweet ache within her. He explored her, tasted her, and trailed soft sweet kisses down her neck, to the soft mounds of her breasts.

Kara whimpered at the delicious sweetness of his lips. They recaptured hers, more insistent. Brent's hard male body demanded satisfaction and her femininity begged to give it. Satisfaction too long denied.

The phone rang. Brent froze. "I have a certain feeling of déjà vu," he said wryly.

"I'll let the machine pick it up," she answered in a husky voice.

"Kara? This is Jenny. I'm so worried."

Brent swore and Kara scrambled to pick up the phone. "Jenny . . . Sorry, I was in the bathroom."

"When did Brent drop you off? He's not back yet. I'm getting worried. I think I'm going to call Dad."

"No! No, don't do that. He said he was going to stop and get you something. There was an accident, going back the other direction. He might be delayed. Give him a little while longer."

"Well, okay," Jenny said grudgingly.

Kara hung up with shaking hands. She looked at Brent.

Fifteen

Brent hurried back home to Jenny from Kara's apartment.

He let himself into his place. It was dark and he heard the television. He walked into the den. Jenny was sprawled out on the sofa, snoring softly, her mouth open.

The coffee table was littered with open Coke cans. Brent started to clean up when something caught his eye sticking out from Jenny's open purse. He pulled it out and his mouth went dry. It was a bottle of Southern Comfort. Empty. He bent down close to Jenny and smelled the unmistakable reek of alcohol.

Two hours later and Jenny still slept. Her parents would start to worry soon, so Brent either had to call them or wake Jenny and take her home.

He set a fresh cup of coffee beside the empty bottle of Southern Comfort liquor on the coffee table. "Jenny, wake up," he said. She didn't stir.

He shook her shoulder gently. "Jenny, you have to get up."

She mumbled and turned her face to the sofa.

Brent shook her more firmly, "Jenny."

"What?" she cried, sitting up in a quick jerky motion. "Why can't you let me sleep?"

Her words were slurred, her eyes bleary. Then her eyes closed and she started to fall over.

"Jenny," Brent said again in a firm voice. Her eyes popped open. He handed her the empty bottle of Southern Comfort.

Jenny shook it. "All gone," she said with a giggle, handing the bottle back to Brent.

"Why, Jenny?" was all he could choke out.

She looked at him unsteadily. "Why not?"

Then she announced, "I'm going back to sleep."

"Oh, no, you're not, I'm taking you home. Drink that coffee," Brent ordered.

"Coffee don't do a damn thing but keep me awake," Jenny said. "And I don't want to be awake."

Brent helped her up and steered her out the door. By the time he got her settled in the car, she was snoring. It was for the best he decided. He'd help her to bed, and say she was exhausted if he saw anybody.

Driving to the Eastman home, Brent was haunted by images of the woman who lost her husband and baby in one stupid drunken instant. Anger flashed in him and burned within his depths.

Getting Jenny to bed had been uneventful. The house was dark, and Brent had seen no one. When he got back home he turned on the TV. He laid down on the sofa, aimlessly flicking the remote, restlessness building inside like the flickering images in front of him.

Without thinking, he picked up the phone and dialed Kara.

"I took Jenny home," he said.

"She wasn't too upset?" Kara asked.

"Noooo, in fact, she was passed out on the couch with a fifth of Southern Comfort."

There was silence on the phone line. "I was afraid she would start drinking again," Kara said.

"Again?" Brent said. "You knew she had been drinking?"

"She was drinking early one morning in your office while she waited for you. I put her in a taxi."

"You should have said something," he said.

"It was really none of my business. She was upset over you."

"It's nobody's fault. Jenny didn't start drinking like this out of the clear blue. She's probably had a drinking problem for a while."

"What are you going to do?" Kara asked.

"Get her in treatment, I guess. Stand by her while she goes through the trial. She needs to pay in some way for what she did."

"Poor Jenny," Kara said.

"I'm tired of hearing about poor Jenny. If she ever decided to take advantage of them, she has plenty of help and resources behind her, not like the man who lost his life and the baby who never had a chance to live."

"She'll get help on her own eventually."

"Possibly. But I wouldn't hold my breath. Jenny doesn't show the slightest sign of being aware of the magnitude of her problem, or even acknowledging she has one."

"Maybe she wouldn't have had one if it wasn't for us," Kara said.

"You keep saying that, but that's bull and you know it," Brent answered.

Kara said nothing.

"I didn't mean to come off cold, but I feel so helpless about Jenny's problems . . ." His voice trailed away. "I'd like to change the subject."

"Okay."

"I wanted to ask if you're available for dinner Sunday," he said.

A pause, a long pause. Brent's hand tightened on the phone.

"What if you come to my place?" she asked.

He couldn't believe his luck. "Great, you're making meatloaf again?" he asked.

"No, probably something a little different. I'll see you around six."

At one thirty Brent rang the bell at the Eastman home. Tiffany opened the door.

"How're you doing, Brent? We just got back from church."

"Did Jenny go?"

"No. She was tired this morning."

"She's still in her room?" he asked. Tiffany nodded.

Brent took the stairs two at a time. The door was ajar; Jenny was lying in bed, in her nightgown. The TV was on, she was watching it, and her hand was moving mechanically between a bag of chips and her lips. Brent saw a glass of orange juice on her bedside table.

Jenny looked up at Brent and back at the TV.

"Oh, hi, Brent."

Brent closed the door and turned off the TV. "We've got to talk."

"Sure, baby, what's going on?" Jenny asked.

"Don't play that with me, you know the deal. How long have you been hiding your drinking, Jenny?"

Jenny blinked. "I have no idea what you're talking about," she said in a level voice.

"You weren't passed out on my sofa with a bottle of Southern Comfort falling out of your purse?"

"I was tired yesterday. I suppose Kara and I overdid it shopping, but—"

"Be quiet." He walked over to the other side of the bed

and picked up the orange juice sitting there. He sipped and grimaced.

"You sicken me," he said.

Jenny's eyes grew wide and she fell forward on the bed, crying hysterically. "How could you say that to me?" she screamed.

"Because of a dead man and his son. Because of a young woman hardly older than you left without her family. Don't you care? Don't you give a damn about anyone but yourself?"

Jenny's screams rose in volume and Tiffany burst in the room. "What's going on?"

Brent thrust the glass of alcohol-laced orange juice in Tiffany's hands.

"Ask your daughter. I'm on my way out."

Brent found himself driving straight to Kara's house. His cell phone started to ring halfway there. With a sigh he answered it.

"What's going on here? My daughter's in hysterics. Tiffany says you just left. We're going to have to call the doctor for sedatives for Jenny," Sidney Eastman said.

"I think Jenny is sedated enough," Brent said drily.

Silence. "Come back and let's talk about it in my office. We'll leave the women out of it. I'll be waiting."

Brent wanted to keep on driving to Kara's, and leave Jenny and the Eastmans far, far behind. However, years of habit and deference to the congressman overrode his need.

"I'll be there shortly," Brent said.

The housekeeper answered the door and Brent went directly to Sidney's office and den, glad not to see any sign of Tiffany or Jenny.

Sidney was waiting for him with a cup of coffee in his hand when Brent entered the study.

"Want some coffee?" Sidney asked.

Brent declined and got directly to the point. "Jenny has a serious drinking problem, one I believe she's had for some time."

To Brent's surprise, Sidney nodded his head.

"You've known about this and done nothing?" Brent asked.

"Of course I didn't know about it. I'm not surprised though. My little girl has always had a hard time with reality."

Brent took a deep breath. "Now that you know about Jenny's drinking, what are you going to do?"

Sidney gave him a sharp look. "Don't you mean what are we going to do?"

Brent looked away. He didn't feel like reminding Sidney again that Jenny was no longer his problem. "I think she needs treatment," he said.

"I'll talk to her therapist, we'll increase her sessions to twice a week, maybe even three times a week."

"She's been in therapy for years and look at all the good it has done her. I'm talking about putting her in an alcohol treatment center," Brent said.

"No, no, the timing's bad, son. With her trial coming up that'd be the same as admitting guilt."

"Isn't she guilty?" Brent asked.

"It was clearly an accident," Sidney said coldly. "An alcohol treatment center is out of the question."

"If Jenny doesn't get help, I don't see how you could live with her drinking problem. I certainly couldn't." Brent stood up to go.

Sidney's stern face softened. He put a fatherly hand on Brent's shoulder. "I know exactly how you feel. But believe me it's not that big a deal. It runs in the family."

Brent frowned. "Are you telling me that Tiffany—?"

Sidney nodded. "For years. We've kept it hush-hush, and see, there's been no problem. She's been a good wife."

Except when you're out cheating on her and she's at home in her lonely bed drowning her sorrows, Brent thought.

He shook Sidney Eastman's hand off his shoulder.

"Maybe I didn't make myself clear when I said I didn't see how you could live with Jenny's drinking problem. The point is I don't see how you chose to live with it."

With those words he turned and left the room. Brent's hand was on the doorknob, when he heard Jenny's voice calling. Brent wanted to walk out of that door. He decided against the cowardly way and turned to face Jenny.

"Brent, Brent, thank God you're back. We have to talk."

"Yes, we do." Jenny followed him into the formal sitting room.

"Sit down," he said. She sat on the couch and he sat beside her.

"It's time we are honest with each other. How long have you been drinking?"

"Drinking," Jenny repeated. "I don't see why you're making such a big deal of it. Everybody drinks. You drink. I wanted to talk about our getting back together."

"All we have to talk about is your drinking. Have you considered treatment?" Jenny's hands balled into little fists at her sides.

"No," she retorted.

"Then we have nothing to talk about. Except this. I'm sorry to be so harsh, but you don't seem to be able to understand that it's over, Jenny. I don't love you, and we are never, ever getting married."

Blood drained out of her cheeks, leaving her ashen-gray. "Any excuse would do, huh?" she said bitterly.

"God, I'm sorry, Jenny. But marriage is a lifetime thing. And it didn't work between us. Couldn't you tell?"

"You promised. You said you wouldn't leave me. But as soon as I'm well—you liar. Liar!"

She flew from the room, leaving Brent with the sound of heartbreak echoing in the room.

Kara hung up the phone from talking to Katey Sunday afternoon. It'd been a depressing conversation. Katey found out the Italian Romeo was married. He wanted to meet her in Paris, but she said she always wanted to go to Rome. He replied Rome wouldn't work because he had too much respect for his wife to meet *one* of his mistresses in the same town she lived in. Poor Katey, she'd had her hopes up so high.

Anthony picked up his phone on the first ring. "Why didn't you tell me Gino's brother, the Italian lover, was married?" Kara demanded.

"You never asked. And he was just for play, not to keep. I can't help it if you had to set him up with one of your friends. Oh, by the way, he told Gino he had a very enjoyable week, he said your friend was hot."

Poor Katey, Kara thought again.

"What are you doing this afternoon?" Anthony asked.

"Cooking. Brent's coming over for dinner."

"Y'all finally resolved the tragic triangle?" he drawled.

"Sort of, I asked him over because I really don't want to be seen with him in public yet."

"Honey, you lay it on him in private, and everything will work out. Try it, you'll see."

Anthony was crazy. When Kara got off the phone she was still chuckling. She got up and pulled some pots and pans down to start dinner. One thing was sure though, her matchmaking days were over.

Sixteen

Kara opened the door, and Brent entered. His eyes were shadowed and his face etched with pain.

"Jenny finally got the fact that it's over," he said.

Kara pressed a hand to her lips. "How did she take it?"

"Not well." He moved to the chair and rubbed the back of his neck. "I should be relieved, but I feel bad, like I kicked a puppy."

"Would you like some coffee?" Kara asked, not knowing what to say.

"Decaf if you have it."

Kara's hands trembled as she busied herself in the kitchen, thinking, now he's here with you. Stretched out in the most comfortable chair in her living room like he belonged there, confiding the most personal matters of his life to her. No, she wasn't going to feel guilty. She'd done nothing to take her sister's man. Jenny messed up big time, and she lost him a long time ago.

With that thought, Kara squared her shoulders, picked up the tray with the coffee, and returned to the living room. Brent smiled at her as he took the steaming mug, and her heart melted.

Somebody who looked that good probably had females all over him since elementary school. At work, lingering glances from the women would follow Brent as he'd walk through the office. All that fine confident masculinity wrapped up with just enough little boy to turn heads and break hearts. He made Denzel look bad.

"Your coffee is getting cold." Brent's voice sliced through Kara's thoughts. She started a little, her skin warming. How could she be lusting over Brent's body with all that was going on? she wondered.

She picked up the cup of coffee and sipped.

"Out of all the people I could talk to and be with right now, it's you. You're the one I want to be with," Brent said.

Kara's eyes lowered as a rush of confusing emotions went through her.

"And a few weeks ago we didn't have a civil word to say to each other," Brent continued.

"It's been strong and strange between us. As if there's no level ground. Every time I'm with you I feel off balance," Kara said. She looked into his eyes. "Even the first time."

"And that was your first time, wasn't it?" he asked.

Kara nodded. "I grew up in a very strict religious sect. For what I did with you that night, I would have been tried before a board of elders and shunned. Even my mother wouldn't have been allowed to talk to me anymore," she said.

"That's crazy. And your mother would have gone along with that?"

"She would have. But my mother's dead."

"I'm sorry," he said. "Do you have other relatives?"

"No, just me and my mother, that was all. My mother's relatives weren't members of the religion, so I never knew them. We only associated with members of the religion."

Kara sat on the end of the couch, her arms wrapped around her knees. "So that's the long story about why I'm a thirty-year-old virgin. Was."

"You still are. We never made love." Brent looked deep into her eyes, and a shiver ran through her body.

"Why did you move to Washington?" he asked.

The question took her aback. She decided to tell him the truth about her, part of it anyway.

"That's an even longer story. Are you sure you want to hear it?" she asked.

"I want to hear everything," Brent answered.

"When my mother died, I wanted to know the reason for her life. The reasons for everything. The old reasons made no sense anymore, and I begged God for new ones. I would pray but the punishing, demanding God I'd been raised with never answered.

"I went to the congregation elders. They said the sin that lies within me was the reason my prayers were unanswered. They said I needed to increase my ministry, and study more religious material. I tried, but it still wasn't enough." Kara unfolded her legs and shot a glance at Brent. He was listening, his finger circling the rim of his coffee cup.

She took a deep breath. "A need to break free, to escape, was the only response to my prayers. I would close my eyes and see a jeweled butterfly, crystalline, radiant, and absolutely beautiful. It escaped its net and was fluttering upward into the clear blue sky. It was joyful, it was free, and it was not afraid." She peeked at Brent. Was he laughing at her? Did he think what she shared was silly? He hadn't moved. His face was open and earnest. He nodded his head and she went on.

"The third time I saw the butterfly, I knew what I had to do. I stopped going to the meetings, and put the house on the market. When the elders came to ask me what was wrong, I told them my questions and doubts.

"Fear filled the older men's eyes when I talked to them, and their only responses were rote answers and quotes from the religious literature the organization published.

"When I saw a member of the congregation in the streets or at the store, they turned away. To these people with whom I'd spent my entire life, I was as good as dead, and no one mourned or cared. The years of service and isolation that my mother went through within the congregation were like nothing; withered to ashes at the voice of doubt and the questioning of their beliefs."

Brent had moved beside her, a tissue in his hand. To Kara's amazement, tears were streaming down her cheeks. She'd given a dispassionate speech about the facts. That was what had happened, and it was over. It shouldn't hurt and she wasn't supposed to cry.

Brent leaned toward her and took her hands in his. "Stone told me you were a member of some small religious group, but I had no idea. You've been through so much."

"Was a member, they put me out." Kara wiped her eyes and blew her nose. "Who is Stone?" she asked.

Brent sat back. "He's a private detective I hired to investigate you," Brent said quietly.

Kara froze in the middle of withdrawing another tissue from the box. "Excuse me? You hired a detective to investigate me?"

"You have to admit the way you maneuvered yourself into a position close to the congressman looked pretty suspicious. It's my job to check out whatever is suspicious."

"And what has this detective found out about me?" Kara asked, trying to sound calm.

"Nothing other than what you've told me," Brent answered.

Relief flooded Kara.

"Wait, he did say he had some information. Something he wouldn't give me details on until he could get hard evidence."

Panic filled Kara and she looked away before Brent could see her eyes. Her mind told her to confess everything to Brent, tell him she was Sidney Eastman's daughter. But, she wasn't ready for the moment of truth.

Brent was waiting for her to say something. To reveal something about her and Sidney Eastman. She couldn't. She just couldn't.

"When is Jenny's trial coming up?" Kara asked.

Disappointment touched Brent's features briefly. "In about three weeks," he said.

"She'll be okay, won't she Brent?" Kara asked. She cared about Jenny.

Brent hesitated. "I don't know. I talked to Sidney today, and he's adamant about her not going into treatment. I learned the problem's roots are deeper than I thought. Tiffany also has a drinking problem."

"What?" Kara breathed.

"Sidney led me to believe she's had one for years. They've hidden, denied, and covered it up all this time. I don't think Jenny is going to be treated differently."

Kara shook her head. "I could tell Tiffany was extremely unhappy when she accused me of . . ." Her voice trailed away. "Not just unhappy at the situation she imagined, but unhappy with her life."

"The family's decidedly dysfunctional. Man, I might drink, too, if I had to deal with a family like that my entire life."

Kara was silent. She wanted to defend the Eastmans. Dysfunctional or not, it was the only family she had. Kara chewed her bottom lip. She glanced at Brent and caught him staring at her. Heat burned in his amber eyes and reflected similar heat in hers.

"I better go," said Brent.

"What about dinner?" Kara asked.

"Do you want me to stay?" The question hung in the air, full of meaning beyond the words. If he stayed he wasn't leaving. They both knew it.

Kara set down her coffee cup and stood up in one smooth motion. The time wasn't right, and the tiny flame burning between them threatened to ignite at any moment. The apartment suddenly seemed much too small and much too warm.

"We can do dinner another time. We have a lot to think about," she said.

She walked him to the door. "I appreciated you being here for me. Talking to you was . . . great," Brent said. He bent down to brush his lips against Kara's cheek.

When his lips touched her skin, trailing fire, Kara's eyes closed. The moment stopped. He moved his lips over and caressed her lips, a tender kiss, full of promise. When he lifted his head, Kara felt bereft.

"Goodbye," he said, and then he was gone.

Fifteen minutes later, Taylor was at the door. "I saw him leave, I thought he was going to stay for dinner."

"Are you spying on me, girl?" Kara asked.

"Yes," Taylor answered, unashamed. "I got to have something to do. My life doesn't have nearly as much excitement as yours. Though I did get a call Friday. I have an interview in Atlanta for a new job. Old one's getting kind of stale."

Taylor, a lawyer, worked for a nonprofit agency for consumer activism. "I can honestly say I don't know what I'd do without you," Kara said.

"You could move to Atlanta, it's a nice town. We could be roomies."

Kara laughed. "You're talking like you've got the job already. It's an interview, right?" she asked.

Taylor gave a sly smile. "If I didn't get the job, it would be a first. I'm psychic remember?"

"Right," Kara said. "You're going to stay for dinner? I made vegetarian lasagna."

"Already working to get Brent off that red meat, I see. Why do you think I came over? I'm hungry."

The next week at the office was uneventful. Kara'd been

jumpy all week. She had a feeling of impending doom, or at least the feeling something was going to happen. It was finally Friday. The empty weekend stretched ahead, but at least she'd be out of the office.

When she returned from getting a cup of coffee, her message light was blinking, indicating she had a note in her voice mail.

"I wondered if we could get away this weekend. I know a great seafood place up at Ann Arbor. Give me a call," Brent had recorded in her voice mail.

Should she go with Brent for a weekend away or tell him she just wanted dinner? Kara twirled a pen in her fingers. Should she or shouldn't she? She'd been browsing in a used bookstore, and seen this book about some rules a woman was supposed to follow with a man. Kara guessed she wasn't a game player, she'd broken most of the rules already.

The book said you were supposed to automatically turn down a weekend date if he didn't ask you some predetermined days in advance. And the main gist of the rules was to make the man wait for sex as long as possible. The book said nothing about what to do if you wanted it as bad as he did.

But look what happened to Katey. Then again, she wasn't Katey and it was a silly book, Kara decided impulsively. She picked up the phone to tell Brent she was free this weekend.

Seventeen

Brent and Kara sped down the highway on an unseasonably warm fall day. Autumn foliage lined the road in tones of gold, red, and brown. The air smelled of woodsmoke and apples touched with the scent of the sea as they neared the bay. Kara's hair blew in the wind.

She peeked at Brent under her lashes. He had one hand draped over the wheel, idly controlling the car. She'd committed herself, there was no turning back. They would spend the weekend together, and the unspoken awareness that they would finally consummate their aching desire tingled between them.

No regrets, no turning back.

The inn on the Chesapeake Bay looked like a large English farmhouse as they approached. The farmhouse notion was dispelled as soon as Kara spied the spectacular gardens surrounding the inn.

When she entered, Kara caught her breath at the luxuriant ambiance. While the exterior of the inn looked like a rambling English home in the country, the interior resembled a palace. Kara's heels clicked on Italian marble, and crystal chandeliers glittered. The inn was perfect for a weekend tryst, intimate and warm in spite of the luxury, filled with antiques and atmosphere.

She wandered into the sitting area while Brent checked

them in, admiring the fire in the marble fireplace that was taller than she was.

"Are you coming up?" Brent asked, holding his hand out to her with a smile.

Kara's heart pounded as they followed the bellboy up to their room. Tonight was the night she would finally belong to Brent. As they entered their room, her mouth dried when she spied the four-poster bed.

"Where's the bathroom?" she stammered. The bellboy gestured toward a door, and Kara fled.

When she returned the bellboy was gone. Brent waited, an amused look on his face. He took her into his arms for a casual hug, but Kara's pulses quickened at the feel of his body against hers.

"The first time I met you, you got nervous and ran in the bathroom, remember?" he said.

"I didn't know if I could go through with it," she murmured.

Brent touched the tip of her nose. "If you're not ready, the inn has vacancies. I can get another room."

Kara shook her head. She was more than ready after thirty years of waiting. She was a little nervous, that was all.

They ate lunch in a seafood restaurant on the bay. There was a casual, family ambiance, but the food and service were excellent. The crab melted in her mouth.

"I rented a boat for the afternoon," Brent said.

Kara's stomach knotted. "I'd rather not. Large bodies of water . . . upset me."

Brent raised an eyebrow. "You don't swim?" he asked.

"Never. Maybe something happened to me when I was very young, I don't remember. I've always had this phobia about deep water."

Kara hated admitting the weakness, but there was no way she was going out on all that water in a boat.

"I don't see you as the type to be scared of water," Brent said.

"I'm not going on a boat," Kara said flatly.

"I'm not asking you to. I was talking about overcoming fear. Have you ever taken swimming lessons?"

Kara hesitated. "No," she answered, wondering what his point was.

"That would be a good place to start," was all he said.

After they finished eating, Kara mentioned there was a movie that she wanted to see. They bought a local paper, and returned to the room. The mood between them had lightened; as if they were good friends, rather than soon-to-be lovers.

Then Brent opened the door to the hotel room. They both paused at the threshold, the door open behind them. The ornate bed loomed and everything changed in an instant.

Their eyes locked, and heat shimmered between them. Kara looked away. Then, with sudden resolve, she walked into the room, he followed, and she pushed the door shut. Brent didn't move. Kara studied him as he stood there.

His chiseled features were stamped with intelligence and sensuality. His tall, leanly muscled, elegant brown body was casually dressed in khakis and a cotton shirt. He was all she ever wanted in a man, all she ever dreamed. She was tired of waiting, and she didn't know how to play games.

She took off her jacket and dropped it in a chair. She walked over and got her bag. "I don't think I want to see that movie this evening. I'm going to get ready for bed."

Brent's face showed bemusement at her words. She grinned wickedly. "Why don't you do your part and order the champagne?" she said before she disappeared into the bathroom.

The pink marble bathroom with gleaming golden fixtures was as big as her bedroom at home. The bathtub was deep and sunken with whirlpool jets. She filled it and studied the array of bath salts and additives the inn provided. Gardenias, she decided. The scent would be perfect.

She sank into the warm scented water with a sigh. She felt confident, relaxed, and happy. The other Kara, the sensuous uninhibited one took over. She sank into the water up to her neck, and closed her eyes, savoring the massaging jets of water.

When she opened her eyes, Brent was standing in the door, a champagne glass in his hand.

She stood up, totally unashamed, water cascading off her brown body. Brent's facial muscles tautened, smoldering sensuality evident in the hard lines of his face. He picked up an oversized bath towel from one of the warmed towel racks, and Kara walked into it.

Her body was aching, quivering, ready for him. He dried her gently and thoroughly, caressing her body through the thick, thirsty terry. Soft murmurs rose from her throat. She wanted him to take her, now. She couldn't wait.

His lips finally touched hers and she shuddered. The tender crush of his lips burned through her. She pulled the towel from between them and it dropped to the floor. She rubbed her naked body feverishly against him, pulling his shirt from the confines of his pants, her fingertips grazing his smooth heated skin.

He groaned. "Don't make me lose it, Kara. I don't want to go too fast," he breathed.

That was exactly what she wanted. She wanted all of him. He gathered her in his arms and moved her to the bed. He trailed kisses down her neck to the mounds of her breasts. She arched against him impatiently seeking his hardness.

With a swift intake of breath, he ground against her, pressing against her sensitive pubic bone, searching and seeking urgent hot fusion.

Suddenly he pulled away and she was bereft. He shed his clothing and he looked like a god dropped from heaven. His maleness, which Kara ached for, was erect and ready for her. She moaned incoherently, reaching for him, and then he was back in her arms. Smooth, sleek skin over hard pulsing muscle, he fit his hot body against hers.

Then he pulled back and pinned her hands over her head. His eyes devoured her. "God, you're beautiful," he whispered. And he lowered his head, raining tender, sweet kisses along her cheekbone, and down the hollows of her neck while he murmured incoherent phrases of adoration and bliss.

Kara's stomach tensed and she gasped as his tongue teased and caressed her breasts. She couldn't breathe, filled with wild, fluttering excitement that rose and rose until she couldn't stand it. Burning and aching, her feminine core begged for him to be buried deep inside. The craving was sweet torture, and she arched her back and moaned.

"Oh God, Brent, please, I can't wait—"

He groaned and muscles rippled through his body as he finally eased himself to the hot slickness between her legs.

The first thrust of his hardness made her gasp and stiffen with the sudden pain. His stroke was swift and sure and he penetrated her fully. He stopped, his eyes dark with passion, his hands caressing her cheeks. "Are you okay?" he murmured.

Kara was beyond speech, she was full, so full of him, and even while she didn't think she could bear the sweet agony of it, she wanted more. She clutched him to her and then he moved and she experienced pleasure so good it hurt. Her body quivered with delight.

The swollen friction of his hardness, his heavy thickness caressed her velvet walls. She whimpered as the deep red waves of pleasure built and eddied higher and higher, with the timeless rhythms of his thrusts. Then the flood gates burst through her body and she died a death of pure shaking rapture. She spiraled down slowly, and felt him shudder his release, melting into her honeyed warmth. And something closed full circle, and she was complete, finally whole. Love too long denied felt as natural and necessary as breathing.

A little later, as they lay in each other's arms, Brent kissed her wet lips with his trembling mouth. Then they fell asleep in each other's arms until they awoke to explore their newfound passions all over again.

Sunday afternoon, Kara and Brent stayed in bed amid a champagne brunch fit for a queen and king. They hadn't left the room since check-in. Kara learned love's many facets from deep red passion to playful games to open, warmhearted giving.

"Umm, try this." Brent fed her a delicious crab-stuffed mushroom, then he licked a fleck away from the corner of her mouth.

Kara smiled in pure satisfaction. She took a swallow of her drink, a mimosa, then kissed him, their tongues entangled and champagne and oranges mingled in their mouths. Brent teased her nipple with his lips, causing electricity to crackle and ignite the flame that never fully went out.

He pulled her on top of him, their bodies fusing with exquisite passion. Later, much later, they remembered they had to get back to Washington and resume the threads of the lives they had suspended for a weekend of bliss.

Even Monday morning couldn't extinguish the warm glow from Kara's first time at love that weekend. She brought the papers from home that she'd stolen from Brent's briefcase the night they'd first met. She stuffed the papers deep in a desk drawer behind other forms, planning to give them back. Hopefully, they could start anew, their initial history put away and forgotten.

As Kara cleared a backlog of work from her desk, her phone rang. She picked it up absently, still studying a memo she was writing about the new computer software to the clerical staff.

"Hi, this is Jenny."

The aftereffects of the blissful weekend with Brent faded away. The sound of Jenny's voice jarred her into reality.

"Have you heard the news?" Jenny went on without waiting for a reply. "Brent broke up with me. He promised he wouldn't leave me, but as soon as I could walk again, he was gone. He was lying all the time. I would have been better off in a wheelchair."

Jenny's voice was bitter and whiny. Kara was shocked at the disregard for reality and lack of self-insight Jenny displayed.

"Are you positive it didn't have something to do with you?" Kara asked gently.

"Of course it had something to do with me. I wasn't exciting or beautiful enough for him. You should see the women he's dated."

It was on the tip of Kara's tongue to ask about Brent's old girlfriends. She firmly put the impulse aside. Jenny was her sister and she needed help. Boy, did she need help.

"Jenny, remember that morning when you were waiting for Brent in his office? When you were drinking that liquor in the orange juice?" Kara asked.

Jenny said nothing.

"Jenny?"

"You've been talking to him. He's blaming everything on my drinking, but he drinks. Everybody drinks. I can handle my liquor. It's just an excuse and I feel sorry for you if you believe it."

Jenny slammed the phone down loudly in Kara's ear.

Kara rubbed her ear to stop the ringing. Irritation at Jenny for her immaturity, her plain stupidity, was overshadowed by another emotion. Guilt. She was raised with the notion that some things simply weren't done. You didn't betray blood. Even if he left her, you still didn't go behind your sister's back with the man she loved.

It was three o'clock in the morning. Tiffany Eastman sat in front of the dim lamp at her antique French Provençal desk. She was alone. A fifth of vodka sat in front of her, alongside an empty glass. She started to open the bottle, hesitated, and closed her eyes in pain. Then with a ferocious movement, she threw it into the fireplace and it exploded into a thousand broken shards.

Tiffany sank into the plush cream carpet in front of the cold fireplace, and the force of her sobs bent her over. She didn't bother to stifle her wails. No one would hear her. Dante was with his girlfriend and Sidney was with his. Jenny was passed out over a bottle of Southern Comfort in her bedroom. Like mother, like daughter.

After a while her sobs subsided. Tiffany stood up, resolute, and walked back over to her desk. She pulled out a blunt-nosed .22, a lady's pistol, the handle daintily inlaid with carved ivory. Laying it on the desk, she sat and stared at it.

These were her choices. She could end this travesty called a life, the miserable life that now infected her daughter. Jenny was just like her. A drunk. A worthless, useless drunk.

Or, she could change.

Dying was easier. She picked up the pistol and caressed it. She thought of the past. When she was Jenny's age, life was full of promise. She'd married an ambitious man, who played and loved as hard as he worked. She was going to have his child.

Sidney continued to rise in the ranks of state government. She was active in society, charity work, clubs, her sorority. When her children were babies, life was good.

When did everything change? When did she and Sidney grow so far apart that he never touched her? That she hardly remembered him ever loving her? When did he turn cruel, his words and actions as painful as blows? When did her children grow away from her and into their own lives?

And when did she take the first drink to escape? She never looked back from that first drink. Solace and oblivion were only vodka martinis away.

Jenny. That failure hurt more than anything. Her baby, so young, losing her life before it even started. Sobs started afresh. Tiffany stared at the gun on the desk. What if Jenny chose this way out? The easy way.

There was no point in going on for herself. Her life was hopeless, she was a failure; her kids were the only good thing she'd ever done.

What would Jenny do after she was gone? She touched the gun and she knew. Tiffany couldn't allow it to happen. She had to go on for her daughter. She had to be strong for Jenny. With shaking hands, Tiffany turned away from the gun and picked up the phone book.

Eighteen

Brent stretched his neck as he ran the razor over the stubble on his chin Monday morning. The jarring ring of the phone made him jump, and the razor slipped. He swore and stuck a piece of tissue on the tiny cut.

He picked up the phone, and the voice of Sidney Eastman boomed out. "Tiffany's gone," he said gruffly.

Brent rubbed his eyes and took another sip of coffee. Setting the cup down, he waited for Sidney to continue, unsuccessfully trying to both hold the cordless phone and resume shaving.

"When I got home this morning, she'd packed a suitcase and taken her purse, but she didn't leave a note, nothing."

You'd think he'd at least spend his week nights at home, Brent thought.

"She's finally left you," Brent said.

"I know she didn't go to her family, and she has no close friends . . ." Sidney's voice trailed away.

"Give her a little time, I'm sure she'll get in touch. Jenny might know where she went," Brent said.

After Brent got off the phone, he thought for once Sidney's primary concern wasn't about how something looked to other people. He'd seemed genuinely shaken.

As soon as Brent got to work there was a message to call Sidney at home.

Sidney picked up on the first ring. "Tiffany left a note

with Jenny. She's checked herself into an alcoholic treatment center. My God! She used her real name. I'm ruined,"
he said.

Ah, now that was the real Sidney, Brent thought.

"Jenny is distraught. In the letter Tiffany left, she raved
on about alcoholism. If you hadn't brought up all that
stuff about drinking, this would never have happened!"
Sidney ranted.

There was a pause, maybe Sidney sensed he had gone
too far.

"Will you find out where she is and go see her? See what
she wants so she'll come back home," Sidney asked.

"That's not my job, Sidney," Brent said.

Sidney sputtered in surprise and indignation for a few
more minutes, but there was nothing more he could say.

Maybe it was time for a change, Brent thought after he'd
gotten Sidney off the phone. He'd been working with Sidney so long, it felt like a habit. A habit that, lately, wasn't
fitting all that well.

Jenny looked up from the pages of a letter her mother
had written her from the alcohol treatment center. So,
Mom was a drunk. Worse, she thinks I'm a drunk, too.
Jenny stared into the brown depths of her drink as if
searching for answers.

She sipped delicately and sighed with pleasure as she
felt the burning liquid slip down her gullet. Southern
Comfort, what an apt name. It felt so good. But she was
not an alcoholic. She never drank in public. Enjoying a
little Southern Comfort in the privacy of one's own room
did not an alcoholic make.

She missed her mother. She missed Brent. The empti-
ness of her days stretched forward. Maybe she'd pull herself together one day and think about grad school. But
not now.

Jenny picked up the phone to call Kara at work. Something drew her to Kara. Exactly what, Jenny didn't understand, since Kara was her opposite in both looks and temperament. Her healthy, well-scrubbed, all-American looks contrasted with Kara's sultry, faintly exotic appearance. Jenny was spring pastels, Kara a palette of winter colors. Jenny's demeanor was sunny and uncomplicated, Kara's reserved and complex.

Still, Jenny really liked Kara, even though it was difficult to crack through her reserve and get to know her. She needed someone to lean on, and Kara seemed to be willing to be that person.

A clerk said Kara was at lunch. Jenny sighed with dissatisfaction and studied the large diamond and sapphire ring Brent had given her for their engagement. He never said anything about her returning it.

Jenny took another sip of Southern Comfort. The bastard. Anger surged through her. He dumped her and there was nothing she could do about it. She would toss his ring back into his face and wipe that self-righteous expression right off. How dare he say she had a drinking problem? He drank all the time.

She called his office. That bitch Katey answered the phone. Even though she called Brent a couple of times every day, Katey never let her through to him.

"Katey, I want to speak to Brent," Jenny said, command in her voice.

"He's out to lunch," Katey replied, sounding weary.

"I won't stand for your excuses, I want to speak to Brent."

"Jenny, he left to meet Kara Smith for lunch over an hour ago. I'll tell him you called."

"You do that," Jenny said, slamming the phone down. Jenny smiled to imagine Katey's wince of pain as the sound reverberated in her ear.

It was a few minutes later when Jenny wondered what Brent was doing at lunch with Kara.

Another perfect fall day, and Brent and Kara had decided to eat in the park. Afterward, they strolled down the walk hand in hand. Kara thanked God daily for the happiness now present in her life. Brent was all she ever dreamed he would be. Tender, fierce, open, and caring, all man with a touch of vulnerable little boy peeking through. She trusted him, secure in the knowledge that he cared deeply for her. For now, it was enough.

Her mind turned to the one blight on her happiness; the Eastman family, Jenny in particular. If the trial next week turned out well, she and Brent would talk to her afterward. Hopefully, they could make her see reason. Brent wasn't meant for her as a husband, but there was someone out there who was right for Jenny. Kara prayed it was so. Maybe, they could all be friends. Maybe, she could help her sister. Kara sighed, knowing how unlikely those scenarios were.

"What are you thinking about?" asked Brent.

"Jenny," she answered.

With a wry twist of his lips Brent said, "Things are complicated when they should be so simple."

"That's the way life is," Kara answered.

They walked in silence a little further.

"Don't ever shut yourself off," Brent said suddenly.

"What do you mean?"

"Let's always be honest with each other. And if there's a problem let's talk it out instead of jumping to conclusions," Brent said.

"All right," Kara said. In the back of her mind dwelled the fear her mouth was making promises her heart couldn't keep.

* * *

Sidney Eastman had been trying all day to see his wife. At first she didn't want to see him and the staff stood firm against his tirades. As the day wore on, Tiffany relented, and Sidney was escorted into a small comfortably furnished room where she waited.

"What's wrong with you? How could you check in here under your real name and put me in an awkward position? If you'd said something, I'd have flown you to the Betty Ford clinic or somewhere!"

Tiffany looked serene and composed. "It's always about you, isn't it Sidney?"

Taken aback, he said nothing, stopped his pacing, and sat in a chair beside her.

"This is for me and my children," Tiffany continued. "It has nothing to do with you."

"Tiffany, come home. We'll talk—"

"I've heard it before. There's nothing more to talk about, don't you understand? I want a divorce."

Sidney blinked. "I can't believe I'm hearing this after all the years I've stuck it out with you."

"Believe it," Tiffany said.

"No. You can't have a divorce. You'd never make it on your own anyway. You can barely make it through a day without a drink. The timing is bad, my political career—"

"I don't give a damn about you or your political career. You give me a fair divorce, or the proceedings will be so ugly the *National Inquirer* won't want to touch it. I promise I'll make your political career a faint memory."

A look of desperation crossed Sidney's face. "Another chance, Tiff. I'll give up the women. We'll spend some time together," he begged.

Tiffany stood up. "Your time was up some time ago. You'll be hearing from my lawyer." She crossed the room swiftly and slipped out the door.

Nights passed in a haze of pleasure. Kara was turning

into a creature of the night. Loving the darkness, loving the love she and Brent shared. She couldn't imagine ever getting enough of him. They sat together on his sofa in front of the TV at Brent's town house, after his now favorite meal of meatloaf and mashed potatoes. His head was nestled in her lap and her fingers caressed the rough texture of his closely cut hair. She drank in his soap and musky male smell.

Brent reached for her face and their lips touched. The tender caress of his lips soon grew more hungry. With a swift motion he turned and pulled her on top of him. His fingers ran under her sweater, over her torso, teasing where her bra lay.

Her nipples were erect and aching, she pressed them against his chest. She needed to feel the flesh of him. In one motion she pulled her sweater and bra off over her head. She pulled up Brent's sweater and rubbed her tender, aching nipples slowly across his lightly haired chest. Brent groaned and cupped her buttocks, pulling her against his rock hard bulge. Kara's hips did a slow grind.

Their eyes met, and they stumbled to the bedroom, leaving a trail of clothing in their wake. They fell on the bed and Brent again held her close, enveloping her small form in a tender hug. Their tongues met and mingled in slow, drugged passion. Kara's hands ran feverishly over Brent's body, seeking, searching . . . Then, her small hand could barely surround the silky warmth of Brent's turgid manhood. He growled and pulled her up to him.

She gave a throaty laugh and leaned down to kiss him, their tongues mingling and meeting in a private dance. In one smooth motion he impaled her and a moan escaped from her lips. Sweet heaven.

She rotated her hips to a sensuous inner rhythm working up and down, milking his shaft. Brent cupped her breasts with both hands, covering them, squeezing them gently, his thumbs rotating over her sensitive nipples, sending electricity to the heart of her. They rocked together faster and faster to the intimate rhythm only they shared. The pressures built within her core to a crescendo, and the movement of her hips became faster, more urgent.

He matched her primal rhythms, his eyes narrowed, his face burning with desire. Now. Right now. Don't stop. Implosion followed, and Kara could only gasp in ecstasy as wave after wave of pure rapture rolled through her.

Brent shuddered and grasped her hips, driving deep within her, to the very womb of her. She felt his explosion of warm life within, and she was complete. This was heaven, everything and all she needed.

They lay together, limbs entangled, in the sweet exhaustion that follows lovemaking. Brent lifted himself up on one elbow and lazily traced Kara's features, running a finger down her cheek.

"This is special. I've had girlfriends, but it never felt like this. I wonder what it is?"

"Barbecue sauce," she replied.

Brent looked confused for an instant, then grinned. "You know I wasn't talking about your meatloaf." He rubbed his stomach. "Though it is pretty special. Barbecue sauce, huh?"

Kara laughed and snuggled in his arms. "Now that you know the secret, I have to kill you."

He held her for a while, their silence comfortable, their breaths matching.

"You belong here with me, Kara. I never want to let you go."

She looked into his eyes, her heart turning to warm, melted butter at his words.

"I never thought I'd hear myself say those words. I was the classic commitment-phobic male. Usually this far into a relationship, I want to jump up and leave, and get on with my life. At the very least, I'd be thinking of excuses to get her out of my place," he said.

Kara rolled over and looked at him earnestly. "That must have really hurt some women who shared their love with you."

Brent swallowed. "It probably did," he said in a distant voice. "I never thought about it in that light before."

A loud crash sounded at Brent's door.

"What the hell?" he said, rolling off the bed and grabbing a pair of jeans.

"Brent, I know you're in there, come and answer this door right now," Jenny screamed.

"Shit," Brent swore.

"Don't let her know I'm in here," Kara said.

Jenny resumed kicking the door and screaming.

"She's going to get the neighbors all upset," Brent said, pulling up his jeans. "If somebody told me a month ago that Jenny'd be carrying on like this, I'd never have believed it," he said as he walked to the door.

Nineteen

Jenny started to burst through the doorway. Brent blocked her way with his body.

"What do you want, Jenny?" he asked.

The calmness of his voice seemed to quiet her. Brent distinctly smelled alcohol. Her hair and clothes were disheveled. His heart sank, she was getting worse. Jenny used to have such control to keep her drinking secret. She'd completely lost it.

She tugged at her engagement ring. "I wanted to throw this in your face, you bastard!"

"You can keep it. It was a gift."

"Why would I want anything that reminded me of you?"

She finally got it off and threw it at him. It bounced on the carpet behind them and laid there gleaming dully.

Then she started to cry. "I don't want to stand in the doorway. Can't you let me in? I want to talk."

Brent looked beyond Jenny, where her yellow car was parked askew from the curb. Alarms went off within him.

"You drove?" he asked, already knowing and dreading the answer.

"What of it?" Jenny asked belligerently.

"Where are the keys?" Brent demanded.

She felt around in her pockets and looked toward the car. "Maybe I left them in the ignition." Brent sighed.

"I've got to take you home," he said.

174   *Monica Jackson*

He stood there for a moment, pondering his dilemma.
He didn't want to let her in, especially with Kara in the
bedroom, but he didn't trust her to wait for him and not
climb back in her car and drive away. In her condition,
driving had been deadly once, and he couldn't risk that
again.

If she got stopped by the police, she would definitely go
to jail. Although, at the moment, Brent didn't think that
was a bad idea.

Jenny tried to push past him. "Let me in!" she cried.

Suddenly her eyes narrowed and her face grew suspicious. "You have somebody in there," she hissed.

This had gone on too long. Brent turned around and
spied his keys on the coffee table. He grabbed them and
grabbed Jenny by the arm. She'd darted inside as soon as
he had moved. He was going to have to take her home.

"I'm taking you home now," he said, loud enough for
Kara to hear.

Tiffany didn't deny her anticipation when her son called
and said he was coming.

She and Dante had grown distant the past few years.
She never worried about him becoming a mama's boy.
Dante had adored his father ever since he could walk. Tiffany remembered him crying out for his father instead of
her when he fell or got hurt. Except his father never came.

That's how it had been until Dante moved out. Dante
needing his father, and Sidney never responding, not caring really. Even when Dante got his law degree and wanted
to follow his dad's footsteps into politics, Sidney shrugged
him away. He spent more time with Brent than with his
own son.

When Sidney got elected to Congress, Dante fully expected to be appointed to the AA position. He'd spent his
summers on Capitol Hill in law school, soaking up the

atmosphere, learning everything he could about the nuts and bolts running of a congressional office.

Only Tiffany knew how wounded Dante was when Sidney gave the position to Brent without even considering his son. Home and family were required ornaments for Sidney, necessary but nonfunctional. Lord knew, he felt the same about her. Sidney sought his feminine pleasures elsewhere, never realizing that he had the same thing at home for free.

Hindsight was often painful. Tiffany hated that she was so weak to have let it go on for so long, hurting not only herself, but her children, too.

She didn't even know Dante anymore. But he stayed in Washington, D.C., when he easily could have left. There was something that wouldn't allow him to sever the family connection.

"Mother," Dante said, interrupting her melancholy thoughts about him.

Tiffany smiled at him. "Come sit beside me," she said.

He kissed her on the cheek. "I heard that you filed for divorce." He looked shaken, uneasy.

"I should have done it sooner. Much sooner," she said, meeting his eyes.

Her son: charming, handsome Dante. She was proud of him. She wished she could break the reserve that he'd locked around himself, so he would confide in her like he used to do when he was a child. Or was that just a fantasy, also? Dante had never really confided in her.

He looked troubled. Her mother's second sense told her something was wrong.

"Are you upset about the divorce?" she asked.

Dante looked fierce. "Not at all," he said. "You're right. You should have done it sooner. And now it'll make it much easier."

"Make what easier?" Tiffany asked.

Dante shrugged. "I hate the son of a bitch. Now, he'll be totally out of our lives."

Tiffany was surprised. She'd never seen Dante show such strong emotion before. And he'd never before spoken disrespectfully of his father.

"What's wrong, Dante? I've never heard you say anything like that about your father before. You used to adore him."

Dante seemed to fold within himself. He smiled, his mask back securely in place.

"I'm sorry, Mom, I was upset."

Tiffany was troubled, but she didn't know how to question him. Dante's relationship with his father wasn't necessarily bad, it was just nonexistent.

So they talked about the food, her treatment, and his job, inconsequential things, impersonal pleasantries. When Dante bent to kiss her goodbye, she wanted to grab his arm, and demand that he talk to her, and tell her what he was thinking.

After he left, she sat staring after him for a while. It was a long time before her uneasiness subsided.

Dante thought that it had been a stroke of genius on his part to search Kara's desk for something incriminating. He suspected the promotions and job changes Brent handed to her, all with his father's apparent say-so, indicated something fishy. Dante'd made it his business to find out what, and he'd struck gold.

All it took was an anonymous packet in the mail to the *Washington Post* containing the papers damning both the Americabanc Corporation and Congressman Eastman. Dad was confident his reelection for a third term was a sure bet, and he was already planning his future senatorial campaign. Now, his father would go down in flames. And as an added bonus, Brent Stevens's political career would turn to ashes, also. Dante would enjoy watching the conflagration.

But nothing had broken in the news yet. What if the papers never reached Dean Riley at the *Washington Post*? What if Dean thought they were fake? Dante couldn't risk this opportunity slipping away. He picked up the phone. He'd have to call Dean Riley himself.

It was past midnight, and Sidney Eastman walked heavily up to his daughter's room, afraid of what he might find. She'd been closeted in there for two days, and he couldn't ignore the situation any longer. He wished he could. Didn't he have enough to worry about without all the problems on the homefront? Damn Tiffany's hide. That was her job and she took off when he needed her to take control of her responsibilities.

He didn't bother to knock. It was his house. He paid the bills. The stink of the room hit his nose first. The acrid stench of old vomit blended with the musky smell of an unwashed body.

Jenny was draped over her bed upside down, her mouth open, an unladylike snore issuing forth. She had nothing on but a filthy T-shirt tangled around her waist. He averted his eyes when he saw that she didn't have any panties on.

The room was an awful mess. Disgust filled Sidney when he saw half empty bottles of Southern Comfort and vodka littered around the room. His fastidious, neat daughter had obviously gone off her rocker. Like mother, like daughter. It was her sorry mother's fault. Tiffany had never measured up to what she was supposed to do. If Tiffany were here, he'd like to beat the crap out of both of them.

He shook Jenny's shoulder roughly. "Get your nasty rear end out of that bed and clean it up."

Jenny opened one eye and moaned, clutching her head.

"Did you hear me?" he thundered.

"Daddy, please leave me alone. I'm sick," she moaned in a little girl's voice.

Sidney's hand ached to knock her upside her head. But he controlled himself. He always did. Cultured men did not beat up their wives and daughters, however much they might want to. Sidney frequently congratulated himself on his self-control.

That self-control was slipping now. He grabbed her by her arms and dragged her off the bed roughly. She screamed. He thrust her in front of a mirror.

"Look at yourself, look at the repulsive slut in that mirror." He shook her in fury.

Jenny screamed again, and tears ran down her face. He shook her one last time and let her drop in a heap on the floor.

"You're just like your mother. I want this room cleaned up, and the funk washed off your nasty butt. If I ever come in here again and see a mess like this, I'll commit you to a mental hospital, where you belong, like your mother."

"Please, Daddy, don't—I'm sorry," Jenny whimpered, curled up in a fetal ball on the floor.

He stared at her, his nostrils flaring. He wanted to kick her, but once he did, he knew he wouldn't stop. She was so much like her mother.

"You disgusting little slut. I'm ashamed you're my daughter," he said, and walked out of the room before he gave in to the impulse to give her what she so richly deserved.

"I can't believe you're going to leave," Kara said, shaking her head.

"I told you I was going to get the job, didn't I?" Taylor said.

Kara sighed. "What am I gonna do without you?" she asked, partially to herself.

"Chin up, girl. I'm not leaving for a month. Anyway, you're probably going to end up in Atlanta yourself."

Kara waved her hand no. "It's getting hot between Brent and me. I'm not going anywhere."

Taylor smiled and plopped on the couch next to Kara. "Pretty good, isn't it?"

"Girl, I can hardly stand it. Why did I wait thirty years for this?" Kara said.

"I don't think you waited for the sex, that was just circumstances; you waited for the man. When it's that good, and believe me it sometimes isn't, it's always the man. He's the right one."

"He is the right one," Kara said, her voice soft. "But it's still messed up. Jenny came over last night while I was there."

Taylor breathed in. "What did she do?"

"I don't know, screamed at Brent, I guess. He had to take her home. She was drunk and she drove over."

"Some people don't learn."

"I feel bad about her, but I don't feel as guilty anymore. I still don't necessarily want her to know about me and Brent yet though. She's so fragile. Brent says she's cracking up, but she won't get help."

Taylor shook her head. "Be careful, Kara. I don't feel that all this with your family is going to be over soon, but it will be over eventually."

"I can't wait."

"You know what it was that saved you?"

"From what?" Kara got a kick out of it when Taylor got into her "psychic" mode. The disconcerting thing was that she was always right. So far, at least.

"From untold disaster and grief," Taylor said matter-of-factly.

"Well, what was it that saved me?" Kara asked.

"That you did no harm. You let your desire for revenge go. Revenge was never your heart's desire."

Kara thought of Brent. "No, it isn't," she said.

That night Brent gathered Kara into his arms and held her close. Their lovemaking over, their hearts beat in unison, and their breathing rose and fell in rhythm.

"I can't get enough of you," he whispered.

Kara sighed in satisfaction. They were spending all their nights together, all their spare time. Pure bliss. She couldn't imagine it ending. She nestled in the crook of his arm.

"Jenny's trial is coming up next week," Brent said.

"I know, she called me. She begged me to be there."

"She left a message for me about it with Katey," he said.

The problem of Jenny wasn't going away. They needed to tell her. Kara was beginning to resent the sneaking around she and Brent were obliged to do to keep their blossoming relationship from Jenny.

"We need to tell her about us," Brent said, seemingly reading her thoughts.

Kara thought about Jenny's reaction.

"After the trial," he added.

Twenty

Jenny put the quarter into the slot of the pay phone with shaking hands and punched in the number again. When the hollow voice of the answering machine came on, a sob of frustration caught in Jenny's throat. Where was Dante? She needed him desperately.

After her father had left the room, she'd picked herself up and stood under the cold water of the shower. She always knew her father didn't like her much, but she never before realized how much he hated her. She threw some clothes into a suitcase, and left by the back door. No car. Brent wouldn't give her Acura back until after the trial. She walked to the pay phone.

She stood there in the cold wind, frigid tears running down her cheeks. A white couple passed, gave her suspicious looks, and walked faster. She supposed she looked like a crack addict who'd wandered into this upscale neighborhood.

Jenny picked up the phone and slowly entered Brent's number. He'd rejected her, but she didn't doubt for an instant that he'd be there to help her. The phone rang until the answering machine picked up.

Despair spiraled through Jenny. "Brent, please God, pick up. I need you," she whimpered into the phone. No answer.

She slowly replaced the receiver. She'd take a taxi to

Kara's. Kara'd let her stay at her place until she got hold of Dante or Brent.

Kara was awakened by the sound of the doorbell. She looked at the clock. It was almost two in the morning. Brent stirred next to her.

"Who do you think it is?" he asked.

"I don't know. Maybe Taylor. Something might be wrong. I'm going to see." Kara slipped her silk kimono over her naked shoulders.

The doorbell rang insistently. Kara peered through the peephole and to her utter dismay, Jenny stood there.

"Oh God, Kara, please let me in. If you don't, I'm going to die. I know it." Kara had never seen Jenny look so bad. Her eyes were red and swollen with crying. Was this never going to end? Were she and Brent continually going to have their sleep and lovemaking interrupted by Jenny's drunken rampages?

Kara cracked the door. "It's so late, Jenny, I have to get up very early."

Jenny leaned against the doorjamb and agonized sobs racked her. A neighbor down the hall peeked out. Kara stood there in a quandary for a moment. Then she opened the door and drew Jenny in.

She eased her in a chair, and handed her a box of tissues. Jenny's cries had diminished to anguished keening.

"I'm going to get some coffee," Kara said. "I'll be back in a few minutes."

"Who was it?" Brent asked as Kara reentered the bedroom.

"Jenny."

Brent turned on the lamp. "Is she drunk again? I wonder why she came over this time," he said, frowning.

"Something's really wrong, I've never seen her like this.

I'll talk to her for a while, then I'll put her in a taxi. I wanted to warn you so you wouldn't come out."

"I'm going to have to do something about her. This can't continue," he said.

Kara made instant coffee, and took a cup out to Jenny. Jenny sat huddled in the chair, her legs drawn up under her.

"What's going on?" Kara asked quietly.

"My mother's gone, my fiancé dumped me, my father hates me, and I'm on trial for murder tomorrow. That's a start."

Kara didn't quite know what to say.

"Can I stay here until I can get hold of Dante or Brent? I can't stay at home anymore," Jenny said.

Anxiety filled Kara. No, Jenny couldn't stay here with Brent naked in the bedroom.

"That would be awkward," Kara said slowly, "I'm expecting company."

"I'm just talking about until morning," Jenny said. "I won't be any trouble."

Damn, Kara thought. There was no way she could allow Jenny to stay. But how could she tell her?

"I'll get you a hotel room," Kara said. She stood up. "I'll call right now, and I'll have a taxi pick you up."

Jenny stared at her, her lip started to quiver, and her eyes grew moist. Kara bit her lower lip. Damn.

Then Jenny's eyes fell on a shining object sitting on the coffee table. Her eyes widened.

"Those are Brent's keys," she said.

Oh God, Kara thought.

Jenny unfolded her legs and moved to the bedroom before Kara could respond. She pulled open the door and stared at Brent lying in Kara's bed. All three of them froze in a tableau that seemed to last an eternity.

Jenny turned to Kara, horror in her eyes. "How could you?" she whispered.

Then Jenny's face transformed. Kara had never before witnessed such naked rage on another human's face. She raised her hand, and before Kara could react, slapped her so hard on the side of the face that she slammed into the opposite wall.

"Jenny!" Brent roared, and lunged toward her.

Jenny dodged him, and ran out of the door into the night.

Tiffany tossed and turned in her bed. Finally she gave up and got out of bed. She hadn't heard from Jenny yesterday, and she couldn't ease the nagging worry from her mind. It didn't help that her recovery was grueling. Her treatment delved to the roots of her reasons for her desire for oblivion, and her need to escape. She was having to face herself and her life. What she saw was painful and her body and emotions ached for a drink.

So far, a day at a time, her mind was stronger. It wasn't her willpower, no. She'd proved time and time again that she had none. Every minute she thanked God for the strength He gave her.

The night nurse tapped lightly on the door and entered the room. "You're awake," she said. "I've got a phone call for you. Your daughter says it's an emergency."

When Tiffany got to the phone, Jenny was incoherent. "Calm down, and tell me what's going on, honey."

"Brent was in Kara's bed and I don't have a place to stay," Jenny cried.

Tiffany took a minute to absorb this information. "Why aren't you home?" she asked.

"My father said I was a no-good slut," Jenny said. "Just like you," she said, as an afterthought.

Then Tiffany knew exactly what Jenny was talking about. She'd love to stick a knife into Sidney's rotten hide. He'd never let his rages boil over onto the kids before. But then, she wasn't there to absorb them.

"I'm not going back there, I hate him," Jenny said.

"Did you call Dante? He'll come and pick you up."

"He's not home."

Tiffany pondered what she should do for a moment.

"Never mind, Mama," Jenny said, sounding defeated. "It doesn't matter anyway."

Tiffany started to speak, to tell her she would leave the hospital and go pick her up, but Jenny had already hung up.

The next morning it was Jenny's trial date and there was still no sign of her. Brent waited at the courthouse for Tiffany and Dante to emerge.

The bereaved widow came out first. She met his eyes and nodded. Brent felt slightly chilled by the satisfied looks on the faces of the family surrounding her.

Then Tiffany emerged, supported by Dante. She looked older than Brent had ever seen her looking before.

"Where is my father?" Dante asked Brent.

Brent looked grim. "Working," he answered.

"My baby is going to go to prison," Tiffany said.

"She came over to Kara's last night," Brent said to Tiffany. "I was there."

"I know, she called me. Sidney went off on her and she wouldn't go back home. She hung up before I could find out where she was. I'm so scared for her," Tiffany said. "We've got to find her. I called the police last night, and they wouldn't even file a missing person's report on her. Since there's a warrant out for arrest with manslaughter on it, now I suppose they'll be looking a little harder," she said bitterly.

"I'll go to the office and get some people on it also." Brent leaned down to kiss her cheek.

Tiffany smiled and patted his cheek. "Thank you, I know you'll do your best."

Nobody but Kara saw Dante's face twist into a mask of resentment that quickly faded away.

Kara rubbed her sore, bruised cheekbone. She'd had to apply makeup heavily and wear dark glasses to cover her bruised eye at work. Jenny had packed a hell of a wallop. The office was buzzing about how the congressman's daughter was missing, and as soon as she was found, she'd go to prison.

Worry and guilt dogged Kara. It was all her fault Jenny missed her court date and had the book thrown at her. Kara should have been honest with her earlier and told her about Brent.

"You look like somebody killed your dog and talked about your mama," Katey said, sitting down next to Kara.

Kara smiled weakly. "I've got a lot on my mind."

"Don't we all. I heard that the congressman didn't even go to his daughter's trial. Her sentence is going to be in the papers tomorrow."

That was the last thing Kara wanted to hear.

"I'm going to get some more coffee, want some?" she asked, praying Katey would be gone when she returned.

"No, I have to get back to work. You should take care of that eye," Katey said in parting.

Kara couldn't wait for the day to be over.

The guilt Kara dismissed earlier flamed, and threatened to grow into a roaring inferno. She and Brent sat in her living room, watching a video, but neither was really seeing it. Brent stared ahead, his eyes unfocused, lost in his thoughts.

The video was simply an excuse for them to be together

without having to talk about what was pressing on both of their minds. The weight of unspoken emotions hung in the room. Brent had said they should talk and work things out. They needed each other more than ever right now. They'd harmed Jenny emotionally, and she could also be . . ." Kara's mind shied away from the thought. They had to talk.

"What are you going to do if Jenny isn't found tonight?" Kara asked. Brent had handled her disappearance as a possible kidnapping, allowing him to involve the federal authorities in the search.

His jaw tightened in response to her question. "There's nothing I can do," he said.

"We should have told her about us sooner."

Brent stared at the television. "The time wasn't right."

"It never would have been right. We should have—"

"Do we have to talk about this right now?" he interrupted.

Kara took a deep breath. "Yes, yes we do. Jenny's been in the middle of our relationship since the beginning."

"*We* had no relationship in the beginning. Jenny and I were once engaged to be married," he said.

It was true, but Kara blinked against the pain of Brent's words.

"We have a relationship now," she said.

"Yes, we do. Now that that's over, can I watch the movie?"

Kara got up and went into the kitchen. A dull ache spread inside her. She poured hot chocolate mix into a cup with shaking hands, filled the cup with water, and stuck it into the microwave.

Brent walked into the kitchen. "Look, I'm a little tired tonight. I'd like to go on home."

Kara swallowed. Earlier, they'd been joking about how they couldn't stand to spend nights alone anymore. But, maybe he was right, maybe they needed a little space.

"All right, I'll see you tomorrow," she said.

"I'll see myself out." Brent left the room. No goodbye, no kiss.

Kara tried to ignore the hollow feeling inside her as she pulled a box of brownie mix out of her shelves. She needed some more chocolate. She hoped Taylor was home tonight to share it with her.

A little later, draped over her couch, Taylor munched on brownies and said, "This is the first night you've been away from Brent in weeks, and you've pulled out all the stops on the chocolate. When are you going to tell me what's wrong? I shared my tale of woe."

Kara sighed and picked up another brownie. Taylor and her married man. She'd finally kicked him to the curb. When Kara first met him, she'd almost sympathized with Taylor. The man was fine, almost as good-looking as Brent. Kara sighed again.

"You hyperventilating over there, girl? Come on, talk."

"It's this stuff with Jenny. I tried to talk it over with Brent—and he left."

"Typical man. You know they have a hard time processing their emotions, the poor creatures."

"I know. It's just that everything was so right."

"The serpent has reared its head in the garden of Eden?" Taylor asked.

Kara nodded.

"Did you fight?" Taylor asked.

"No, but—" Kara's words were interrupted by the ring of the doorbell.

She looked out the peephole and the object of their conversation stood outside the door. Kara's fingers shook as she unlocked the door to let Brent in.

"I'd better go," Taylor said, making a hasty exit.

The door clicked behind her and Kara and Brent stood, looking at each other.

"I'm sorry. I shouldn't have left like that," he said.

Kara made a soft sound as Brent drew her into his arms.

That was all she needed to hear. His mouth covered hers and she sank into the velvet warmth of his kiss. Pleasure radiated through her at his tender caress. His tongue traced the softness of her lips, and his lips seared the silky skin of her cheek, trailing fire down her neck.

He pulled her closer to him, and her body tingled with the contact. "You're right, we need to talk," he said.

"We can talk later," she breathed.

Brent grinned.

"You rat," Kara said as she hit his chest, and it turned into a caress.

"We'll talk," Brent said, his hand dropping to cup her buttocks, nestling her against his hard readiness. "Later," he finished.

Twenty-one

In the delicious moments after the lovemaking, Kara and Brent lay entangled in each other's arms.

Brent tightened his arms around Kara and lightly kissed the tip of her nose.

"You're almost perfect, do you know that?" he asked.

"Almost?" Kara asked, raising an eyebrow. Then she laughed, kissing Brent back on his firm lips.

"I'm crazy about you, too," she said. Then her smile faded. The "L" word hovered so near, yet so far away. She wouldn't say it first, though she felt the truth of it. She loved him. Wholly, fiercely. She didn't want to live without him, and without a doubt she'd fight to keep him.

She didn't dwell on the hint of insecurity that touched her. Did Brent love her, too? Their relationship was growing; there still was time. She had to be certain of his love before she told him she loved him, and that was one rule she couldn't break.

"It's hard for me to talk about Jenny. I feel so damn bad about how things turned out," Brent said.

Kara waited for Brent to continue. The words were hard coming, but he needed to get them out.

"I wanted you from the moment I first saw you. I wanted Jenny to disappear from my life, but I couldn't shake her off. She was driving me crazy. I made a terrible mistake, but when I asked her to marry me, I never imagined feeling about any woman the way I feel about you now."

Indescribable joy flared within her. Then, Brent turned to face her, his face shadowed.

"It was unfair to Jenny when I decided not to rock the boat and marry her in spite of the fact I never loved her. And when she saw me lying in your bed . . . I don't deserve"—Brent's jaw clenched and he looked away—"what I have here with you."

Kara wanted to cry. She wanted to tell him that what she had done to Jenny, her flesh and blood, her sister, was just as wrong.

"We've got to get past this. It wasn't fair to Jenny, but it's not fair to us. We didn't plan this," she said.

Brent kissed her. They melted into one another, their mutual heartache turning into longing. Tongues intertwined, sleek skin rubbed against skin, quickened breaths mingled. Tender caresses grew into damp, sweaty urgency.

She arched to meet his silk hardness as he glided into her. She sucked in her breath, drowned in bliss, his fullness filling her up completely. The sweet friction began, and she shuddered.

She ground her hips against his hard column, her universe constricting to the tiny fiery bud between her legs. When the rapture caught her in its rolling waves, she clutched his shoulders and pulsed around him, spinning into ecstasy as he spilled himself inside her.

The phone rang, cutting into Kara's mists of sleep. She answered the phone in a haze, squinting at the clock that read just past midnight.

"May I speak to Brent Stevens?" an authoritative male voice asked.

Kara shook Brent gently on the shoulder. He sat up and took the phone, instantly awake. He listened intently.

"Thanks for calling," he said, handing the phone back to Kara.

"What happened? Is it Jenny?" she asked.

"They picked her up in a hotel in Dupont Circle. She used a credit card to reserve the room," he said.

Pure relief washed through Kara. She didn't think she could've coped with it if permanent harm had come to Jenny. "Thank God," she said.

"They've taken her into custody. She's not dealing with it very well. They're transferring her to a hospital for psychiatric evaluation," Brent said.

The cold rain came down in sheets. Kara and Brent dashed into the inn through the downpour. They both had Monday off and they'd planned a long romantic weekend, in the place where they'd first made love, to unwind from the stress of the previous week's events. The lobby was almost deserted of weekend guests in the bad weather.

"Is room 211 available?" Brent asked. That was the room they had stayed in before. Much to Kara's delight, it was available. The bellboy ushered them into their room, and Brent tipped him.

Kara sighed in satisfaction, hanging up her trench coat. "This is perfect weather," she said.

"Huh?"

"We have the perfect excuse for never leaving the room. We can order room service and lie in bed and never even get dressed," she said.

"Sounds good," Brent said, smiling.

Kara spied a brochure on top of the VCR. "We can rent movies. Look here, they have new releases that are always all rented out by Friday night at home. See, I told you this was perfect. With luck it'll rain until Sunday."

Her voice trailed away as she spied Brent pulling off his shirt. "I'm going to take a shower then get into some dry clothes. You can order up that room service if you want, I'm hungry."

So was she, but not for food.

She waited until she heard the water run in the shower then took her clothes off.

Brent started when she pulled open the door to the shower stall. His eyes widened as he took in her nakedness and his body evidenced an immediate response.

"I thought I'd volunteer to wash your back," she said, stepping into the shower stall with Brent.

"Be my guest," he said, his voice husky.

Much to Kara's delight, rain was forecast through Sunday. She'd called for three videos of new releases she was dying to see.

They ordered breakfast from room service, pancakes and waffles, fresh fruit and eggs. She and Brent fed each other, not moving from the bed.

Saturday, the sun came out around noon.

"We're going out to eat today, I called for reservations." Brent was getting cabin fever, Kara thought.

"The concierge recommended we eat on this yacht that's been converted to a restaurant. We can cruise the Chesapeake bay and dine at the same time."

Kara's eyes widened. "I don't want to go on any boat."

Brent looked puzzled for a moment, then comprehension dawned on his face.

"I'm sorry, baby, I forgot you told me you were afraid of water. But think about it, it's a large boat. I think it would be a good first step."

"You made this reservation on purpose, didn't you?" she asked, feeling testy.

"No, honestly, I forgot. But this would be a good opportunity for you. I dare you," he said, grinning.

At thirty years old, he wants me to get on my first boat, she thought.

"You'll love it," Brent promised.

When Kara boarded the boat, she didn't look down at the water. It was a silly phobia, she thought, fear of boats. Why couldn't she be afraid of heights or airplanes or snakes like everybody else?

The cabin was large and spacious, a band played soft jazz in the background, and the food was delicious. The boat rocked gently, but Kara found she could ignore it. As long as she didn't look out the portholes to the water she was fine.

She had the bluefish, Brent had the crab. The bluefish tasted like the end of summer, as if it had been cooked on a fire on the beach. Corn on the cob and tiny boiled new potatoes accompanied it.

She turned to look out the porthole and it was fine—she could hardly tell they were on the water. A riotous sunset flamed across the horizon. The view was glorious.

"Happy you came?" Brent asked.

"Happy I came," she answered.

They shared a piece of chocolate mousse cake, sinfully rich and heaped with whipped cream. Afterward, they were sipping their coffee when Kara sniffed.

"It smells like something's burning," she said.

As soon as she said the words, they heard a whompf and the boat shuddered.

Cries of alarm ripped through the dinner guests, and a siren started to sound. The sensation that traveled through Kara was more primitive than panic. She was on a boat, and it probably was going to blow up. She hoped she didn't wet her pants.

"We have things under control. Please line up by the

exits and the staff will escort you to the decks," a man announced. "It is imperative that everyone remain calm."

Remain calm? The words echoed through Kara's head. She was on a boat that was going to blow up any second, and this man told her to remain calm?

"I'm going to panic now," she told Brent.

He grasped her firmly by the arm. "Don't. Let's go."

Kara's feet weren't obeying the commands from her brain, because if they had been she would've run over the water right about then to get back to the shore. Brent half-shoved, half-dragged her to the exit.

When they got on deck and Kara saw all that deep water surrounding the boat, she gave an anguished moan. They had moved away from the shore. Why had she assumed that they were tied safely to a pier?

The staff was handing out life jackets and instructing the guests on how to put them on. It was cold, and a gusty wind blew off the water. Kara saw a thin stream of black smoke come from the other side of the boat. She moaned again and started to slump. Brent pulled her up and put the life jacket on her, then he put his own on.

"Pull yourself together," he said gently. "See, they're coming to get us. Kara looked in the direction he'd pointed and saw a collection of even tinier boats speeding toward them.

So the choice was between getting in one of those tiny boats or going down with the ship.

The staff spoke reassurances over the loudspeaker, saying it was only a small kitchen fire they would soon contain, but in the meantime they were going to take the precaution of evacuating the boat.

"This is exciting," a blond exclaimed, her eyes glittering. Kara longed to slap her. She closed her eyes against the sight of deep water. If she lived through this, she would never ever get on a boat again, she vowed.

Then they were supposed to climb down teeny chain

ladders to the Coast Guard cutter. Kara's knees locked and her legs refused to move. The thin stream of smoke had gotten larger.

Brent finally had to pick Kara up over his shoulder and carry her onto the boat. She kept her eyes shut, trembling uncontrollably.

Her eyes remained squeezed shut as they sped over the water to shore. She couldn't move to get off the boat, so Brent had to carry her to shore.

Once off the boat, she leaned over and threw up.

"Are you okay?" Brent asked. She refused to talk to him and they returned to their room in silence.

"That was an adventure," Brent said. He watched her, concern on his face.

Kara grabbed her suitcase and started throwing clothes into it. "I want to go home," she said.

"You're okay. Everything turned out all right," he said.

She wanted to slap him.

"That was one of the most horrific experiences I've ever gone through in my entire life, and it's all your fault. Take me home right now."

"I thought dinner on the yacht would be a good idea; I had no idea there was going to be a fire in the kitchen," he said, contrite.

"That is not the point," Kara ground out. "I told you I was scared and you should have respected my fears. If you won't take me back, I'll get a train."

Brent scratched his head. "I'll take you back."

She wouldn't talk to him on the drive back.

"I'm respecting your need to be outraged," Brent said, his tongue in his cheek. It didn't help.

When he dropped her off at home, he said, "I'll come by tomorrow."

"I'm going to catch up on my laundry and wash my hair. Don't bother."

Brent chuckled and kissed her lightly on the lips. "Hope you're cooled off by then, my prickly pear."

Actually she'd forgiven him already, but she did have to do laundry.

She put on a load of laundry and saw there was a good movie on TV. Kara made popcorn and settled into the movie. Unfortunately it was a mystery thriller about a woman and a man on a yacht. Kara supposed she should learn to swim. She'd check into swimming lessons on her day off tomorrow, and she'd whip up the best biscuits Brent ever tasted. She missed him already.

She picked up the phone to call him.

"What are you doing?" she asked

"Laundry," he said. "You aren't the only one who's let it pile up."

"I'm sorry I was so grouchy. It's just that I was so scared."

"I know, baby."

"I'm going to cook brunch tomorrow. I'll expect you."

"I miss you," he said.

Kara's heart melted.

"I miss you, too," she whispered.

Monday morning, Kara stretched on the bed, feeling good. She'd slept late. She brushed her teeth and put on the coffee. She planned to putter around today, and after she and Brent ate brunch, maybe they'd go shopping.

She opened the door to get her morning paper to go with her coffee. She poured herself a cup and settled down at the kitchen table, unfolding the paper. Then she froze in shock as she saw the picture of Sidney Eastman accompanying the headline, "CONGRESSMAN IMPLICATED FOR IL-LEGAL FUNDING."

The lead sentence read: "Evidence has surfaced implicating Congressman Sidney Eastman for receiving loans from Americabanc Corporation in the face of upcoming sweeping legislation in the banking industry."

Brent answered the phone yawning. "Have you seen the paper yet?" she asked.

"Nope, I'm still in bed."

"Go get it, I'll hold on."

There was silence for long minutes.

"How could you do this without letting me know? I trusted you," he said when he returned to the phone. His voice was steely.

"I didn't release the papers, Brent. I was going to give them back to you, but I forgot. I don't know what happened."

"I'm going to the office." He hung up abruptly.

With a sinking heart Kara got dressed to go to work also. She'd find the papers she'd shoved in her desk and put them in Brent's hand today.

Twenty-two

Sidney Eastman was mad enough to kill. He didn't bother to call to alert the staff of his arrival like he usually did. He stormed through the office to find Brent. The woman at the desk outside Brent's office was busily applying lipstick and eyeing herself in her compact. Sidney rapped on her desk and she started.

"I'm paying you to work, not beautify yourself," he snapped.

He walked to Brent's office and pushed open the door. "Uh, he's not in, he has the day off," Katey said.

Sidney frowned. "Get him on the phone and tell him to meet me in my office. Remind him I'm not a patient man."

"Cancel my appointments," he snapped at Velma as he entered his office.

He tossed his coat and hat in a chair and poured a drink with shaking hands. His life was crumbling before his eyes. His wife had deserted him and exposed herself as a lush for all the world to see. His sorry daughter had gotten herself thrown into the loony bin. Now, it was Brent's fault his career was on the line.

He had asked Brent to handle that loan. Brent had screwed up by turning the money over to the party campaign funding committee where Sidney would have to jump through hoops to get his hands back on it. He had raked Brent through the coals for that one. Sometimes Brent pretended he was so damn naive.

Now, Brent had leaked the news of the source. For a long time he'd trusted Brent to run his office and handle all the day-to-day duties, freeing him up so he didn't have to worry about them. Those days were over. Brent obviously couldn't hang in there and play with the big boys. You needed money, big money, to win a campaign, and sometimes Brent acted as if he forgot that important fact.

His hopes to run for a Senate seat and win had gone up in smoke with this leak. Sidney took another swallow of his scotch and shrugged. Bigger fish than him had done worse and survived. Maybe they'd just make him pay a fine, and another party member would "lend" him the money.

He doubted he'd be that lucky though. Capitol Hill was an exclusive club and even with his ten years of tenure, blue eyes, and all, he was still an outsider. Minorities didn't have the Teflon coating some did. His head would roll, no doubt about it.

Fury filled him as he paced the room. His entire life was filled with incompetents and people who were against him. He brought people up to where he was now, and then they refused to carry their own weight. Well, he was going to put an end to this foolishness right now.

His extension buzzed.

"What?" he barked at Velma.

"Brent Stevens is here to see you now, sir."

"Send him in."

Brent entered looking grim. Sidney felt a qualm go through him. What he had decided to do now would not be easy.

"The media did not get the information about the Americabanc loan from me," Brent said, cutting directly to the point.

Sidney almost admired the boy. He would miss him.

Brent had always been so efficient. Maybe if he groveled enough, Sidney would give him another chance.

Sidney opened his mouth to speak, but Brent held up his hand.

"I've been with you for a long time, Sidney. I admired you. I wanted to follow in your footsteps."

The boy was getting a good start on the groveling, Sidney thought.

"But that was then," Brent continued. "I don't admire the man you've turned into. Our goals and work styles are no longer compatible. It's time for us to part ways. I'm re-signing."

Sidney stared at Brent in disbelief. The boy had the gall to quit before he fired him?

"You can't resign," he sputtered.

"I can and I just did. My office will be cleaned out within the hour."

Fury built within Sidney. He stood up and advanced on Brent. "I made you everything you are, boy. I pulled you out of the gutter. I paid for that fancy law school degree you have. I was the father you never had!" he yelled, jabbing Brent with his finger in the chest at every point. "How dare you desert me!" Sidney tossed the drink in his hand in Brent's face.

Brent blinked, sighed, and pulled a handkerchief out of his pocket and wiped his face.

He started to say something, but instead looked at Sidney Eastman and shook his head. As he turned to leave, Sidney launched himself at the younger man with a growl.

"What the hell?" Brent muttered, easily holding Sidney off him with one hand.

Sidney yelled obscenities and swung at Brent. He never landed the punch. The next thing he knew he was lying on the floor, Brent bent over him.

"You need to get a grip, Sidney," Brent said, before he left the office.

* * *

Kara walked straight to her desk. She pulled open her deep file drawer and felt behind the folders where she'd stuffed the papers she took from Brent. They weren't there. She pulled out the entire drawer, disbelieving, and set it on the floor.

An hour later, she was still going through the papers, not wanting to face the fact that they weren't there, but rapidly unable to escape the reality.

Katey came by her cubicle, and did a double take when she saw Kara sitting on the floor, hunched over a stack of papers.

"Looking for something?" she asked.

Kara looked up. "Katey, who has keys to the office after hours?"

"Well, the cleaning staff . . . Velma, Brent, and all the department heads, including myself. Didn't you have one?"

Kara nodded. "I'm missing something from my desk. The only possible explanation is that someone removed it. I know it didn't happen during office hours, so I was wondering . . . Are you sure nobody else has keys?"

"I'm sure Sidney Eastman and his family do. But that's it."

Kara tried to replace the heavy drawer. "Help me with this, would you?"

Once they got the drawer in place Katey sank into the chair beside Kara's desk.

"I came by to give you the news. You won't believe it."

"Umm," Kara said absentmindedly, her thoughts on the papers and who could possibly have removed them.

"Brent quit."

Now Katey had her full attention.

"What?"

"It must have had something to do with that article in

the paper this morning. You saw it, didn't you? The congressman is in a heap o' trouble. It's bad timing for that sort of thing to come out."

"You were telling me about Brent," Kara said.

"Oh, yes. Sidney Eastman stormed in this morning. He about gave me a heart attack. When Brent came in they were closeted in the congressman's office. Velma said there was whooping and hollering like you wouldn't believe.

"Then Brent packed up his things and left. He didn't take very much, just personal stuff; he said I could have the rest, or give it away. I'm going to keep his desk set, it's . . ."

Katey's voice faded. Brent had quit. Kara couldn't believe he'd made a move of that magnitude without talking to her about it. Was the reason really that the papers had leaked the news about the loan? Did Brent have something to hide?

"I've got to go, Katey."

Kara stood, slung her purse over her shoulder, and headed out the door.

Dante's hand clenched as he read the article again. He barely controlled his frustration. The story had hit the papers but the public received it with a blasé indifference that showed how accustomed they were to politicians behaving badly. The story barely rated a mention on the evening news. There was no justice in the world.

His father might be the subject of a hearing or two. He might get a fine or be slapped on the wrist. It would probably hurt his chances for reelection, but that was it. He was a fool to wish for more. What was a little corruption in a town already hopelessly corrupt?

He'd heard Brent had quit. That only made Dante envy him more. At least Brent could walk away. He had the good fortune not to be born with Sidney Eastman for a father.

Tiffany had a pass to leave the alcohol treatment center for the day to prepare for her upcoming discharge. She looked forward to discharge with trepidation, knowing she would have to start all over again. She had to find a place to live, a job, friends, an entire life. And she had to do it by herself, one day at a time, without the crutch of alcohol. She prayed she was up to the challenge. For today, she was.

The housekeeper let her into the house. "I'm just going to look around for a while, maybe pack a few things," Tiffany said. The housekeeper nodded and went back to her work.

Tiffany wandered the rooms with a sense of nostalgia. How excited she'd been when she and Sidney first bought this home, confident he would win reelection and be in Washington a long while. How pleased she'd been when Anthony finished the interiors. It had been her dream home. But it hadn't been enough.

Their home in Atlanta had been rented out for years. The lease was coming up for renewal, and maybe she'd move back home. She'd had enough of Washington. Tiffany pulled out her notebook from her purse to make notes on what she wanted shipped to Georgia.

She stopped when she reached Jenny's bedroom and pressed a hand to her mouth, willing herself not to cry. Jenny would be hospitalized for a year in lieu of prison. It was a good thing, Tiffany reassured herself yet again. Jenny had been on a downward spiral, and now she was forced to accept help. Jenny would be paying the Bailey family back for the rest of her life though. She'd heard that their lawyers were going after Sidney's money. Good, Tiffany thought. She hoped they'd get it.

Sidney loved position and money. Losing it would certainly hurt him more than the loss of his family. But she had to face her own desires for those things. She'd stayed with Sidney for the security of money and marriage to a powerful man. Lord knew that financial security and status were all Sidney had ever offered her.

She heard the door slam shut and she shivered. It would have to be Sidney. What was he doing home this time of day? She steeled herself and went down the stairs to meet him.

He looked wild. His usually smooth white hair was ruffled, his tie was askew.

"What are you doing here? I thought you were still locked up with your daughter in the funny farm," he snapped.

Tiffany stiffened. Sidney's insults no longer had any power over her. "I'm cataloguing the things I want shipped to Georgia. I'm also going to pack a few clothes."

Sidney cocked his head. "Now what is wrong with this picture?" he asked. "Oh, I can hardly recognize you when you're not drunk. You're not going anywhere. As soon as you get out of the funny farm, you're coming home where you belong. I've put up with you not holding up your end of this marriage long enough," Sidney said.

"I take it you haven't heard from my lawyer yet?" she asked.

Sidney waved a hand. "I disregarded that crap. Everyone knows how crazy you are now that you've checked yourself into the loony bin. It's no secret what I've been putting up with," he said.

Tiffany's eyes widened in anger. "It's true. I've been crazy to put up with you all these years. But it's over now. I'm getting a divorce and starting my life over. It can be amicable or nasty, it's up to you."

"Sorry slut," he snarled. "Everything I've done for you is down the drain. What do I get in return? You're no better than that sorry Brent I just fired."

"You fired Brent?" she asked faintly.

"Damn right. And I'm sick of your foolishness. If you think you're going back to the insane asylum, you're mistaken. They put all this foolishness in your head. Get your butt into the den and make me a drink. You know what I like. Get one for yourself while you're at it, I liked you better drunk."

He glared at Tiffany standing there, frozen in place. "Don't you hear me, woman? Move!"

This was the crap she'd put up with for too long.

"Kiss my black ass," she said in measured tones, and turned to walk out the door.

Sidney roared and grabbed her by her neck. Tiffany gave a strangled scream as Sidney started to drag her up the stairs.

"Who the hell do you think you're talking back to, slut? I'm going to teach you a lesson you won't forget."

Twenty-three

"I've got an urgent call for you on line two, Mr. Eastman," the receptionist said. Dante picked up the call wondering who it was. Jenny?

"Mr. Eastman, something is going on here. I think you'd better come over right way," his parents' housekeeper whispered.

"What's wrong?"

"Well, your mother came home, then your father came home, and they're both upstairs. Screaming and crashing's going on and I'm frightened for your mother. She's not used to that sort of thing," the housekeeper said.

Alarm rose within Dante. Had his father finally snapped? It must be terrible for the housekeeper to call him at work.

"I'll be right there," he said.

The housekeeper was waiting outside the door. Dante's tires squealed as he braked at his parents' house.

"Your father just left," she said.

"Did you check on my mother?" Dante asked.

"Your daddy will fire me if he finds out—"

Dante bit off an oath and dashed into the house. He heard the strangled edge of his mother's sob. He flew up the steps and burst into his parents' bedroom.

His mother was lying in a heap on the floor alone in the room. Her shoulders heaved with the force of her sobs.

"Mom, what happened?" Dante touched her gently on the shoulder, and her entire body trembled.

"Mom?" Dante said again.

Tiffany looked up at him and Dante gasped at the sight of her bruised and bloody face.

"My God, I've got to get you to a hospital."

Kara had been trying to call Brent for the past two hours. He wasn't answering his car phone or his pages. She'd left messages. She was starting to worry.

She took a taxi to his place. His car was parked in the driveway. "Wait, please," Kara asked the driver and approached the door. If Brent's car was here, he had to be home. She rang the doorbell and waited for long minutes. She banged on the door. "Brent, I need to talk to you. Please."

Brent opened the door and Kara waved the taxi driver away.

"You shouldn't have had him go," Brent said. "I'm not in a talking mood."

"Don't do this," Kara said quietly. She walked past him into the room. "I heard you quit."

"I didn't have the stomach for dealing with Sidney anymore. I don't have much stomach for dealing with anyone I don't trust," he said.

"Are you speaking about me?"

"If the shoe fits," he answered.

"That's not fair. The papers were missing from my desk. Someone who had a key must have taken them after hours. Why would I release the documents now? It doesn't make sense."

"Why would you steal them in the first place?"

Pain sharp as a knife struck Kara and for a moment she couldn't breathe, couldn't speak.

Brent sighed and rubbed his eyes. "At this point I don't

care about the release of the papers. It's a matter of trust. There are too many unanswered questions between us. My instincts tell me that you haven't leveled with me, and I trust my instincts."

Kara knew it was the time to tell him about her connection with Sidney Eastman, and the motivation for her actions. But she was afraid. If he reacted like this now, how would he react once he learned she was Sidney Eastman's daughter? She didn't want to lose this man.

"Listen, Kara, I'm tired. I'll call a taxi, and why don't you go on home. I'll call you tomorrow."

Rage sprang up, quickly followed by despair. He was blowing her off. Was he cleaning house, getting rid of all the old things, along with his job, to make way for the new?

"Don't bother, I'll call one myself." And with those words she walked out the door.

Tears blurred her vision as she walked down the street. Was this the beginning of the end? The pain of the thought numbed her and she put one step in front of the other, the rhythm of her steps a soothing mantra.

She spied a coffee shop on the corner, and walked inside. The cheerful, sunny shop did little to dispel the anxiety that gnawed at her. She ordered a latte, then a dark shadow fell across her. She looked up and a man stood over her, very handsome, with caramel skin and his hair a cap of smooth tight curls. He smiled and asked, "May I join you?" Kara couldn't place his accent. Maybe African?

Kara nodded assent, anything but be alone with her thoughts right now.

He was a graduate student at Georgetown, an Ethiopian, and drop-dead handsome, but she barely listened to his conversation, hoping it was enough that she smiled and nodded at appropriate intervals.

The echo of Brent's words, "My instinct tells me you haven't leveled with me," reverberated in her ears. What would he do when he found out he was right? God, how was she going to tell him?

She stood up. "I have to go now," she said, and without a backward glance walked out of the coffee shop.

Brent slowly closed the door after Kara left. He'd been hard on her. He was letting his own emotions and circumstances affect their relationship. Sure he felt Kara was holding something from him, but he was the one who always said they should talk things out—and he'd practically thrown her out of his house.

With sudden resolve he grabbed his jacket and keys. He was going after her. On foot, she couldn't have gotten far.

A few minutes later he pulled up to the Sunflower Coffeehouse. Kara was sitting inside, bent over a cup of coffee, looking meditative. He parked the car and started to go in, but pulled up at the sight of her smiling and nodding to some guy who joined her.

Brent shook his head and got back into his car. Obviously she wasn't too upset. He'd talk to her later. Maybe what they both needed was a little space.

Kara paced her apartment. She'd picked up the phone a dozen times to call Brent, then put it down and willed him to call her.

The words, "I don't have much stomach now for dealing with someone I don't trust," resounded in her mind.

How could you make someone trust you? By being honest, a tiny voice within answered.

And the awful part was that Brent was so very right.

Kara grabbed her purse and coat. She was going back to the office. She needed something to do.

* * *

With each passing second, the wait grew more frustrating and Dante approached the emergency room information desk. "May I speak to Tiffany Eastman's doctor? I'm her son."

"One moment," the receptionist said and picked up a phone. She spoke into it and said, "Go through those doors and check in at the nurse's desk."

Once inside the emergency room, Dante leaned over the desk, trying to get someone's attention.

"I'm Dante Eastman," he said to a pleasant-looking nurse hurrying through.

She barely glanced at him. "We'll get to you in a second, we're busy right now."

He looked around in frustration, then spied his mother's name on a board with room numbers listed. He turned and headed for that room.

He died a little when he saw his mother lying on the stretcher looking small and incredibly fragile. He approached and slipped his hand around hers. Her eyes opened.

"Dante," she whispered.

"I'm here. Have you seen the doctor yet?"

She nodded. "I'm okay, just a little sore," she said, her lips so swollen she could barely move them.

Dante wanted to cry.

"Did my father do this to you?" He wanted to hear it from her.

Tiffany looked away, then nodded.

Rage filled Dante, interrupted by the quiet entrance of the doctor.

"Hello, are you a relative?"

"I'm her son."

"It looks like she's going to be all right. She does have some hairline rib fractures. I'd like to keep her overnight for observation," she said.

Dante nodded. "Mom, I'm going to let them get you settled in your room, then I'll be right back."

Dante headed to the car with one thought only. That bastard was going to pay for what he had done.

"Velma, is my father in his office?" Dante asked.

Velma nodded, bemused; she'd never seen Dante look angry before.

"I'll tell him you're here," she said.

"Don't bother," he said, and strode into his father's office.

Sidney was on the phone. He gestured for Dante to sit down.

Dante ripped the phone out of his father's hand and threw it against the wall.

"That was uncalled for. I was talking to Senator Janforth," he said.

"You lousy son of a bitch. Do you know where my mother is?" Dante roared.

Sidney raised an eyebrow. "Why, back at the loony bin, I suppose," he said.

Dante advanced on Sidney. Rage ignited red sparks in front of his eyes.

"I'm going to kill you," he breathed. "No matter what happens to me, it will be worth it to know that scum like you no longer walks the face of the earth."

"Stop right there, boy," Sidney commanded.

Dante stopped when he saw the small but deadly gun in his father's hand. "Don't make me use this, boy. It would be self-defense."

Sidney sank back into his chair, the gun still trained on Dante. "Your mother deserved that little butt whipping I gave her. Sometimes a woman needs to be set in her place. You'll learn."

Dante's nostrils flared.

"I'm a little disappointed in you, boy. Now that's not unusual, but I thought you'd be smarter than to come busting in here like this. Makes no sense."

"I will destroy you if it's the last thing I do," Dante said slowly and carefully. "I gave those papers to Dean Riley about the Americabanc loan, and that's only the beginning. I'm going to get you in the only place that you hurt. Your power. I believe Jenny's already taken care of your other love, money."

"What did I do to deserve two such worthless children?" Sidney said, setting the gun on his desk and picking up a drink.

With a snarl, Dante launched himself at him. Two explosions sounded in his ears and he stumbled. His body crumpled and the edges of his world darkened and faded to black.

Kara looked up from her desk as the two loud reports sounded. That couldn't have been gunshots, could it? Then, she heard screaming from back by the congressman's office.

When Kara and the other staff members reached the congressman's office, Velma was screaming hysterically. Sidney Eastman stood over his son with a gun.

"It was self-defense," he said, to nobody in particular.

Somebody who had nurse's training tried to staunch the river of blood flowing from Dante's body. Kara pressed her hand to her mouth, tears filling her eyes. This was her brother, his life leaking away.

It seemed it took only seconds for the ambulance to arrive and the office to fill with police and federal authorities. She heard Sidney Eastman say again as he was led away in handcuffs, "It was only self-defense."

Kara returned to her desk in a daze. The office mood seemed to be similar, subdued. The staff hardly believed what they'd witnessed. The police took a statement from Velma. Katey said that some of the staff members were already calling around to renew their job contacts.

Dante was in critical condition, fighting for his life. Cecile, the press secretary, came around. "Attention, I have an announcement. The hospital has put out a call for Dante's blood type, O negative. They desperately need more and it could save his life. If anyone can help, please call or go on in to the hospital."

Kara's lips tightened, but it took her barely a second to make the decision. "Katey, can you give me a ride to that hospital?" she asked.

Arraignment was nearly instantaneous and bail very reasonable if you were a United States congressman, even when the charge was attempted murder, Sidney thought. He had nothing to worry about. It was clearly self-defense. He wondered if Johnnie Cochran was available for his trial though.

He'd just settled down with a glass of scotch, when the door bell rang. He'd already sent the housekeeper home, and he just wanted to relax. It'd been a tiring day.

With a frown he got up and answered the door. His eyes widened when he recognized the man standing there accompanied by secret servicemen.

"Come in, gentlemen," he said, his voice betraying a slight stammer.

They followed Sidney into the sitting room. "I wanted to do you the courtesy of coming and talking to you in person. I'm going to get right to the point, Sidney. In the light of your personal and family problems, I think your responsibilities as a United States congressman are too heavy."

"Not at all, sir, and my recent troubles will be resolved shortly. I was merely defending myself this afternoon."

"Regardless, you've been charged with a felony. The point is, I'm telling you, not asking you. I expect your resignation tomorrow."

Sidney paled. "But—but—" he started to say, panic and disbelief filling him. The man stood up and his companions followed his action.

"Good evening, Congressman Eastman. I'll let myself out."

Twenty-four

"I'm here to donate blood for Dante Eastman," Kara said. The nurse typed on the computer. "Are you aware of his blood type?" she asked.

"Yes. I have the same blood type."

The nurse gave her forms to fill out, and told her to go to the lab.

Kara walked to the lab, where a cheerful lab technician drew a blood sample, and told her to wait. About twenty minutes later a nurse entered.

"There's no time to lose, please follow me."

In a few minutes, Kara was flat on her back on a stretcher, her life blood flowing into a bag.

"We need the maximum amount of blood. There might be side effects. We'd like to run in intravenous fluids simultaneously."

"Of course, anything," Kara said.

"How are you acquainted with Mr. Eastman?" the nurse asked.

Kara hesitated a moment. "He's my brother," she answered.

She closed her eyes and relaxed, drifting into sleep. When someone gently shook her shoulder, she opened her eyes. Tiffany stood over her. Kara gasped at the sight of Tiffany's bruised and swollen face.

"What happened to you?" she asked.

Tiffany bit her lip. "Nothing that matters now," she said.

"Is Dante all right?" Kara asked, almost afraid to hear the answer.

"He just got out of surgery. The doctors think he's going to make it."

Kara exhaled a breath of relief. "Thank God." She frowned. "What possible reason could there be for Sidney to shoot his own son?"

"With the events of the past month, I think something's snapped within him. He's a disturbed and vindictive man, and he's lost control," Tiffany said.

Tiffany darted a glance at Kara. "I came down here to thank the woman who helped to save my son's life. Getting that blood was critical. Imagine my shock when I saw it was you and they told me you were his sister." She frowned. "Would you like to tell me what's going on?"

Now, Kara looked away. "I'm Dante's half sister," she said slowly. "My mother died recently and before she passed, she told me my father was Sidney Eastman."

"Does he know?" Tiffany asked.

Kara grimaced. "No. Nobody knows. I blackmailed Brent to get a job so I could have access to Sidney Eastman."

"Goodness. For some reason, I can't imagine Brent allowing himself to be blackmailed. You must have had something very serious."

"I had the papers that are now in the news about the Americabanc loan." A considering look crossed Tiffany's face.

"What did you want from Sidney?" she asked.

"At first I wanted to hurt him for what he did to my mother. But, I think underneath it all I wanted a father and the family I never had."

Tiffany nodded. "Being Sidney Eastman's child is not necessarily an enviable position. He always was emotionally distant and cold with his children, and . . . and I wasn't there for them either."

Tiffany's eyes filled. "I'm sorry I attacked you and made those groundless accusations at lunch that day. I wasn't thinking straight. I haven't thought straight in a long while."

"That's okay," Kara said softly. This was overwhelming, she thought. That's why everything was fuzzy and unfocused.

"I have to go to the bathroom," she said.

"Do you need help?" Tiffany asked.

"No, I'm all right." Kara swung upright in a smooth graceful motion and stood. Suddenly, the room tilted and crashed into nothingness.

She awoke in a hospital room. Taylor was at her bedside thumbing through a magazine.

"What happened?" Kara croaked, her mouth dry.

"I told them I was your sister, and nearest relative, so I could get the scoop. They took too much blood from you," Taylor said. She took Kara's hand. "Especially from someone in your condition."

Kara closed her eyes. She'd been feeling tired and drained lately. This was where she learned she had leukemia or something.

"What's wrong with me? Give it to me straight," she asked, bracing herself mentally for the worst.

Taylor squeezed her hand. "You're pregnant," she said.

"Hello," Brent said.

"Tim Redman here. I have news from the office I think you'll be interested in."

Brent didn't see how he'd be interested in anything happening at Sidney's office. "Yes?" he said politely.

"Sidney Eastman shot Dante."

"You're kidding," Brent said.

"I do not lie. I saw it all. His son was lying on the floor bleeding, and Sidney stood over him with a gun."

"My God," Brent said. "What happened?"

"I don't know. Velma said they had an argument. But that's not all. Earlier today he beat up his wife and put her in the hospital. She's pressing charges."

"How is Dante?"

"Critical condition. He's in surgery. With this happening on top of his daughter being convicted of two counts of voluntary manslaughter, I think you got out in the nick of time."

Brent put the phone back on the hook slowly. Sidney had become totally unhinged. Brent had been connected to the Eastman family a long time. He needed to go and stand by Tiffany and her children. It was the least he should do.

Brent had put on his jacket and was looking around for his keys when the doorbell rang.

He opened it and his friend Stone stood there. "Hey, I didn't know you where going to be in town. Come on in."

"I had some business to take care of, and I was going to give you my news in person. I called your office, and they said you no longer worked there. What's going on?"

"I quit. I don't want to even get started on what else right now. I was on my way out to the hospital. Do you want to ride with me?"

In the car, Brent turned on the radio as they pulled onto the highway. "Congressman Sidney Eastman has been taken into custody for shooting his son, Dante Eastman, in his Capitol Hill offices. Details will follow this brief message."

Brent turned the radio off.

Stone whistled. "Damn. I suppose all this has something to do with your leaving the job?"

"Not really."

"My news about Kara pales in comparison to the drama going on in your life now," Stone said.

Brent glanced over at him. "What do you have?" His casual words belied his sudden tumult of emotion.

"Her mother dated Sidney Eastman. It was hush-hush because she was from the wrong side of the tracks. She disappeared, then resurfaced in Tyrone, Georgia. A few months later she had Kara. She refused to say who Kara's father was, but all the evidence points to Sidney Eastman. That's why she was willing to go all out to get close to him."

Brent's knuckles whitened on the steering wheel. "Why did she lie to me all this time?" he asked himself aloud.

"I don't know, man."

Brent nodded, lost in his thoughts, as they sped to the hospital.

Kara turned her face to the wall, the news of her pregnancy hitting her like a physical blow.

"I'll leave you alone for a while. I'm going to the cafeteria," Taylor said.

Remembrance of Brent's rejection racked her. What would he do once he found out the extent of what she'd hidden from him? He'd probably reject the baby, also. History repeats itself, she thought bitterly, remembering her mother's love for Sidney and his cold withdrawal when he discovered she was pregnant.

Kara didn't think she could bear suffering the same from Brent. The thought of terminating the pregnancy touched her mind, and instantly her body and soul rebelled. She was going to have Brent's baby. Any other option was out of the question.

She would have to be strong and raise this baby alone. Her mother had done it, and she was capable of no less.

Her fingertips grazed her lower abdomen. A baby. Images of an infant nestled against her breast flashed before her. She was going to be a mother. How terrifyingly wonderful.

"You have a call from your mother, line three."

Jenny left the dayroom where she was watching TV, and walked to the tiny cubicle where patients could receive calls.

"How are you doing, baby?" her mother asked.

"I'm okay."

"I have disturbing news for you. Your brother was shot this afternoon."

Something squeezed her heart and hot tears started to fall. "Is he . . . is he alive?" Jenny whispered.

"Yes, baby. The doctors think he's going to make it. But I have more to tell you. You're going to hear it on the news that your father shot him."

Jenny wasn't all that surprised. "I hope they put him in jail," she said.

"They did. But I just heard he's already out on bond. You might hear something else on the news. He beat me, and I'm pressing charges."

"Are you all right?" Jenny asked.

"I'm all right. I wanted to be the one to break this news to you, rather than you hear it on TV. Concentrate on your recovery. That's so important, baby. You won't have a life if you continue to be enslaved by alcohol."

"I know, Mom." Jenny's voice turned fierce. "I hope they lock him up and throw away the key. I hate him."

"I believe that Sidney is finally going to have to suffer some consequences. There's one more thing. I hate to hit you with all this at once, but like I said, I'd rather you hear it from me. Do you remember Kara Smith?"

"How could I forget her?" Jenny said, a tinge of bitterness in her voice.

"I just learned that she's your half sister."

Jenny absorbed this news in silence.

"Give Dante my love. Mom, I gotta go now," she said.

"Jenny, are you dealing with this all right?" asked Tiffany nervously. "Do you need to talk?"

"I'm okay, Mom. Goodbye." Jenny replaced the phone.

So, Kara was her sister, and she'd come into her life to steal her man and destroy her chances for happiness. Well, her father was finally getting what was due him and she prayed that Kara Smith wasn't too far behind him.

Brent and Stone walked into the hospital. Brent glanced over at Stone. "You said you had business in Washington?"

"It'll wait. I think I'll stick around for a while. We've been friends for a long time, Brent."

Brent was grateful for Stone's presence. His tumbled emotions mirrored the events of the day, wobbling on the edge and about to career out of control.

"I'm here to see about Dante Eastman," Brent said at the information desk.

The volunteer entered the name into her console. "Surgical waiting room, third floor, to your left," she said crisply.

Tiffany was sitting in the room by herself. Brent thanked God that he'd come. At least he could support Tiffany, the woman had been through so much.

Tiffany's face lit up when she saw him. "I'm pleased you came, Brent. It means a lot to me," she said.

"This is my friend, Stone Emerson, from Atlanta."

"Nice to meet you," said Tiffany.

"How's Dante?"

"Better. They say he's going to make it. He lost a lot of blood but with transfusions, he made it through surgery. He's in the recovery room now."

Brent looked at her closely. "Are you all right? Your face is badly bruised."

"Sidney attacked me. That's why Dante went after him."

"My God." Brent sank into a chair.

"Your girlfriend, Kara, was instrumental in saving Dante. She has the same blood type and she donated quite a bit of blood. She got dehydrated and lost consciousness in the process. They admitted her."

Tiffany looked at Brent and waited for him to say something. When he didn't, she continued, "It was quite a surprising revelation when she admitted that she was Sidney's daughter. Why did you keep it hidden for so long?"

"I didn't keep anything hidden. I didn't know either until today," Brent ground out.

"Oh," Tiffany said.

"I'm going to the cafeteria," said Stone, looking uncomfortable. "Anybody want anything?"

Since nobody wanted anything from the cafeteria, Stone took his time getting his food. He was hungry, and the food looked halfway decent for a hospital. His tray laden he looked around the dining room for a seat. A slim, attractive woman with dreads was sitting at a table, reading a paper while she ate. Something about her appealed to him. Stone made his way to her table.

"Mind if I join you?" he asked.

She glanced up, about to refuse, he thought, then met his eyes and slowly nodded.

"I'm Stone Emerson. I'm visiting from Atlanta."

She folded the paper briskly. She was really quite attractive, he thought again, a bit different from the BAP's he'd dated.

"Taylor Cates. I've got a new job in Atlanta. I'm moving next week."

Stone's interest quickened. "Let me give you my card. Can I ask where you'll be working?"

"I'll be a lawyer for Helping Hands, a nonprofit agency to aid abused women."

Stone nodded. "I'm familiar with their work. Give me a call when you get settled. I'd really like to show you the town."

Taylor nodded, taking his card. "I've got to get back to my friend. Nice to meet you," she said.

Stone watched the sway of her hips as she walked away. He sincerely hoped she'd call, but even if she didn't, he'd be sure to find an excuse to drop by Helping Hands.

Twenty-five

How could Kara live out a lie while he held her in his arms? Brent struggled in a tarry pit of betrayal and anger. He'd told her there was nothing they couldn't work out. He'd made love to her and loved her the best he could, and it felt as if she'd kicked him in the gut.

She'd kept a secret of such magnitude from him that at first he couldn't credit the truth of it. Kara was Sidney Eastman's daughter. Jenny's sister. No wonder she felt so guilty.

And the sad part about it was he still wanted her. That husky ripple of her laugh. The little growl she made when they made love. The way her tongue peeked out of the very corner of her mouth when she was concentrating on something.

Brent leaned his head against the wall, his eyes closed.

"Are you all right?" Tiffany asked.

"Yeah. I'm going to step out for a moment. Maybe go see Kara. Do you know her room number?"

Tiffany told him and he paced the halls. He didn't want to face her. He would have to end it. The thought pained him, but how could he continue a relationship that had been based on deceit and dishonesty from the beginning? He had been willing to overlook everything and start anew if she'd only leveled with him from then on out.

He should go and see her, but he dreaded it. What would

he say to her? Hi, honey, I've just found out you've been lying to me for months, but that's all right.

No, it was over. He couldn't spend his life with a woman he didn't trust, who wouldn't be honest with him. That's what it came down to. Spend his life with . . . The thought jarred him. That's what he'd been building up to with Kara, and now that the promise was gone, he felt bereft.

He walked with heavy steps toward Kara's room. The door was ajar and he pushed it open. The room was empty. He asked a passing nurse, "Do you know where Kara Smith is, the patient in this room?"

"She's been discharged," she said. Relief rippled through him. He didn't have to face her just yet.

It had been two days since Dante had been shot by his father, and Kara still hadn't heard from Brent.

"So, what are you going to do?" Taylor asked.

"Be the best mother I can, and raise my child in a peaceful, happy home," Kara said.

They were sitting on floor cushions in Kara's apartment, the plates from the dinner they'd shared between them.

Taylor nodded. "When are you going to tell Brent?" she asked.

Kara drew her legs up and wrapped her arms around them.

"I'm afraid. When my mother told Sidney about her pregnancy—look what happened. Brent was so cold the last time I saw him. And I haven't heard a word from him since. He said he doesn't trust me. What if he found out that I didn't tell him about being Sidney Eastman's daughter? I don't want to repeat my mother's history."

"Kara, listen to me. Every time you've acted and reacted out of fear, especially with Brent, it's been hard on you. If you don't release your fear, you may lose everything."

Kara shook her head. "I can't help it. When I try to tell him, I just can't. I'm afraid if I tell him—"

She stopped, and put her hand on her stomach. Her eyes filled with tears. "I'm so afraid. And it's probably too late anyway."

Taylor's face darkened. "Words are powerful," she said. "Stop saying you're afraid. You're a strong, competent woman. You proved you could break old patterns when you left Tyrone and remade your life here. Snap out of it, Kara."

Kara stared at Taylor, her eyes narrowed, and then she grinned. "Blame it on my hormones running amuck. You never let me get away with a damned thing, do you? God, I'm going to miss you when you go."

"Then come with me," said Taylor.

Kara's grin faded. Leaving Washington meant leaving Brent. And even with her fear standing between them, she didn't know how she could leave Brent.

"I can't leave Brent."

"Then go to him," Taylor said.

A cold, gusty wind blew as Kara stood in the doorway facing Brent's home. The lights were on and his car was in the drive. She rang the doorbell. Brent opened the door. Her heart skipped at the sight of him. He looked tired but so fine.

"May I come in?" she asked.

Brent nodded and stepped aside. He didn't smile. Kara sat in his living room. He sat across the room. The silence lengthened. He wasn't going to make this easy for her.

"I came by, since I haven't heard from you, and I think we need to talk. I was hoping you'd call," she said. That didn't come out right. She didn't want to start out by mentioning how he didn't call. The words just slipped out.

"You're right, we need to talk. It isn't something I'm looking forward to and I've been avoiding it," Brent said.

Uh-oh, Kara thought.

"I've learned that you're Sidney Eastman's daughter," he said.

The blood drained from Kara's face. But to be honest with herself, she had to admit she'd expected this. Once she told that nurse she was Dante's sister . . . it was only a matter of time.

"Sidney Eastman got my mother pregnant thirty years ago. Then he had no further use for us. I didn't learn he was my father until my mother told me while she was dying."

Kara twisted her purse strap, reluctant to meet Brent's eyes.

"I've thought about us quite a bit in the last few days, and what I still don't understand is why you didn't level with me, especially once we'd become close. Especially once I let you understand how important honesty is to me," he said.

"I'm sorry, but I was afraid," Kara whispered.

"I'm sorry, too, but it isn't good enough. I need to trust the woman I share my life with and you've let me down too often and too badly. Do you understand what I'm saying?" he asked.

"It won't happen again."

Brent stood up. "You're right. It won't happen again."

Kara stared up at him, and a look of ineffable sadness crossed his face. She wouldn't cry. Not here in front of him.

"I have to go to the bathroom," she choked out.

Once there, wave after wave of nausea racked her. She turned on the water to drown out the sound and heaved over the toilet bowl. Silent sobs shook her after she finished. It was over. Finis. Brent had just dumped her. She would not grovel, she would not beg. Her hand massaged the curve of her belly. Kara wiped her face, and touched up her makeup. She straightened her shoulders and left the bathroom.

"I'd like to call a taxi and go home now," she said.

"I'll take you home," Brent answered.

The drive was a strained and silent one. He finally pulled up to her apartment.

"Well, goodbye," Kara said, feeling wretched, knowing it was the last one.

"Goodbye," Brent answered.

Kara slipped out of the car. She willed herself not to turn and watch Brent drive away. She stumbled into her apartment, not bothering to turn on the lights, and threw herself on the bed.

The pain became a blanket of numbness permeating her being. She couldn't even be angry at Brent for rejecting her. It was all her fault. All her fault because of her fear; Taylor was right. Kara curled into a fetal position. She'd gone over to tell him about the baby. Now, they'd have to live without him. The choice had been taken away, because he no longer chose to be with her.

Poetic justice. She wondered if Jenny had felt like this when Brent said goodbye. Had her pain run this deep? Had she felt this helpless? Finally, sobs shook her, and she didn't know the moment when she passed from grief into the twilight realms of sleep.

Dappled drops of golden sunlight crept through the curtains of Kara's room. She lay in bed, staring at the ceiling, a headache threatening to erupt from the edges of her sorrow. She'd taken off work for the day to help Taylor pack.

She swung her legs over the side of the bed, and trudged over to Taylor's apartment. Her door was open. Taylor was standing on a stepstool, taking dishes out of top kitchen cabinets. She swung around when she heard Kara approach.

"You scared me," she said. Then she looked closer. "You look awful."

"Not as awful as I feel. I went over Brent's last night like you suggested and he dumped me."

Taylor came down off the step ladder. "Did you tell him about the baby?"

"I didn't get that far."

Taylor shook her head.

"I'm not going to tell him. Telling Brent I'm pregnant would simply force him into something he doesn't want."

"It's his child, he deserves to know," Taylor said.

Kara's hands curved protectively around her belly. "It's my child," she said fiercely. "Brent Stevens made it very clear that he doesn't want to share his life with me, and at this point, me means *us.*"

Kara glanced around at the disarray of Taylor's apartment. "Is that offer to join you in Atlanta still open?" she asked.

Tiffany knocked gingerly on the door of Kara's apartment. The door creaked open at her knock and she peered at the boxes everywhere.

Kara appeared from the bedroom. "Tiffany, come on in. It's good to see you. I called the hospital about Dante, and they said he was stable. I hadn't gotten by yet because I've been busy." She gestured around the apartment.

"It looks like you're moving," Tiffany said.

"Taylor and I are heading to Atlanta."

Tiffany's face brightened. "So am I. The tenant's lease was up on our old house, and I thought I'd go on home."

"That's wonderful; I'll know someone in Atlanta besides Taylor."

Tiffany gazed around Kara's apartment. "May I ask where you two are going to stay?"

"We were going to get a hotel room until we found someplace. We're going to room together."

"You know, if you girls would like, you could stay with me until you get settled. It's a huge house, so you'd both have plenty of privacy, and frankly, I'd appreciate the company. I haven't lived alone for years."

"That's very generous. Let's go over and talk to Taylor and see what she thinks," Kara said.

They were all going to live together in Atlanta. A warm glow filled Kara at the thought. She wasn't going to be alone, just her and her baby. Taylor and Tiffany felt like family, and they'd help see her through.

There was something she had yet to do, something she'd been dreading. She needed to go see Jenny, and set things straight if she could. Jenny had reacted badly when Tiffany told her that Kara would be staying with her in Atlanta, Tiffany'd said.

They searched Kara before they let her into the visiting area. The place was cold and institutional, with concrete brick walls painted nauseous green. Kara shivered. She couldn't imagine spending a year here.

A stocky female guard entered with Jenny, nodded at Kara, and then withdrew to stand outside the door. Jenny stared at Kara with open resentment.

"It wasn't enough you took the man I loved, you had to take my mother, too," she said.

"You know there is no way I could ever replace you in your mother's affections. You are always on her mind, and she talks about you constantly," Kara said.

Jenny sank into a chair, hostility still shining in her eyes.

"I'm sorry," Kara continued. And she was. She'd do anything to go back and make it right, but even if she could rewind that particular tape, she knew she'd still love Brent. No matter what. "I didn't mean to fall in love with Brent. It just happened. We tried to fight it, but we couldn't." Kara's voice faltered at the painful memories.

"What do you want from me?" Jenny asked, her voice hard.

"Forgiveness."

"Sorry, sister. Right now I'm fresh out," Jenny said.

Tears stung the corners of Kara's eyes. It was no less than she deserved.

"Before I go, I want to tell you that I know how you felt when Brent said he no longer wanted to be with you. He said the same thing to me. I'm pregnant with his child and he doesn't want either of us."

And with those words, Kara went and knocked on the locked door for the guard to let her out.

Twenty-six

In the weeks since Brent had last told Kara goodbye he'd gotten into the habit of driving by her apartment. He picked up the phone to call her a dozen times a day, only to put it back down again. What did he want? A glimpse of her? To hear her voice, to feel her touch? He wanted all of that and more. The longing for her would pass, he told himself daily. The problem was that it hadn't, not yet anyway.

He went to visit Dante, who'd recovered nicely, and would be discharged from the hospital soon.

Dante was watching a game on TV when Brent entered. "Pull up a chair, man," he said.

They watched the game in silence for a while. "Mom's moved back to our old house in Atlanta," Dante said.

"A change will probably do her good."

"Mom, Kara Smith, and her neighbor, Taylor, are one big, happy family in that house to hear her tell it. I'm just happy she's not alone."

"Kara moved to Atlanta?" Brent croaked.

"You mean you didn't know? I thought you two were pretty hot and heavy for a while."

He couldn't believe she'd packed up and left town without letting him know in some fashion. Unfinished business between Kara and him echoed within him.

"No, man. I didn't know," was all Brent said to Dante.

Brent stayed with Dante until the game was over and then went home to his empty apartment and ordered a pizza. He was getting to be on a first name basis with the pizza delivery guy. He fell sleep on the couch to the blare of the television.

He woke the next morning feeling empty, remembering Kara was gone. He got up and went to brush his teeth. There was the matter of the job offers, Brent thought. They'd poured in from Capitol Hill. He'd mulled them over and realized that he didn't want to work in politics anymore. What once had been exciting to him had soured.

There was no big rush. He could take his time and consider his next move. He'd never been a big spender and he'd invested his money wisely over the years. The problem was he was bored, and lonely for Kara. Bittersweet memories of her touched his mind and he smiled. Then the smile faded. He'd lost his temper with her. Had he been too rash? He missed her so much.

He poured cornflakes in the bowl and looked in the refrigerator. No milk. He grabbed some potato chips and a can of beer and went and sat in front of the TV. Then he remembered he'd forgotten to check his mail yesterday.

On top of the stack was a scented letter on pink stationery from Jenny. He sat back on the couch and took out the papers filled with Jenny's blockish schoolgirl handwriting.

"Dear Brent: I hope you are doing well. All these events unfolding . . . I'm thankful that Dante is doing well. I'm happy that my father is finally getting what he deserves. It's a hard thing, to take responsibility for myself and my actions, but I'm slowly getting there.

"When I heard Kara Smith was my sister, and was moving in with my mother in our old family home, I was upset. Then, she visited me and asked for my forgiveness. At the time, I didn't have it to give, but I've had to lean on God a lot lately, and in the forgiveness and grace He grants me,

I've finally found release from my bitterness. We'd never have been completely happy together."

He was truly happy Jenny was finally over him and finding peace. He read on.

"Kara confessed her pain to me. I'm asking you to reconsider, Brent. Things happen for a purpose. You and Kara shared something special. And now that she's having your child, you have a responsibility."

Brent's hands trembled as he read the words, "having your child." He read them again and again until his eyes burned. Then he picked up his jacket. He was going to have to speak to Jenny himself.

Tiffany had orchestrated the move with the precision and authority of an officer putting her cadets through their paces. She was in her element, unpacking boxes, organizing cabinets. Kara and Taylor both were only too happy to let her handle it. Taylor was busy with her new job, and Kara was taking lessons.

She'd enrolled in courses for driving, swimming, prenatal care, infant care, computers, word processing, and desktop publishing. It was a little excessive, but she was determined to be a strong and competent mother, and that meant conquering her fears. She wanted to gain skills to work at home so she could spend maximum time with her baby.

Also, staying busy meant less time to think about the loss of Brent. She'd only been gone three weeks, but she still missed him so badly it ached, and only the fact that she carried his child made it bearable.

Kara loved Cascade, the affluent, tree-lined African-American neighborhood. The house was on a large lot, surrounded by trees and brush. A pool and large deck were enclosed with a privacy fence. Inside was tons of space, rooms and rooms for Anthony to work his magic on.

He was coming next week, Tiffany said. He'd extracted a promise from Taylor and Kara that they'd go out and party with him.

They each had a suite of rooms complete with kitchenettes, teenage havens that had once belonged to Dante and Jenny. Kara sensed that Tiffany was grateful for their presence. She was attending AA meetings daily, and planning to start a job search. Tiffany was outside, firing up the grill right now. It was an unseasonably warm day, and Tiffany said she craved barbecue.

Kara would bet money she was going to ply Taylor with barbecue to entice her from her vegetarianism. Kara knew Taylor wouldn't be swayed, and went downstairs to make sure Tiffany threw some vegetables or tofu on that grill.

"What's up. How're the driving lessons?" Tiffany said. Kara noticed Tiffany had white and sweet potatoes, corn on the cob, and eggplant ready to put on the grill along with the cuts of meat.

"They're going. I think I'm going to buy a car next week. I really need one here in Atlanta."

"What do you want to get?" Tiffany asked, moving around looking for something.

"Something safe for the baby. Probably a minivan. You need some help?" Kara asked.

"That's strange. The charcoal starter fluid is missing. I made sure there was some yesterday. A whole gallon was right here."

"Want me to go get some for you? I was planning to walk down to the video store anyway."

"Please. Thanks, baby."

Kara had started down the front walkway when Brent pulled up into the drive.

She froze, poised to flee. What was he doing here? Brent

saw her and stopped the car, got out, and headed for her. He didn't look happy. She tried to compose herself.

"Is it true? Are you pregnant? Were you going to have my baby without letting me know?" Brent asked in the soft, dangerous voice he used when he was particularly upset.

Kara looked away. "Maybe we should go in the house to talk about it."

Brent looked even grimmer, if that was possible. "Maybe we should," he said.

They walked into the house. Kara walked to the back and called out the door, "Tiffany, Brent's here." So she was a coward. She needed a third party to defuse this situation until Brent calmed down. He looked like he wanted to kill her.

Tiffany came in immediately. "Hello, Brent, it's wonderful to see you."

"Same here," he said. "Would you excuse Kara and me? We have some serious talking to do."

"Of course," Tiffany said, looking over at Kara. Brent's eyes locked with hers, daring her to say differently. Tiffany went back outside.

"So is it true?" Brent asked again after Tiffany had left.

"Yes, yes I'm pregnant," Kara stammered.

"Damn it all!" Brent exploded and paced the floor. Then he stopped. "You are going to have the baby?" he asked.

Kara was confused, hadn't she just told him that? Then she understood. He was asking her if she planned to terminate the pregnancy. Indignation filled her.

"I'm having the baby," she said flatly.

Brent looked relieved. "Thank God," he murmured.

"I'm going to take a job here in Atlanta," he announced. "I'm going to provide for you and the baby."

Kara's eyes burned with unshed tears. In her fantasy this

was where he was supposed to swear his undying love for her and beg her to marry him.

"I don't expect anything from you. I'm quite capable of providing for my child," she said.

"It's my child, too, and I have the right to be a part of his or her life."

It simply wasn't fair. How could she bear Brent being a part of her life, loving him without love, only obligation in return?

She couldn't stop the onrush of tears along with the onslaught of emotion. "Why did you have to come here and ruin everything? I hate you!" she cried, and fled up the stairs to her room.

They said he was all washed up. They had taken his seat in congress, his money, and they said they were going to put him in jail—for defending himself. But they would regret trying to destroy Sidney Eastman. He couldn't stay down. Like a phoenix he would rise from the ashes. He giggled to himself at the vision.

They would be sorry. Everything was Tiffany's fault. It'd all started when she left him. Once that slut Tiffany was dead he'd be free to start all over and get everything they thought they'd taken from him back. Her death was the key.

He'd hire Brent back. He'd have won a Senate seat and Brent had always run his office so well. Sidney had hardly ever had to do anything himself. He liked that. Brent would forgive his little outburst of temper. Brent would understand the pressure he was under.

He'd get a new wife. A decent one this time. No more kids though. Once he cleansed the earth of the worthless whelps he had, that was it.

He shifted in the underbrush and unscrewed the top of the flask of scotch, taking a swallow. He could see the back of the house very well from here. He saw his slut of a wife out on the deck and longed to feel his hands around her neck squeezing the life out of her. No, what he craved was to hear her screaming in agony. He caressed the can of starter fluid. That would be even better.

Night was falling soon, and he could hardly wait for the fun to begin.

Twenty-seven

It had been a long, challenging day. It would be good to get home, Taylor thought. Pulling in, she saw Brent's car parked in the driveway. She hoped Brent had the sense to do the right thing, which was throw himself on his knees, declare undying love, and present Kara with a diamond the size of a robin's egg.

But she had yet to meet a man who had enough sense to get it right the first time. Oh well, despite all the angst, they'd get through this eventually. She grabbed her dry cleaning and ran up the steps into the house. She was starving.

"Hey, Taylor." Tiffany greeted her when she entered the homey country kitchen.

Brent slumped on the couch, looking morose. He stood when he saw her, and attempted to brighten. "It's good to see you again," he said.

Taylor nodded pleasantly. "Where's Kara?" she asked, knowing the answer.

"Holed up in her bedroom," Tiffany replied. "She's upset at Brent."

Taylor glanced over at him, and he looked even more miserable.

"Give her a little time, she'll get over it. What's on the stove, Tiff? It smells great," Taylor said.

"Barbecue, but plenty of grilled vegetables and potatoes

for you. Here, take this tray up to Kara, then we'll sit down and eat."

Taylor carried the tray up the stairs and tapped on Kara's door. "It's Taylor. I've got food for you and that other mouth you have to feed," she called.

"Come on in," Kara called out.

She was seated on her bed, staring out the window. She looked up and smiled as Taylor entered, but Taylor saw the deep sadness shadowing her eyes. Taylor set the tray on the dresser and sat by Kara.

"He's downstairs looking as down as you do right now."

Kara looked out the window at the setting sun.

"He found out I'm pregnant. He's furious. He said he would provide for me and my baby. Well, we don't need his provision," Kara said.

"You need his love," Taylor answered.

Kara's eyes filled with tears and Taylor wanted to banish her pain. She handed her a tissue.

"He dumped me. He thinks I'm dishonest and untrustworthy and he said he didn't want to share his life with me. The only reason he's here is because of the baby. I don't want him in my life under those terms. I don't think I can bear it."

"I don't think he's here just because of the baby. And anyway, he's not going anywhere until he convinces you otherwise. Sleep on it and talk to him tomorrow when your emotions are a little more under control."

Kara shook her head. "I want him to go away."

"He's not going away. You're going to have to deal with him. Relax, girlfriend, everything's going to work out."

Kara gave her a weak smile. "Thanks for the tray," she said.

Taylor closed the door behind her. "I only hope everything works out soon," she said to herself, crossing her fingers.

She started to go down the stairs, but a premonition hit

her so hard, she sank to her knees. Danger and death. Taylor closed her eyes and moaned, when she opened them she saw fire. Cold flames danced around her, and the banisters and the stairway burned. Smoke formed images of an evil face whose features she couldn't make out. A waking dream. She whimpered, and the flames flickered and went out. The smoke dissipated into nothingness. Only the hard knot of fear within her remained. The vision was true, but, oh God, when?

"Aren't you hungry?" Tiffany asked both Taylor and Brent.

Brent shook his head. "I guess I have too much on my mind," he said. And he did. His thoughts were upstairs in that room with Kara. He wanted to go upstairs and knock down the door, drag her out, and make love to her until she saw reason. She said she hated him. He didn't want to believe it, but the fear lodged in the corner of his mind, what if is was true? What if she really just wanted to be rid of him?

Too bad. She was going to have his baby, and he wasn't going anywhere. She was his and he'd camp out here until she realized it. And that was the way it was going to be whether she liked it or not.

Tiffany was clearing the table. "I feel that dinner was a flop," she said.

"No, it was delicious," Taylor protested.

"I have too much on my mind to eat right now, but it was good," Brent added. "Here, you cooked, let me clean the kitchen," he said, happy to have something to occupy his hands.

"I'll get your room ready," Tiffany said.

Brent was finishing up the pots and pans when he decided Kara's friend Taylor was wacked. Now, she was pacing the perimeter of the entire house with a lit blue candle and muttering under her breath.

She'd just finished digging through all the kitchen drawers looking for batteries and checking every smoke alarm in the house. There she goes again with the candle and the chanting. Weird. Brent nodded as she passed, but Taylor ignored him. Ah well, different strokes for different folks.

Tiffany tapped on Kara's door, and stuck her head in. "You need anything, baby? I'm going to turn in."

"I'm okay. Thanks," Kara said.

"Brent's staying. I don't think he's going to leave until you and he come to an understanding."

"You could throw him out," Kara said hopefully.

Tiffany laughed. "I'm not going to do that. Brent's practically part of the family."

Back in her bedroom Tiffany chuckled again. Those kids would work it out. Brent was crazy about that girl, and her love for him was written plainly all over her face.

She and Sidney had never felt like that for each other. She was flattered when he first asked her out. He'd gone through all the motions, but the depth of feelings behind them was never there. She never remembered Sidney showing any emotion except occasional rage.

She couldn't even pity him. Sidney deserved everything life had dealt him. She didn't know when he had transformed from merely self-centered to the level of malevolence that would allow him to shoot his son with no sign of guilt.

He was out of her life, permanently, and she was building a new life slowly and surely. She'd scheduled a job interview for the next day. A man from an AA meeting had asked her out. She'd refused, but the fact he'd asked was a pleasant surprise. It'd been so long since she thought of herself as a sexual being. There was some life in her yet, and she wanted to enjoy every moment of it.

* * *

Kara didn't see how she would get up and go to her classes tomorrow. Emotionally, she was a wreck. Brent had intruded into her life asking questions and making demands. She hated it. She hated it that she loved him so much. . . . Hated the fact that he was in the same house with her, making her want what she couldn't have. He'd made it very clear what he thought of her, and that he no longer wanted her in his life. She had followed her mother's example and gotten out of his life.

And now, like Sidney Eastman when he proffered his check in that letter he wrote her mother thirty years ago, Brent offered her protection and support. She'd torn up the letter and the check, the only concrete proof she had that Sidney Eastman was her father. The act was symbolic; she wanted no part of her father. How could she accept the same treatment her mother had rejected? Like Sidney Eastman, Brent offered duty and obligation, but he didn't offer love. She wanted no part of him either.

But is that fair to your baby? a tiny voice asked. Brent was offering to be an ongoing part of the child's life, something her father never considered. Did she have that right to deny her child access to his or her father?

Kara groaned and covered her head with the pillow. Why did he have to come and complicate her life? Why did he have to come and offer her a part of what she wanted but not all? She was going to have to do what was right for her baby. She'd have to settle for what Brent offered. She'd have to spend the rest of her life longing for what she didn't have, maybe watching him marry, start another family. Hot hears leaked from her closed eyelids. She'd made that bed herself.

Sidney slipped into the dark house, silent as a wraith. Tiffany, as stupid as usual, had failed to have the locks changed or install an alarm system. The foolish slut had made it very easy for him. He hefted the gallon can of starter fluid, very easy indeed. In the other hand, he carried a duffle bag with his tools.

He needed to see Tiffany's face when she recognized him, when she writhed in pain, her features slowly charring and turning unrecognizable. That would be the best part.

He was hungry. Sidney went to the refrigerator and studied the contents lit by the cold appliance light. There was a ziplocked bag filled with some leftover grilled steaks. He got one out, took a loaf of bread from the bread box, and made a sandwich in the dark. He slowly savored the charbroiled flesh. Imagine Tiffany tied to the grill, the coals nice and hot.

That would be much slower and deliciously agonizing than the pyrotechnics he'd planned. Charbroiled Tiffany. Sidney stuffed the last of the sandwich in his mouth and giggled. Too bad he couldn't do it. The neighbors would probably complain.

He grabbed the can of starter fluid and the bag and soundlessly climbed the stairs to Tiffany's room. He heard a sound off to his left and slipped into the shadows in the hall. His so-called daughter, Kara, was wandering the halls, reflected in the window from the moonlight filtering through and conspicuous in her white robe.

"Who's there?" she whispered.

Damn, Sidney thought in surprise. He would've sworn he made no sound. He hoped he had enough starter fluid for both of them, setting the can down as quietly as he could. She moved closer. Sidney was delighted. He willed her to come even closer.

In one swift movement the gun was at her temple, and he was whispering in her ear, "One sound and I'll blow your head off." She inhaled with what could be the beginning of a scream anyway. "There's a silencer on this gun,"

Sidney said conversationally, still in a low voice. "So it doesn't really matter if I shoot you now or not." He cocked the gun and the girl exhaled without a sound.

"Lead the way to Tiffany's room." She started to turn in the wrong direction and Sidney chuckled. "I used to live here, remember? I know where it is. Every second that passes you're getting more useless to me. I might as well shoot you now."

The girl moved quickly toward Tiffany's room. Halfway down the hall he said, "Stop right there." The girl stopped. "Turn and face the wall." The girl's eyes widened and she trembled visibly. "You heard me," Sidney said. When she didn't move Sidney sighed and released the safety of the gun. She turned.

"I could blow off the back of your head, and if you make a sound I will," he said, pulling out a roll of duct tape from his toolbag. He reached around and covered her mouth with it, tearing the length off, after wrapping it completely around her head. "You can turn around," he said. "Hold out your arms," he said, and deftly wound the tape around her arms.

Tears were rolling down her face. He wasn't an unjust man, he thought. "If you behave, I'll go easy on you. Okay?" The girl was unmoved. Sidney was a little irritated. Ungrateful slut. "Okay?" he asked again, soft and deadly.

She nodded her head. Good. He might put a bullet through her head instead of burn her after all. He probably didn't have enough starter fluid anyway.

"Lead the way," he hissed.

Twenty-eight

Tiffany stirred as they entered. He'd have to be fast. "I'll kill her in a heartbeat if you give me any trouble," he said to the girl. Tiffany opened her eyes, and he was at her side before she could scream. She focused on the gun pointing at her face, then on Sidney.

"Don't say a word," he said, then hit her hard on the head with the butt of the gun. Tiffany slumped and the girl made a strangled sound through the duct tape.

Sidney swung the gun toward her. "Lie down," he ordered. The girl laid down on the floor. He quickly applied duct tape around Tiffany's face, being careful to leave her nostrils free. He didn't want her to suffocate. That would be too easy. He wound tape around her wrists and ankles. When he was sure she was secure, he turned to get the can of starter fluid.

The girl was gone. He heard the thud of her feet as she ran down the hall. He should have shot her instead of looking forward to the pleasure he'd get from her reactions to Tiffany burning. He swore, picked up the gun, and started after her.

Kara fled the madman—her father. She ran to Brent's room. Unable to make a sound or free her hands, she kicked the door. Then she heard Sidney coming after her, and she ran toward the west wing, to the stairs leading to the basement.

Her heart pounded as she heard him gaining on her. She was making too much noise as she ran through the house, she had to hide. Running down the stairs to the basement, stumbling and almost falling, she cast about wildly. An open closet door? No, too obvious.

There was an old empty steamer trunk in the back utility room she was sure was unlatched. Running to it, she heard him coming down the stairs. It wouldn't open. Frantically, she tried to unlatch it with her foot.

"Where are you, Kara?" Sidney called with a singsong voice. "I've got something for you."

The trunk opened. She fell into it, and used her toe to draw it shut.

"I've got a big, fat bullet with your name on it," he yelled. He was getting closer. She feared he could hear the frantic beat of her heart through the walls of the trunk.

"There you are," he said. Pure panic rippled through her, then she heard him pull open the closet door and rummage around. Tears leaked from under her lashes. She thought of her baby . . . of Brent . . .

Brent woke to a thud on his door. He rolled out of bed and pulled the door open. In his customary cotton pajama bottoms, he walked into the hallway. He thought he heard the echo of running feet. He started to follow the sound, but then heard a moan from Tiffany's room. Her door was ajar.

"Tiffany?" he called. Another moan was his only response. He clicked on the light switch. The room flooded with light, and Brent gasped to see Tiffany gagged and bound with duct tape.

"What's going on?" Taylor asked, coming into the room.

A strangled scream escaped when she saw Tiffany bound on the bed.

"Call 911, free her, and you both get out of the house," Brent told Taylor. "I'm going to check on Kara."

He ran to Kara's room. Dread clutched his heart with icy fingers when he saw the empty bed. He hesitated only a moment before running toward the west wing, where he had first heard the footfalls.

Brent stopped and listened, his breath coming in harsh gasps. The faint resonance of a male voice sounded from the basement. Creeping down the stairs, so as not to startle the intruder, he heard someone rummaging around in the storage room. Brent crept toward the sound.

Sidney was bending over an old steamer trunk. A gun was in his hand. Brent tackled him and they fell to the floor, the gun spinning free. Sidney lunged for it and Brent grabbed him, knocking him to the floor again. They struggled, rolling on the floor. Brent pinned Sidney down, dismayed at the madness he saw in the man's eyes. "Why, Sidney? In God's name, why?"

In answer, Sidney spit in his eyes, and there was a sharp pain in his side. Brent grunted in surprise, and grasped his side. A small knife stuck from his flesh and warm, wet blood leaked through his fingers. Sidney scrambled away and ran up the stairs.

These people were really getting on his nerves, Sidney thought as he raced up the stairs. The only thing that mattered was that he finish what he'd started. He had to kill the slut Tiffany or he'd never regain what he'd lost. He'd definitely never win that Senate seat. That was how it was supposed to work.

Running to her room, he screamed when he saw her bed empty, festooned with tatters of duct tape. "No, no, no," he wailed.

Grabbing the can of charcoal starter fluid, he ran back to the basement stairs. He splashed a generous portion over the wooden stairs and threw a match. The flames were really lovely. Too bad he couldn't stay to enjoy the screams of anguish that would soon come from the basement. Sidney danced throughout the house, scattering fire. The flames danced and bathed his face with diabolical light.

Brent gasped in pain as he pulled out the knife. He pressed his fist to the wound, holding pressure, trying to staunch the flow of blood. He struggled to stand up. Dizziness hit him like a physical blow, and he swayed. He willed himself to stay upright, and not to lose consciousness.

Then he smelled something burning. The alarm blared, and the basement started to fill with black, heavy smoke.

"Kara! Kara, where are you?" Brent listened but heard nothing but the crackle of flames. The smoke was growing thicker and he knew he had to get out. But he couldn't, he wouldn't leave without Kara. With every fiber of his body, he knew she was down here somewhere.

The smoke thickened. He bent down close to the floor and tried not to gasp for air.

"Kara!" he yelled. He heard a faint knocking. He groped his way toward the sound through the blinding smoke, his lungs burning. A moan reached his ears, and he knew it was her. Reaching the trunk where he'd first seen Sidney, he threw it open and almost sobbed in relief. He gathered her up, warm, vital, and alive in his arms. He touched her face and felt the tape covering her mouth. He tore it off.

Kara coughed and sputtered. "Go to your left, and stay against the wall," she gasped. "There's a deadbolted sliding glass door. A chair is about three feet in front of it."

He half carried, half dragged her through the choking

smoke. She was limp in his arms, and his lungs burned, every breath a misery. Where was that damned door? They couldn't come this far and not make it. He finally felt the smooth glass surface.

"Chair—straight back," Kara said faintly. Thank God, she was conscious.

With his last remnants of strength he groped for the chair, picked it up, and swung it with all his strength against the door. Glass exploded outward, and he pulled Kara through to the blessed night air. He cradled her in his arms, rocking her as they both gasped the life-giving oxygen.

She was alive, she'd be all right, he thought, realizing what he knew all along. There was simply no point in living without her.

Brent woke in the hospital, and Kara sat beside him. He smiled. "Hello," he said, feeling almost dizzy with love.

Kara folded the newspaper she'd been reading. "You've slept for almost twenty-four hours. You lost a lot of blood, and they had to give you a transfusion."

"Are Tiffany and Taylor all right?" he asked.

"They're fine; they got out, like you told them. The house burned to the ground. Sidney Eastman burned with it. They pulled his body out of the ruins." Kara looked away. "I'm ashamed to be his daughter. He was a monster."

"He was a sick man. But never be ashamed of who you are. You're not Sidney Eastman's daughter, you're Kara Smith. I almost thought I'd lost you and the baby," Brent said. He reached for her hand.

"Thank you for . . . everything," she said, her voice almost a whisper.

Brent caressed her hand. She drew it away. "Don't tease me," she said. Her eyes were bright with unshed tears. "I'd been thinking that night, before . . ." She hesitated, cleared her throat and continued, "I decided that I couldn't deprive my baby of a father. If your offer still stands to be a part of my child's life, I accept it."

Brent stared at her. "Is that all you want, Kara? I want to give you so much more," he said.

Kara shook her head as if she didn't hear him right. "You talked about duty and obligation, not love."

"I was stupid and angry. I've been self-righteous, not understanding your fear. I'm sorry I rejected you instead of trying to work things out. I regretted it almost from the moment I did it. I've missed you so much."

Brent grasped her chin. "Look at me," he said. "You obviously have no idea about how I feel about you. I love you, Kara. I love you so much that I'd rather have died myself than have lost you. I love you so much that if you won't marry me and share the rest of our lives together, life won't be worth living."

Tears fell freely down Kara's face. Brent's lips kissed her tears away, each touch a caress full of promises and love.

"Yes," she whispered. She'd been blessed with her heart's desire. The God of grace and love that she'd learned to know, smiled, and the jeweled butterfly of her spirit, finally free, took flight.

Dear Reader:

I hope the story of Kara and Brent touched your heart. Look for Taylor and Stone's story next year. Along with the romance and passion, it's liberally spiced with mystery and a hint of the paranormal. What else could you possibly expect from a psychic and a detective?

I'm hard at work making the principles of Kwanzaa come to life in a book that sizzles with passion and adventure laced with the enduring love and hope that family represents. It should be on the shelves by December 1998.

There is nothing I'd rather do than weave stories and characters and watch them spring to life under the click of my computer keyboard. The best part is the opportunity to share my stories with you. I'd love to hear what you like to read, what moves you, and what doesn't. Include a SASE if you like and write to me at P.O. Box 654, Topeka, KS 66601.

Sincerely,
Monica Jackson

About the Author

Monica Jackson has always loved stories. Reading them is good, and writing them is even better, but sharing one of her stories with you is the best. Monica is a registered nurse who likes working with children. She lives in Kansas.

COMING IN AUGUST...

BREAK EVERY RULE, by Francis Ray   (0-7860-0544-0, $4.99/$6.50)
Dominique Falcon was known amongst the elite for her wealth and beauty. But behind the glamorous image was a lonely dreamer who had fallen for a money-grubbing charmer. She vowed that her next lover would be richer and socially her superior. But then she meets the unrefined Trent Jacob Masters, falls in love and breaks every rule.

CHARADE, by Donna Hill   (0-7860-0545-9, $4.99/$6.50)
Tyler Ellington enrolled in film school and fell for filmmaker Miles Bennett. But his deceit fled her back to her hometown where handsome photographer Sterling Grey entered her life in an opportune moment. He is everything that Miles is not, and she finds herself falling in love. For career reasons, she must return to New York, where Miles awaits to shower her with apologies. Will Miles' charade blind her to the true love that awaits her with Sterling?

ONE SPECIAL MOMENT, by Brenda Jackson (0-7860-0546-7, $4.99/$6.50)
To salvage her brother's struggling cosmetics company, schoolteacher Colby Wingate seeks superstar actor Sterling Gamble to endorse her brother's new perfume. Sterling thinks she is answering his ad for a woman to bear his child. He is deeply attracted to her and is determined to convince her to agree to his proposition. He didn't expect to fall deeply in love with her. Now he must prove his love is genuine.

IT HAD TO BE YOU, by Courtni Wright   (0-7860-0547-5, $4.99/$6.50)
After many sacrifices, Jenna Cross became a successful lawyer at a prestigious law firm in Washington. Her ambition will not let her stop until she becomes a judge. When love threatens to intervene, she pushes it away. She wants nothing to divert her focus from her career—not even her gorgeous senior partner Mike Matthews. He vows to show her that love does not threaten her career and that she can have it all.

Available wherever paperbacks are sold, or order direct from the Publisher. Send cover price plus 50¢ per copy for mailing and handling to Kensington Publishing Corp., Consumer Orders, or call (toll free) 888-345-BOOK, to place your order using Mastercard or Visa. Residents of New York and Tennessee must include sales tax. DO NOT SEND CASH.

LOOK FOR THESE ARABESQUE ROMANCES